"A beautiful homage to a mother's bravery and the grace and grit that is our inheritance. *An American Immigrant* is a clarion call to water our roots and refuse to allow those we love to be lost in translation."

—ALICIA MENENDEZ,
MSNBC anchor and creator and host of
Latina to Latina podcast

"In a yearning and humbling journey to the place of her mother's birth, a fictional Miami journalist discovers her innermost worth by yielding to family truth, creative courage, and cultural clarity—which she needs to give both her heart and the hard world her authentic best. An enchanting, brave, and uplifting story of discovery, family love, and determined hope."

—PATRICIA RAYBON, Christy Award–winning author of the
Annalee Spain Mystery series and
*My First White Friend: Confessions on
Race, Love, and Forgiveness*

"In *An American Immigrant*, Johanna Rojas Vann delivers a powerful exploration of the risks we face in pursuit of a better life. By weaving a compelling and emotional tale, she offers readers a fresh examination of identity, truth, generational sacrifice, and the real meaning of home. Ideal for book clubs, this story will have people talking."

—JULIE CANTRELL,
New York Times and *USA Today*
bestselling author of *Perennials*

"Johanna Rojas Vann takes readers on a journey that brings about knowledge, empathy, relatability, connection, and empowerment. The food and culture made me want to dig up recipes and follow in Melanie's shoes in *An American Immigrant* and celebrate the blessings God brings us. Readers don't want to miss this uplifting story!"

—TONI SHILOH,
Christy Award–winning author

"Not only does *An American Immigrant* celebrate tradition and cultural exploration, but it is a captivating journey of self-discovery that serves as a powerful reminder that it's never too late to go after your dreams on your own terms. Melanie's story is a must-read for anyone wanting to understand the power of family and the true meaning of home."

—COURTNEY DYKSTERHOUSE,
media personality and former news anchor

"I don't usually read fiction, but Johanna's storytelling gripped me from the start, and I wasn't able to put *An American Immigrant* down. I highly recommend this book!"

—JORDAN RAYNOR,
bestselling author of *Redeeming Your Time* and
Called to Create

AN AMERICAN IMMIGRANT

AN AMERICAN IMMIGRANT

A Novel

JOHANNA ROJAS VANN

WATERBROOK

A WaterBrook Trade Paperback Original

Published in the United States by WaterBrook, an imprint of Random House, a division of Penguin Random House LLC.

WATERBROOK and colophon are registered trademarks of Penguin Random House LLC.

Library of Congress Cataloging-in-Publication Data
Names: Rojas Vann, Johanna, author.
Title: An American immigrant : a novel / Johanna Rojas Vann.
Description: First edition. | Colorado Springs : WaterBrook, 2023.
Identifiers: LCCN 2023002288 |
ISBN 9780593445556 (trade paperback ; acid-free paper) |
ISBN 9780593445563 (ebook)
Subjects: LCSH: Colombian Americans—Fiction. |
Self-realization in women—Fiction.
Classification: LCC PS3618.O5357 A83 2023 |
DDC 813/.6—dc23/eng/20230320
LC record available at https://lccn.loc.gov/2023002288

Printed in the United States of America on acid-free paper

waterbrookmultnomah.com

1 2 3 4 5 6 7 8 9

Book design by Edwin A. Vázquez

To my mother.
Thank you for your sacrifice.
My life is sweeter because of it.

PROLOGUE

ANITA

She clutched the leather duffel bag on her lap.

The flight attendant walked by and asked if she could store the bag for Anita in the overhead compartment. Anita shook her head. She wanted to make sure the contents inside didn't get flattened or crushed on the long flight home.

From the exterior slip pocket, she pulled out a journal and brushed the front cover with her hand. Spreading it open over the creases of the bag, Anita continued transferring memories from her head onto the page. Since arriving at the airport early that morning, she'd hardly let her pen rest.

She made this trip yearly, but it was the first time she'd had to travel with a few treasured possessions to store in her mother's home. With the divorce, she'd decided life in a new state would be the fresh start she and her three kids needed. But their new apartment lacked the space to store anything beyond necessities. Her mother's home was the only place she felt her things would be safe.

When she finally stepped foot through her mother's door after the long journey, she took a deep breath. Since moving to

America, returning to her childhood home had become the breath of fresh air she waited for each year.

Alba peeked her head into the front hallway, and when she saw her daughter standing beneath her doorway, luggage in tow, she scrambled toward her with arms wide open.

"*Hola, mi amor,*" Alba whispered, arms around her neck.

Anita's shoulders relaxed beneath her mother's embrace.

Alba stepped back and looked her daughter up and down. "You look skinny. Come, let's eat. I have plenty."

"Of course you do." Anita smiled and followed her mother into the kitchen, where she was met with the familiar aroma of strong coffee and sweet bread.

"I wish you would have brought the kids with you. They're getting so big. I'm afraid I won't recognize them the next time I see them," Alba said.

"If only I could convince them. They're not interested in coming here, *Mamá*. I asked if they'd like to come, but every one of them had something they just couldn't miss," Anita said, using air quotes. "Some camp, some birthday outing for a friend . . . who knows. Their dad is staying with them while I'm here."

Alba shrugged. "Well, hopefully the next time you come, they'll want to tag along. Or you could just tell them they *have* to come with you."

Anita shook her head. "I don't know, *Mamá*. I don't want to force them to come. I want them to *want* to come here. It's not you, *Mamá*. They miss you, of course. But it's like they can't stand the idea of leaving the States. They think that's all there is to see in the world." She took a sip of coffee and stared into the mug. "I hope I didn't make a mistake raising them there."

Alba reached out her hand and grabbed Anita's wrist, gently massaging it.

"I just want them to be proud of who we are," Anita said, looking into her mother's eyes.

"They're still so young. Don't worry about all that. Just keep speaking to them in Spanish and talking about our culture. They don't have to grow up in this country to learn those things and be proud Colombians."

"But what if that's not enough? They stumble on their words when they speak Spanish, and so they revert to English. They're more comfortable in English. I try to force them to speak to me in Spanish, but it just aggravates them. Alex doesn't even know what these are," Anita said, raising a *pandebono* from her plate. "I'm not doing enough, *Mamá*. I'm failing them."

"*Todo en su tiempo, mi amor*. Everything in its time, my love. You're not failing. You're a wonderful mother. Have faith and do your best. There's not much else you can do." Alba dusted her hands on her apron and stood. "Now finish up so you can get some rest."

When the round wooden table in her mother's dining room was cleared, Anita gathered her belongings from the front of the house and took them to the very back, where her old bedroom was. Alba hadn't changed a single thing since her daughters left.

She dropped onto the bed she once shared with her two sisters. One look around brought back fond memories of staying up late braiding one another's hair and gossiping about the boys in school. She let out a deep sigh. Never once did she imagine the three of them would be scattered around the Northeast in America, raising their kids hours apart from one another.

She lifted the leather tote from the ground, placed it on her lap, and peeked inside.

I won't leave you here forever. Just until I can afford to get us a bigger place.

She walked to the closet and wiped the dust from the shelf

inside with the washcloth her mother had left on her bed. Then she closed the leather bag with the gold-plated clasp and stuffed it as far back on the shelf as she could, hoping it would be safely hidden there.

Back on her bed, scooted against the headboard, she opened the journal she'd been writing in at the airport, her pen still stuffed inside. It'd been years since she'd written, but the journal still had a few empty pages to fill. There was a large gap of time and events missing from this journal, but perhaps with a little more dedication, she could fill in those holes with all that had happened since the day she left this home.

And what better place to document those memories than where it all began.

PART 1

PART 1

CHAPTER 1

2018
MIAMI

MELANIE

"**M**mm, it's still warm," Melanie whispered as she brushed a copy of the *Miami Herald* across her cheek.

"What are you doing?"

She jumped and turned around to find Rick, the overnight security guard, sitting up from behind the receptionist's desk.

"Rick! You scared me. What are you doing kicked back on Amanda's desk?" Melanie folded the newspaper and tucked it underneath her arm. "She'll be in any minute and I do not want to know what she'd do to you if she saw your grungy boots near her Chinese money plant."

Rick kicked his feet off the desk and meandered across the lobby to a less comfortable post. "Ah, she doesn't scare me. So, do you always sniff newspapers when you think no one's looking?"

"Do you always take naps at Amanda's desk when you're on the clock?"

"Touché."

"I won't tell Amanda what I witnessed if we never speak of this again," Melanie said with a wink. She reached for her badge, which she kept attached to the belt loop of her pants at all times.

The day HR handed her this badge was the day she became the first to arrive and the last to leave the newsroom each day. It was her first year on the job, and she had a lot to prove. This year especially would be crucial to her future success—there's no way she'd allow another rookie reporter to outperform her.

"Deal."

When she opened the door, a gust of air from the frigid newsroom tousled her cola-colored pin-straight hair—the perfect accessory for a confident strut to her desk.

Could this morning get any better?

She wore her favorite pair of black twill pants—the ones she'd bought at the J. Crew Factory the day she signed her offer letter—and had even splurged on a vanilla latte from Starbucks. The occasion warranted a fancy coffee drink, despite her having a slim thirty-five dollars in her bank account.

It didn't matter. Not when this was the morning she'd been waiting for. All her hard work had paid off, and now it was time for the best part: to see her byline closer to the front page of the *Herald*. Her articles—usually local stories no one else wanted to cover—were often published somewhere between pages ten and fourteen. But not today. She'd overheard the page editors discussing placing her article closer to the front because of the big interview she'd landed with the attorney general.

When Melanie reached her desk, she laid out the crisp newspaper on top. She smoothed out the front and slowly flipped through the various pages. Every part of her wanted to find her name as quickly as possible, but she knew better than to turn the pages with too much force.

Melanie loved the way a newspaper felt in her hands. The gentle weight of it. The crinkling sound that reminded her to be careful. The way it bent to the rhythm of her fingers. Opening a fresh copy each morning was like a meditative practice that never got old.

Only, suddenly, she felt pulled away from this calming ritual. She'd come to the middle of the newspaper and hadn't found her article.

She furrowed her eyebrows and tilted her head.

Maybe it's a little deeper in.

She turned a few more pages.

After another skim, she still came up empty.

Maybe I missed it. I must be so excited I'm missing it right before my eyes.

Okay . . . let's start again from the beginning.

When, again, she didn't see her story, she took a deep breath and decided to look through the entire paper once more.

Nothing. No headline. No byline. No story.

Her heart rate sped up and her cheeks became hot to the touch. She reached for her phone underneath the newspaper, launched her browser, and went to the paper's website to find out if the digital version of her article was missing too.

No trace of it online either.

Her arms stiffened and her hand formed a fist. To protect the paper, she had to step away for a moment or she might crumple it in her hands and toss it in the trash. She backed away from her desk and marched toward the bathroom while her mind raced with all the possible reasons her article could be missing from both print and online.

In the privacy of a stall, she retraced her steps in her mind.

Did I forget to give Ignacio the updated version? No. Can't be. I remember putting the hard copy on his desk two hours before the deadline.

Ignacio—her boss and the editor in chief—was old-school

and still demanded hard copies on his desk to review each day. It was one of many things Melanie admired about him. While newspapers everywhere were hyperfocused on meeting the demands of a "new kind of reader"—not to mention downsizing because newspapers just didn't make the kind of money they used to—Ignacio fought to keep at least a few traditions alive.

She paced in a circle inside the handicap bathroom stall.

Maybe he forgot to look at it. Or maybe it got lost. . . . He has so many stacks of paper on his desk.

Or maybe my revision wasn't good enough. No, no, no. That's impossible. I checked everything off the list.

Stop jumping to the worst-case scenario, Melanie. You always do this and everything turns out to be fine.

There's a perfectly logical explanation. There has to be.

I bet he pushed the pub date to tomorrow or another day this week. A more time-sensitive story probably took precedence. Yep, that's it.

But there hadn't been any breaking news overnight, and she didn't notice anything in the paper that hadn't been discussed in last week's editorial meeting. So, what could it be?

There must be something else she missed.

Fear set in. Even as a full-time reporter, she didn't always get her own byline. Most days, she assisted other reporters on their stories, which meant she had to share a byline. What could this mean about her performance? Her future at the paper?

She walked back to her desk, closed the newspaper, and stuffed it into the top drawer of the file cabinet by her chair. Then she sat down, bowed her head, and prayed there was a simple, logical reason why her article hadn't been published. And, more importantly, that her job was safe. That all the planning and preparation she'd done had not been in vain. That her hard work would pay off and keep her from a life of hardship and scarcity like the one she'd grown up in.

When she finished her prayer, she looked up and spotted Genesis walking over.

"Finally," Melanie said aloud.

Genesis was tall and slender with shiny blond hair and the biggest, brightest blue eyes she'd ever seen. Her hair was so blond and her eyes so blue that people often found it hard to believe she was 100 percent *Cubana*. Even Melanie had the same doubt when she first met her. But all it took was breaking out her Cuban slang for Genesis to set them straight. There was no denying authentic *Cubanismo* when you heard it in Miami.

"Good morning! How's it going?" Genesis pulled out her office chair, which was tucked under the nook of her desk.

"Genesis, my article isn't in the paper." No time for pleasantries. Melanie needed help from her only friend at the paper as soon as possible.

"I'm doing great this morning, thanks for asking," she responded with a smirk.

"I'm sorry, Gen. But this is serious. I need your help. What am I going to do? Do you think I'm fired?"

"*Ay, tumba eso.* You always get so worked up. Have you asked Ignacio yet?"

In this high-stakes environment, it was rare to meet a free-spirited journalist. Melanie had coined the oxymoron after working on a few stories with Genesis. Her friend's carefree attitude often helped calm Melanie's not-so-carefree personality, and she appreciated that. Only today, she needed someone who would allow her even a tiny meltdown. Her missing article was a big deal, and she needed Genesis to see that.

"No, I haven't seen him come in yet." Melanie had watched the doors ever since she hadn't found her article. She wanted to be the first to speak with Ignacio before anyone else could catch him and sour his mood.

"Oh, that's right. I think he has a meeting with the publisher again. They're probably at some fancy hotel in Brickell. He should be here by lunch." Genesis turned on her laptop and stared at her screen as if what she'd just said was no big deal.

"What?" Melanie braced a hand to her forehead and tried to calm her rapid breathing. The room closed in. Was the air getting thinner? Before she could start hyperventilating, she looked down toward her chair and drank in deep breaths, wishing now more than ever that she'd paid more attention in those yoga classes her college roommates used to drag her to.

Then she turned to look back at Genesis with her eyebrows scrunched together. "How am I possibly supposed to wait until lunch to find out what happened?"

"*Ay, mija, calmaté.* Everything's going to be fine." Genesis turned and placed her hands gently on Melanie's shoulders. "C'mon, relax your face a little—you look like the queen Frida Kahlo herself. Just find something to keep you busy until you can talk to Ignacio—oh look, your mom is calling."

Melanie looked down at her vibrating phone and let out a deep sigh. This was not a good time for her mom to call—but then again, her mother's calls never seemed to come at a good time. She picked up the phone anyway, desperate for a distraction.

"*¿Q'hubo, mija?*" Melanie felt her shoulders tighten as she listened to the familiar greeting on the other end of the line. While she heard from her mother at least once most days, it wasn't always welcome.

It's not that Melanie didn't like talking to her mother, who still lived back home in Maryland. She only wished conversations with her were easier—more enjoyable and less like a chore. Her mother, Anita, was a good mother—kind, funny in her own quirky way, and sweet as *dulce de leche*—but English was her second language. Melanie had grown up speaking Spanish in her home, but English would always be her native tongue—the only language in which she could fully express herself. This meant conversations with her mother required endless explanations.

"*No entiendo,*" her mother would say to just about any topic Melanie spoke of. "I don't understand. Tell me again. What do you mean?" Conversations never seemed to flow seamlessly back and forth, and at times, their phone calls felt more like a teaching session than a conversation between a mother and her daughter.

With as worried and, frankly, scared as Melanie felt, not knowing what had happened to her article, it was the worst time to enter into another one of those teaching sessions. So rather than being honest about how her morning was going so far, Melanie greeted her mother as nonchalantly as she could.

"Hey, Mom. Nothing much. What's up?"

"*Nada.* I was just wondering if I could come visit you for a day or two on my way home from Colombia. I'm going this weekend, remember? So, I was thinking . . . since I have to fly through Miami anyway, maybe I could stay one night? I still haven't seen your apartment or your work. I would love to see your life there. If I can."

Melanie opened her mouth to speak but paused when her gaze drifted to the cabinet where she'd stuffed the newspaper.

"Mom, it's not a good time. I'm really busy with work. Plus, where would you sleep? I don't have a couch or guest room. You know I live in a studio apartment."

"I don't care about that. I can sleep anywhere—on the floor, even!"

Melanie wanted to say yes. She wanted to make an effort with her mom, but her offering to sleep on the floor brought back painful memories of the years Melanie spent sleeping on the floor of her mother's bedroom with her siblings in the summer. Anita's room was the only one with air-conditioning. She also remembered overhearing friends at school giggling about Melanie's "bedroom" being in the dining room. When Melanie and her sister couldn't stop bickering and begged for their own rooms, Anita moved Melanie's bed into the dining room and closed off the space with a four-panel room divider. Melanie never again invited a friend over after she heard the rumors about her "dining bed" at school.

When Melanie first moved into her studio, she had a feeling her mother would take her having her own place as an invitation to visit whenever she wanted. But that wasn't why Melanie chose to spend twice as much on rent rather than share with a roommate. She wanted her own space, no matter how much more it cost her.

"Mom, no. I don't want you sleeping on the floor. How about another time? Maybe in the winter when you can get a hotel room at a cheaper price. I'll even stay there with you if you want."

Melanie tried to sound convincing, but the truth was, a visit in the winter wasn't probable. She'd keep putting it off and putting it off. There wasn't a life for her mom—or any of her family—to see here anyway. Her life consisted of long workdays, even on the weekends. But that's what needed to happen right now. These first few years post college were crucial to her long-term plan. Every day mattered.

Anita didn't say a word for a moment. Melanie could tell her mother was hurt by her response. She leaned back in her chair and rubbed her forehead.

Great, now I've got this guilt to deal with on top of my career being on the rocks.

I just wish she could understand how important my job is. I can't afford to take my foot off the gas.

"Mom, I'm sorry. There's just so much going on right now."

"*Bueno,*" Anita responded before changing the subject. "Your sister's baby is just precious. I can't believe he's already going to be six months old. You should come meet him. Before you know it, we'll be celebrating his first birthday."

There it was—more guilt rising.

"I know, Mom. We FaceTime a lot. It's just hard right now to take time off when work is so crazy."

"*Ay, mija,* work is always going to be crazy. Trust me. Life never slows down. But you don't get back any of these special moments that you miss."

Once again, she doesn't understand.

Melanie took a breath. "Okay, Mom. I'll be home for Christmas this year for sure. I promise. But I have to go now. I'll call you later." She said those last four words every time she got off the phone with her mother, even though she knew she wouldn't have to call her. No matter what she said to her mother, there would be a call from her the next day.

Anita was that way. Accommodating. Docile. Well behaved. Someone who always came running back.

CHAPTER 2

The inside of Melanie's brain felt like a loud, obnoxious pinball machine. No matter what she tried, she couldn't settle her thoughts. She had to speak to Ignacio, but he still hadn't arrived.

What more could she do to kill time? She had already scrolled through more online newspapers than she had since her first month on the job—the training period when you're not yet writing but learning the ropes. Melanie pretended to skim most of the articles, but it was impossible to focus on anything except what she would say to Ignacio.

One look around the newsroom filled Melanie with envy. All the other reporters looked at peace. Of course they were at peace—they weren't on the brink of losing their jobs.

Time ticked by more slowly than it ever had before. If it weren't for Genesis swooping in to save her from her misery, she might have started plucking hairs out of her scalp.

"Hey, I'm starving." Genesis pulled off her doughnut-sized headphones. "Want to get an early lunch?"

"Absolutely." Melanie grabbed her purse, which hung from her desk chair. She was halfway to the employee entrance before Genesis had a moment to gather her things or suggest where they should eat. There was no time to waste—Melanie needed fresh air.

"Mel! *¡Espera!*" Genesis yelled in the parking lot when she spotted Melanie charging toward her car in the far back row. "Come, let's take my car. Clearly, you're in no position to drive right now."

There was no use arguing with her friend. She needed to escape to a place where she could really air her grievances as soon as possible.

"I think the mood you're in calls for some Cuban sandwiches," Genesis said as they climbed into her black BMW X5. Any other day, Melanie would have counted in her head how many years it would take her to reach the kind of salary required to buy this luxury car. The kind of car you didn't need to hide from anyone.

She still parked at the back of the *Herald*'s lot. So far back that she added an extra ten minutes to her commute because it took her that long to reach her desk from where she parked.

The habit began many years earlier, before Melanie even had her driver's license. She'd never forget the day she saw the cute blond with the Justin Bieber haircut—the one in her English class—jump out of his father's shiny black Hummer the first week of school. What was it like to have parents that rich?

From that day on, her mother's minivan—the one that dropped chips of teal paint everywhere it went—was not allowed in her school's drop-off lane. Instead, Melanie insisted her mother drop her off at the far end of the lot, where no one would see her. Where no one would be able to laugh at her family's lack.

She'd saved enough during her four years at Northwestern to buy herself a car her senior year, but all she could afford was an old Ford Focus the color of rust. She didn't have a choice but to drive it when she moved to Miami. As much as she didn't want to be seen at the *Herald* driving that car, it was better than relying on the bus.

El Tropico on Northwest Thirty-sixth Street was always packed at noon. But because no one had time to kill on their lunch break in this warehouse district, tables usually opened up within minutes of a new group arriving. Melanie and Genesis were seated in an emerald-green booth behind a glass block wall that must have been installed during the seventies from the looks of it.

The smell of buttered Cuban toast and *cortaditos* enveloped the whole place. It still shocked Melanie how many people in Miami ate buttered toast alongside shots of espresso that had more sugar than caffeine. How were more people not falling over from heart attacks on the regular?

The hostess handed them each a menu and informed them, in Spanish, that their waitress would be right with them. Then she ambled away.

Even eight months into living in Miami, Melanie still hadn't gotten used to being surrounded by Latin culture on every front. Having Colombian parents didn't shield her from experiencing culture shock when she moved to Miami. Back home and in college, her immediate family were the only Latinos around. And she certainly never had to speak Spanish anywhere but home— she preferred it that way. Even though her parents spoke only Spanish to her, the language felt uncomfortable on her tongue in public.

Miami didn't seem to care about her preference. Living here felt like living in another country. In this city, it seemed the primary language was Spanish, and nobody fought it. She couldn't hide here either. Back home, Melanie was used to people consid-

ering her looks exotic, but most never assumed she spoke anything but English. Here, no matter where she went, people spoke
in Spanish first. Her dark hair and tawny-brown skin made her
heritage obvious.

The waitress approached their table, gripping a pitcher of
water that sweat profusely. *"Buenos dias, niñas. ¿Agua?"*

"Sí, gracias. Y dos cubanos, por favor," Genesis said. "Two
Cuban sandwiches, please."

Melanie looked up at the waitress and added, "No mustard
on my sandwich, please."

The waitress froze and stared at Melanie as if she'd spoken
Mandarin. After Melanie offered nothing in response, the woman
turned to Genesis.

"Uno sin mostaza, por favor," Genesis translated with an en-
dearing smile. The waitress gave a nod and turned to walk
toward a terminal to punch the order in.

"You always do that," Genesis said when the waitress was
out of earshot.

"Do what?"

"Anywhere we go, you respond in English. Why? Your
Spanish is perfectly good. I've heard you on the phone with your
mom."

Melanie shrugged. "I don't know. I'm just not used to it. I
only ever speak it with my mom."

"Well, you better get used to it, *chica*, because I won't always
be around to save you when you get a non-English-speaking
waitress. Besides, it's part of who you are. You should embrace
it. Especially in a place like Miami, where you don't get much of
a choice."

This wasn't the first time someone had said something like
this to Melanie. It always made her jaw clench, and she never

knew how to respond but to shrug. Why did everyone care so much about whether she chose to use her Spanish outside her family circle anyway?

"I know, I know. I'm still new here, okay? Give me some time to adjust," she said. "Can we talk about the real issue at hand? Why do you think Ignacio didn't publish my article?"

"Who knows? There could be a million reasons. Why don't you just try to forget it until you can talk to him? There's no sense in worrying yourself to death about it when it could be nothing."

"Gen, it's not nothing. You've seen the edits I've been getting back from Ignacio. There's always something wrong, and he doesn't explain what it is. And now he finally decided that instead of editing, he just wouldn't publish it. That has to be what happened."

"I don't know, maybe. Sure, I guess that could be a possibility. But I still think you should wait until you can talk to him and not waste time being anxious over it until you do."

"But you don't understand." She squeezed the edges of the table in search of something stable to steady her. It took everything in her to keep her tears inside their ducts. "I can't lose this job. I just can't. What would I do without it? Where would I go?" Her voice quickened as her heart began to accelerate. "I worked so hard to get here. I planned everything me-ti-cu-lous-ly. I prepared and studied in every waking moment that I had. I gave up friends, holidays, even boyfriends to get here. Man, and I spent sooo much money on that stinkin' life coach to help me craft the perfect ten-year plan. All so that I could create this life, you know? Create a future where I'm a journalist and earn good money and can buy the same things everyone else has."

She bit her tongue before she could continue. Her cheeks

burned from the heat they gave off. No doubt her face was as red as a strawberry right now. Genesis probably thought she sounded ridiculous—like a child. Melanie cradled her face. All she wanted was to curl up in a ball and cry.

"*Calmate.* Calm down, *mija.* I didn't know it was this bad." Genesis reached out and tapped a finger to Melanie's wrist until she lifted her head. "It's going to be okay. Take a deep breath. Go on, take a few."

Melanie looked her in the eyes and followed her instructions. She trusted Genesis more than she trusted anyone else in Miami. There was certainly no one else on the planet she would cry in front of.

"Let's just talk for a minute," Genesis said. "There's no need to panic—you haven't actually been fired. *Mira,* it takes time and practice, and life experience, to hone your voice as a writer. To get the hang of things. I laugh at the stuff I wrote when I was fresh out of college."

"But did any of your articles ever not make it into the paper?" Melanie asked with black mascara dripping down her cheeks.

Genesis glanced at the table before answering. "No. That never happened." Melanie's head fell backwards. "But that doesn't mean there wasn't a huge learning curve in the first few years of my career. And, by the way, my career today looks very different from how I thought it would look when I started more than ten years ago. And that's okay. I'm so grateful for where I am now. You have to be a little more flexible, *mija.* Life and work are full of challenges, and we have to be able to bend and sway . . . like the palm trees, you know?" Genesis smiled at her corny comparison. Melanie would normally appreciate her desperate attempt to try to lighten the mood, but today it was lost on her. There was too much to fret over.

"Says the girl who was hired at *The Boston Globe* fresh out of college." Melanie folded her arms on the table and rested her head on top.

The *Herald* was great, but it didn't hold a candle to *The Boston Globe*. And not only did Genesis get an offer to work there at twenty-one years old, but she achieved more in her three years working there than most journalists achieve in their entire career. Awards, promotions, and even multiple bylines on the *front* page.

"And look where I am now. . . . You may think getting to a place like the *Globe* is the ultimate goal for a journalist, but trust me, it's not. I spent my entire young adulthood rambling on and on about how I couldn't wait to get out of Miami. People think this is paradise, and I guess it is, but when you grow up here, all you dream about is living in a place with changing seasons, traffic that doesn't bring out your ugly side, and just a little less humidity.

"That's why I accepted the job at the *Globe*. But, man, after three years there, I'd had enough. Never in a million years would I have thought that I'd end up right back here after just a few years. But I missed home. I missed my city, my people. . . . The stories I get to cover here matter to people like me, and being at the *Globe* made me realize *this* is where I could make the most impact. A decade later, I still feel the same way."

"That's so great for you, Gen, but I don't have options like you do. There's no plan B . . . no other place for me to go. I have to succeed here or my future as a journalist is over. Who's going to hire me when I get fired from the *Herald?*"

Before Genesis could respond, the waitress dropped off two steamy sandwiches. It would be a shame to let the sandwich go to waste, but Melanie could stomach only half—her nerves filled up the rest of the space. Her friend, on the other hand, nearly licked her plate clean.

"Mmm, I never get tired of these. Anyway, I have a feeling the *Herald* isn't done with you yet. Let's be a little more positive, okay?"

Melanie nodded.

"You ready to get back?"

"Should I be honest or positive?"

Genesis gave her a wry smile. "All right, c'mon. Let's get it over with."

CHAPTER 3

"Oh no, is that Manuel?"

Too deep in thought, Melanie didn't hear Genesis or follow her sudden change of direction. She walked straight into Manuel's path and collided with his bulky left arm. The to-go coffee she'd bought at lunch went flying into the air and crashed onto the gray striped carpet, leaving a large wet spot right at the entrance to the office. But Manuel, the publisher of the *Herald*, didn't seem to notice, or maybe he didn't care. He brushed off his blazer and continued toward the elevator that would take him up to his corner office.

Genesis ran to the closest break room, grabbed a roll of paper towels, and came back to where Melanie stood to help her clean up the mess.

"What was *that* about? Did you not see him or something?" Genesis asked.

Melanie dabbed sweat off her forehead with the back of her hand before patting the carpet dry. "What else can go wrong today?" she grumbled. "What's he even doing down here? I thought he didn't venture through desks of writers on the lower rungs?"

"Who knows, but Ignacio does not look happy." Genesis

tipped her head in the direction of his office, where he sat behind his desk.

"Oh no, I was going to try to get to him first . . . before anyone could put him in a bad mood." How could Melanie's plan already be falling to pieces?

They stood and walked to their desks.

"He's not that scary. Just go talk to him," Genesis said as she sank into her chair.

"I don't even know what to say. I've been thinking about it the whole way back here, but I don't know if there's even a good way to start this conversation. I should just do him a favor and pack up my things and leave."

"*Ay, tumba eso ya*, Melanie. He's not going to fire you. Relax. Just go in there and get right to the point. You know he doesn't like it when people dance around a topic. Ask him what happened straight up and what you need to do to get better. There's really not much more to it. You'll be fine. I promise."

Melanie frowned. "You make it sound so easy."

"*Dale*. Go . . . now, before you change your mind." Genesis flicked her wrist to shoo her away.

A deep breath filled Melanie with the sliver of confidence she needed to swivel around in her chair and walk toward Ignacio's office. She prayed for a miracle. Maybe, just maybe, contrary to what Genesis had said, his meeting with Manuel had been a happy one.

Or maybe not.

What's Manuel doing back down here? Oh no, why is he walking toward Ignacio's office?

Melanie wouldn't be able to keep up with his long and heavy strides. And she didn't have to. Before she could reach his office, Ignacio stood from his desk and followed Manuel out into the newsroom.

Her pace slowed to a crawl, and her gaze followed them. It was clear that something big was about to happen.

There was only one place in the newsroom that wasn't crowded with desks and file cabinets. Manuel and Ignacio planted their feet in the middle of the large open area that featured a wall of televisions airing the twenty-four-hour news cycle from every affiliate imaginable. Even Spanish-language news had a dedicated flat-screen TV. Usually, reporters gathered there to watch breaking news hit or for the occasional town hall with corporate. Not today. Manuel yelled into the newsroom for everyone to gather where he stood.

Reporters, photographers, sales reps, and even copy editors looked up from their posts to confirm they'd heard correctly because the entire team hardly ever gathered in one place. Manuel's crossed arms and wide stance were enough to communicate to everyone that this was serious business and they'd better not make him wait too long. Headphones were removed, calls ended, and sentences left unfinished as everyone within earshot moved to gather around him.

Melanie looked for Genesis—she always provided additional commentary and context, when necessary, during meetings.

"Do you know what this is about?" Melanie asked Genesis when they found each other in the crowd.

"Who knows. . . . To tell us how terrible we are?"

"I don't like the look on Ignacio's face," Melanie whispered.

"*Pobrecito.* Feels like Manuel has been out to get him since he joined the exec team."

Behind Manuel, Ignacio looked like a scared child. Melanie had only ever seen him as the confident boss in charge. Sure, he was tough and didn't accept substandard work, but only because he cared about the reputation of the paper—something that was obvious from his high expectations. How strange to see him in such a vulnerable position.

Manuel didn't start the impromptu all-staff meeting with a greeting, an inspirational story, or any kind of recognition about the odd nature of this gathering on a random Friday afternoon. Hard facts: That's what he was good at.

"As you know, subscriptions to our paper are still down twelve percent year after year. At this rate, half of us in this room could be gone in three years. Is that what we want?"

Genesis leaned closer to Melanie. "Only if he's included in the half that leaves."

Melanie raised her eyebrows and nodded. "I just wish his tone wasn't so . . . brash."

"He puts so much pressure on everyone, especially Ignacio," Genesis responded. "If you ask me, trying to increase subscriptions by twenty percent over five years is a lofty goal. Even before Manuel came, subscriptions were taking a nosedive. That's not something we can fix overnight."

Manuel went on to discuss all that the team needed to do to keep the *Herald* from filing for bankruptcy. He said a large piece of the puzzle would be changing the kind of content they published.

Genesis continued, raising her voice just a little higher than Melanie felt comfortable with. "You know what, though? It's really frustrating that he constantly comes in here yelling about the standard of our work when he has no real experience in journalism. Who is he to tell us what works and what doesn't? He's just another business type who's read one book about the industry and now assumes he knows everything about how to do our jobs."

Melanie nodded while grinning—she loved how fiery Genesis became when she got worked up.

After a few more impassioned words from Manuel, Melanie's anxiety started to rise again. She slipped her hands into her pockets in an attempt to dry the moisture that had gathered on her palms. She knew about the decrease in subscriptions over the past few years—everyone did—but she had no idea it was this bad. So bad that the publisher had to fly in and talk to the team directly. Despite having his own office in the building, his visits had been infrequent until recently.

No matter what Genesis said, with her own work struggling, there was no doubt in Melanie's mind she'd be one of the first layoffs whenever those began. What would be the point in keeping her? She didn't have seniority, didn't have her own beat, and couldn't write an article good enough to print.

Maybe there was enough time to salvage her job and her place at the *Herald*. Maybe if she studied other articles a little bit harder and asked Genesis to review her work before turning it in to Ignacio, she could improve in time to save her spot here.

Manuel continued on a long spiel about not reaching millennials or Gen Z, not thinking creatively enough, and relying too much on ancient practices rather than innovating and getting ahead on trends. "If we can fix these things, I know we can get our numbers up," he said.

They'd all heard this sermon before—from someone who didn't work out of the *Herald* office on a regular basis. It was no wonder the eyes around the room seemed to glaze over with everything he said. It was easy for him to ask more of the team when he'd never rolled up his sleeves and taken a seat at the same table.

You could sense the morale being wrung out from the room like water from a soaked towel.

When he finally dismissed everyone, Melanie looked around at the crowd of employees and noticed an endless sea of slumped shoulders and long faces, including Ignacio's, wandering back to desks stacked with manila envelopes and cold coffee. It was a stark reminder that this was a tough business to be in.

But Melanie hadn't chosen it because it was an easy path to success. She knew journalism would be tough to break into, but she wanted it anyway.

From a very young age, she knew she could write. Words spilled out of her. It wasn't like math or science, which she struggled to pass. Writing came easy to her. Whether journalism wanted her or not didn't matter; she had to find her place in this business. There were no other options to help her secure a stable future.

She'd have to push Manuel's speech to the back of her mind. Now that Ignacio had returned to his desk, she had to find out what had happened to her article. This was the worst possible time to ask, but she couldn't wait a second longer to find out what she'd done wrong. She also felt an urge to reassure Ignacio that she would fix whatever she had to. And not only that, but that she was, in fact, capable of contributing articles that could help save the paper from its peril.

So rather than walk back to her desk with the rest of the melancholy reporters, she puffed up her chest, lifted her chin a bit higher, and cleared her throat.

Fake it till you make it, Melanie. It's now or never.

CHAPTER 4

Ignacio picked up a white mug with the *Herald* logo from the Keurig machine in the back right corner of his office. When he turned around to walk to his desk, he jumped at the sight of Melanie standing in the doorway. Manuel's talk must have made him extra jittery.

Some of the coffee splattered onto his shirt—at least it was a black shirt. Ignacio only wore black.

He looked up at her and back down at his shirt. "Great, now I have to—"

"Oh, I'm so sorry, Ignacio. I didn't mean to scare you. Do you need some napkins?"

"No, I'm fine, Melanie. What's up?"

She was off to a poor start. Her nerves increased tenfold and her mind went blank. What was the advice Gen had given her? But there was no time to think. Ignacio looked irritated, and he stared at her like he might assign her to the classifieds—or worse—at any moment.

Spit it out, Melanie!

"Just a quick question," she responded, trying to stay composed on the outside. "My article on the verdict of the Miller case was supposed to be in today's paper. I didn't see it there, and it's not online either. What happened? I'm sure I submitted the edited version on time." Melanie had a terrible habit of rambling when under stress. No exception now. "I looked through my checklist, and everything that needed to be in the piece was there. I even landed that important—"

"I didn't publish it." He dabbed at the wet spot on his shirt with his sleeve.

"Oh," she said, pausing so he could continue with an explanation.

No such luck. Ignacio stayed quiet as he walked back to his desk, swiped a finger over his trackpad to wake up his sleeping computer, and shuffled some of the papers scattered about.

"Um . . . is there a reason you didn't publish it? I wish you would have told me something was wrong with it. I would have stayed late to fix it." She felt like a complete fool standing in front of him. Why was he so short with her? He didn't act like this normally. While he wasn't your average happy-go-lucky guy, over the past few months he'd at least made an effort to guide and mold Melanie's work.

"It just wasn't up to par. You would have had to rewrite the whole thing, and there wasn't enough time for that before the deadline to send to print."

"Rewrite it? I don't understand. . . . I made all the revisions you requested the first time around. Did I miss one? I went through each one very carefully, I can assure you—"

"It wasn't enough. Your lead was still weak. The whole thing was weak. Sure, you got the attorney general to comment— that's great. But the whole thing felt sanitized. And, quite frankly, kind of boring."

"Is it possible to make education reform fun?" Melanie shouldn't have said this, but it just came out.

"It doesn't have to be fun. It does have to be engaging. Give people a reason to keep reading. We've talked about this before, about injecting something new and different into your work that will stand out from other papers. We can't keep writing like everyone else if we're going to stay relevant.

"And I can't keep spending this much time on your work, Melanie. I'm very busy. I've tried to be patient. I've tried to make time to sit with you and walk you through changes, but it's been almost a year, right?" He turned his body to face her directly and looked her straight in the eyes. "I can't spend more than thirty minutes on your articles anymore. You're a professional. And if your work requires more than that, then I'm going to move on. I'm sorry, but that's how it has to be."

Melanie nodded her head, waiting for the words to come— any words that would make for an acceptable response.

"Um . . . okay. I understand. I'll try harder." It was the best she could come up with.

"I'm not sure you need to try harder. You need to try something different. Sometimes I feel like you're trying to impress an Ivy League professor . . . or my grandfather. You need to start writing like you're talking to real people. Your work has gotten more stuffy and overly formal."

She squeezed her eyes shut for a moment and turned her head toward her shoulder.

"No matter your subject, you have to write your stories in a way that draws people in. Otherwise, why would readers choose our paper over any other? We've all got the same stories, so we have to give people a reason to choose us."

After a long, awkward silence, Ignacio turned his gaze back

to his computer, typed a few words, and turned his computer screen to face Melanie.

"When I hired you, I thought I'd be getting work like this." Ignacio had pulled up the email Melanie had sent him when she applied for the position. He clicked on the link to her online portfolio and found the story he referenced.

"This is the writer I wanted on this team," he said as he pointed to his screen. On his computer was an essay Melanie had written when she applied to the journalism program at Northwestern. It was about the struggles of being a cross-cultural child.

What is that doing on my website? I could have sworn I took that one down.

"Melanie," he said. He must have noticed her gaze drifting away. "What happened to this writer? That is not the same writer who wrote this." He shuffled papers around on his desk until he found the article she'd left the day before—the one he didn't publish.

"Who are you trying to imitate here?" Ignacio continued. "Did you pick up newspapers and start copying what other writers are doing? Just because something is published doesn't mean it's good."

Melanie's eyebrows drifted closer together as she stared at Ignacio in disbelief. Was he accusing her of the worst crime in journalism—plagiarism?

"I can assure you those are all my words. I didn't steal content from anyone."

"That's not what I said. Since you've started here, your work looks more like the mediocre stuff out in the world and less like this." He pointed at his computer screen again. "This has life and soul. It's filled with passion. It's writing that evokes emotion and allows the reader an opportunity to get lost in a story—truly lost. It's fun. Entertaining. Full of life and deep. After I interviewed you, I connected the two. I saw a writer who was full of life and who translated that onto a page. I don't know what's happened, but your work lately has not reflected that."

"Okay. I'll do better." She still didn't understand what she had to do better, but she had to say something to make him stop talking. How much longer could she stand the criticism?

Ignacio checked his watch, then closed his laptop. He stood up from his desk and walked past Melanie. "I'm late for a meeting. You can do better than this."

But Melanie was too jarred to move. Even if she'd wanted to lift her legs, she wouldn't have been able to. They'd become two oversized tree trunks with roots deep down into the earth.

Did that just happen? Is this a nightmare?

Ignacio's words bounced around in her head, causing a ringing in her ears.

Sanitized . . . Boring . . . Spending hours on my work . . . Weak?

Could all that be true? How could it be when she spent every waking hour of her life perfecting her work? Even her weekends were spent in the library reviewing archives of the *Herald*. She'd always written her articles by the book, so how could Ignacio disapprove of them?

Before she could continue spiraling, she heard a familiar voice behind her.

"Mel? What are you doing?" Genesis's voice confirmed the unfortunate truth that she hadn't dreamt any of Ignacio's words.

"What just happened?" Melanie asked, still facing Ignacio's desk.

"What? What are you talking about, Mel? You're being weird. What's going on?"

Her friend's presence brought air back into the room, allowing Melanie to breathe and move again. She turned to face Genesis. "Ignacio . . . My work . . . I'm gonna get fired any day now."

"Fired? What's going on? Are you okay?"

When Melanie didn't respond, Genesis walked over to her and put her arm around her shoulder. "Come. I'm sure you're not fired. They only fire people on Mondays. Let's get you back to your desk. Feels weird to be in here when Ignacio is not."

Melanie sat down at her desk, but before Genesis could join her, she was pulled into a small huddle by two other reporters. There wasn't any time to wait for their impromptu meeting to end. She grabbed her satchel and searched inside for a white three-ring binder that traveled to work with her each day. It was her vision binder, as she called it. Inside it lived one divider separating archived pieces of her work from the work of other writers. Writers she admired. Writers whose work she'd spent hours reading and rereading, dissecting every word, hoping to somehow unlock the secret to their brilliance.

Whenever she was assigned a piece similar to one she had saved, she'd open the binder in search of inspiration. She'd carefully study how the writer before her had structured the story, taking note of the questions they must have asked to get those answers from their interviewee. And the specific images they described in the scene or the way they used analogies and metaphors to bring the reader into their subject's world.

As she would reread these articles she'd saved, she'd take notes in the margins—*described the kitchen for three lines, included the dog who barked outside, waited three paragraphs to introduce the subject,* etc. She investigated every line, determined to be as great as the folks who'd been somehow lucky enough to get a byline in these prestigious publications.

She didn't just study their work; she studied their lives. On nights when she couldn't sleep, she'd grab her phone and search the names of some of the writers in her binder. She wanted to learn how they had reached their success. Late into the night, she'd look up where they went to college, what they studied, where they worked after graduation, how long they worked there, what stories they published there, and the entire list of jobs they had before their current position.

At one point, Melanie even considered taking a waitressing job on the weekends because she'd noticed in a few research sessions that various prominent writers waited tables on the side when they first started out. Could that be where they found inspiration?

If there was a time when she needed insight into their classified world, it was right now.

She laid out a hard copy of her article next to the binder. Ignacio had used many callous words to describe her latest work, but she needed more specifics.

Where did I go wrong? Where exactly?

First, she reviewed the checklist she'd created and laminated—the one she intentionally placed after the cover.

The lead is not buried? Check.

There are at least two interviews to provide sufficient perspectives? Check.

There are no misplaced commas or passive voice? Check.

There's a good mixture of short and long sentences? Check.

I didn't insert my opinion or imply it? Check.

Check, check, check.

Technique-wise, everything in the article was pristine. Was it her word choice, then? Her lack of humor? But again, how could one make education reform humorous?

"What are you doing?" Genesis asked when she returned to her desk. "What happened back there anyway?" She leaned in and moved closer to Melanie's seat.

"It was intentional. Ignacio didn't publish my article because apparently my writing isn't good enough to print."

"He said that?"

"Not in those exact words, but yes. My writing is not up to par." She bit her nails to keep from grinding her teeth. "So here I am, trying to dig deeper into what in the world is wrong with my work lately. He told me my article had no life, but what does that even mean? I thought maybe I could find the answer inside here." She lifted the open binder with her fingertips and let gravity bring it back down to her desk.

Genesis reached for the binder to get a closer look. She flipped through the laminated articles, her eyebrows dancing with each turn of a page. "What is this? Some kind of shrine for other writers?"

"Well, some of my work is in there too, but yes. I like to read them when I'm working sometimes."

"Do you think that maybe this has something to do with it?" she said with her eyebrows still raised.

"Has something to do with what?"

"With what Ignacio said. Maybe there's no life in your work because you're preoccupied with trying to match other people's rather than writing from your own voice."

Melanie flinched as if the words themselves had tried to strike her.

"I'm just looking at their work for inspiration . . . ideas . . ." She reached for the binder, closed it, and placed it back in her satchel.

"And there's nothing inherently wrong with that. I'm just saying, maybe you're trying so hard to be like other writers that you're missing out on the excellent writer who's already inside you."

Melanie's gaze drifted as she thought about what Genesis had said.

Could she be right? What was *her* voice anyway?

Her eyes landed on the giant clock above their pod. She released a deep sigh. "It's time for the pitch meeting. You think I'll be allowed in?"

"There's only one way to find out. *Vamos.*"

CHAPTER 5

Melanie stroked her twill pants, hoping to dry her palms again. Her knee bounced while she worked to avoid eye contact with every reporter stuffed inside the conference room.

The afternoon pitch meeting used to be her favorite part of each day. The room always oozed with passion and energy. It was fast-paced and exhilarating, and Melanie loved to watch seasoned reporter after seasoned reporter toss out updates on their work and pitch unique angles on stories from around the world. It still felt like a dream to be among so many brilliant journalists who could easily work at any major publication.

They were all so confident. She envied that—especially now. Perhaps some of them considered her to be confident like them. But deep down inside, she was a mess of nerves and insecurities, wondering whether she would ever truly measure up to Ignacio's standards.

Sure, Melanie walked around with her head held high, and she was one of the only general-assignment reporters who spoke up in meetings. It was what she felt she had to do to prove herself. To prove she deserved a seat at that table. That she hadn't been offered a job at the *Herald* for any reason except that she was a good writer, a good reporter—like everyone else. She hated feeling like she still had to convince people of that. Wasn't her badge enough to prove she belonged here? It didn't feel like it.

She had to do better. She had to try harder. She wouldn't allow herself to go down this easily.

You will figure this out. You're not done here yet. Show them what you're capable of.

Ignacio leaned back in the chair at the head of the table—so far he could have taken a nap. Each reporter made eye contact with him as they provided an update one at a time. Occasionally, someone would jump in with a suggestion of whom the reporter should interview or offer a connection that might help them get a piece to the story that no other paper would have. Despite the journalism industry being such a cutthroat business, this meeting always made Melanie feel like they were a harmonious team all working for one mission.

"Okay, great work, everyone," Ignacio said, wrapping up the updates portion of the meeting.

Except for me.

Ignacio sat upright. "Let's hear pitches for next week now."

Jordan, the senior sports reporter, pitched an update to a story the paper had covered ten years before. Claudia, who covered immigration, wanted to travel to L.A. to cover the state sanctuary law that was about to go into effect. The arts and entertainment reporter, Danny, took the story on the anniversary of the opening of Versailles—a beloved staple in Miami. Michelle, who covered local and state government, volunteered to attend the press conference with the governor downtown. And Caroline, who normally covered health and fitness, wanted to look into a story about a nine-year-old boy undergoing the first ever gene therapy surgery to restore his vision.

People pitched stories both near and far, and when there were no more pitches to go around, Ignacio ran down a list of general-assignment stories he needed reporters to pick up.

Melanie's stomach churned. She sat quietly, waiting for the perfect opportunity to volunteer for a story. But nothing stuck out to her. She needed something that would impress Ignacio and put her on an uphill trajectory at the paper. While she wasn't sure where she stood after their conversation in his office—who knew if he would even allow her a story this week—she had to try.

"Okay, the last story I need someone to take is an international one. Mike will be on his honeymoon, so I need someone else to cover the Latin America beat. Rise in crime and deaths suspected from an increase of cocaine smuggled in from Colombia. I need someone in Bogotá early next week to cover the president's address. Who wants it?"

The room was quiet, but after a few moments, Claudia spoke up.

"Melanie, aren't you Colombian? You should take this story. You'd offer an interesting perspective."

Melanie and Genesis locked eyes from across the glass table. Genesis tilted her head and pursed her lips. Before Melanie could respond, Claudia spoke again.

"You've been there, haven't you?"

Melanie looked back at Genesis once more before responding. "Um, yeah. I'm from there. I'd love to take the story, Ignacio. Maybe my mom can even help me land some interviews since she grew up there."

She couldn't believe what she'd just done, but there was no

turning back now. Ignacio touched the base of his neck and looked around the room. Melanie scooted back in her seat and sat up straighter. There was an awkward silence that only made her bouncing knee pick up speed.

"I'll help her," said a familiar voice. Melanie turned and looked at Genesis with squished eyebrows and a quick head shake.

What are you doing? she wanted to say.

There was no denying it—Genesis had just thrown Melanie a life preserver in the middle of raging waters. But did she realize, in doing so, she'd thrown herself into the deep as well?

Genesis and Ignacio stared at each other for what felt like an eternity. Melanie didn't take another breath until Ignacio broke the silence. "Fine," he said as he squared up the sheets of paper he held in his hands before standing to walk out of the conference room.

Melanie took a deep breath. Ignacio had allowed her to take this story, which meant she still had a job—at least for another week.

When the room cleared out, Melanie and Genesis stayed behind. From the look on Genesis's face, Melanie could tell she had a lot of questions for her.

When every colleague was out of earshot, Genesis swallowed and looked down at the floor before speaking.

"Okay, am I crazy or do I remember you telling me when I first met you that you've never been to Colombia?"

"You're not crazy." Where was her water bottle when she needed it? She already knew what Genesis was about to say. She'd made a serious error in judgment, but could Genesis blame her? Desperate times call for desperate measures.

"And you didn't think you needed to mention that when Claudia assumed you'd been there?"

"I don't know, Gen. People always assume I know everything about Colombia just because my parents were born there, and I usually just go with it—it's easier than explaining. Plus, it all happened so fast. And when Ignacio didn't immediately reject the idea of me taking the story, I panicked. It was the last story he offered. It was my only option.

"I've got to produce something new . . . something big if I'm going to get back in his good graces. And then you jumped in offering to help. What was I supposed to do? Should I have—"

"I get it. I get it. But one surefire way to lose your place here is to lose Ignacio's trust, and you're dangerously close to doing that. It's too late to do anything about it now. At this point, it would only make things worse."

Melanie had never seen Genesis so upset, especially at her. Since Melanie's first day on the job, Genesis had been like her fairy godmother—always helpful, always encouraging, and always available to listen to her woes. Right now, she was more like a school principal than a friend.

"So, what should I do now?" Melanie asked.

"What do you mean what should you do? The only thing you can do. Write a really good story and hope this never comes up again."

Melanie closed her eyes and pinched the bridge of her nose. "I shouldn't have done that. That was so stupid of me. If I get caught—"

"Don't even go there. Listen, we've all been there, especially early on in our careers when we're just trying to prove ourselves. I know you're in a tough place right now and it's hard to see beyond today, but this business is a relationship business. I think the best thing to do now is move on. What's done is done. Get your head straight and write a story Ignacio can't deny is good, okay? You never know—maybe this story is exactly what you need to find that X factor you've been missing. And maybe you'll even have a little fun while you're there. I think you could use some of that."

A brief smile emerged on Melanie's face, but she made eye contact for only a moment before looking back down.

"Hey . . . *¡anímate!* I know you can do this. You're capable. You're a great writer, and few people have as much *chispa* as you. And you know I'll always help you however I can."

"I feel like I just put your job on the line here. What if I don't nail this story? He's going to ask you about it, no?"

"*Ay,* don't worry about me. I'll be fine. Just focus on the story."

They walked back to their desks and sat down.

"Why don't you get your travel booked while I start some preliminary research?" Genesis said.

Perfect. An assignment that didn't require much thought. Melanie needed a little more time to come to grips with what she'd done. She slipped on her earbuds, hoping calming music would help her relax.

It took only about an hour to book her flights and reserve a hotel room and car service to and from the airport.

She took out her earbuds and noticed her phone vibrating in her back pocket. It was her mother again. Melanie needed a refill on her coffee, so she stood up and answered the call on her way to the break room.

"*¿Q'hubo, mija?*"

"I'm working, Mom. What's up?" She tried not to sound frustrated at the fact that her mother would think it okay to call twice in one day during work hours.

"Listen, I forgot to ask you . . . Do you have anything you don't wear anymore that I can take with me to Colombia? Maybe you can meet me quickly at the airport during my layover to bring me anything you have?"

Melanie often got this type of call from her mother whenever she traveled to her home country. One never traveled to Colombia empty-handed—it was a grave sin, her mother always told her. It's just what you did when you visited, no matter your personal financial situation. While Anita wasn't considered wealthy here in America—by any means—she had a great abundance compared to the people she knew and loved in Cali, Colombia.

Melanie grabbed the industrial-sized pot of coffee off the hot plate and poured what looked like black tar into her mug. She took one look inside her mug before pouring the drink out into the sink. There was no telling how old that coffee was. She pinned her phone between her ear and shoulder while she prepped a new pot to brew.

"Sure, Mom. I'll look around." Before her mother could respond, Melanie let the details of her trip slip. "Oh, wait a minute. What time is your layover? I'm actually traveling to Colombia too. But I'm going to Bogotá."

"*¿Que?*"

Melanie immediately regretted having told her mother about her trip. She already knew there would be some kind of request coming next. But it was too late now. The news was out, so she might as well share the rest.

"I'm going to Bogotá," she repeated. "For work." Every conversation required repeating what she'd said at least once. She'd learned early on to keep the details to a minimum—the vaguer she was, the less she'd have to explain.

"*Ay,* then why don't you come to Cali with me first? It's your grandmother's ninetieth birthday and she would love to see you. It's only like an hour flight to Bogotá from there."

"What? No, I can't, Mom. I'm going for work. This isn't a vacation." This was so like her mother—trying to turn a business trip into a vacation. Melanie's job was already on the line, and there was no way she was going to do anything to make it worse. She wished her mother could understand that.

"Just come for a few days. You don't have to stay the whole week. The party is tomorrow. Stop by, say hello to everyone, and then you can fly to Bogotá. Juan Carlos can give you a ride to the airport. Your grandmother only turns ninety once, and you haven't seen her since she visited for your *quinceañera*. That would be the best birthday gift for her. Plus, she's not well, *mija*. We just don't know how much time she has left. Why do you think I've been visiting more than normal? Every trip I take, I wonder if it will be the last time I see her alive."

Melanie took a pained breath, closed her eyes, and rubbed her temples.

Her mother had a point. Her grandmother had heart failure, but she'd been diagnosed many years ago and she seemed to be doing okay. She still worked the little general store she set up in her living room a few hours a day and even sewed clothes for people in her community—she was a gifted seamstress. So, while her health wasn't perfect, she always seemed to be doing fine. But then again, she was turning ninety. How much longer could she live with a failing heart?

Still on the phone, Melanie walked back toward her desk and stopped in her tracks when she noticed Genesis laughing with Danny, who sat on the other side of her. She marveled at how much fun Genesis seemed to have while working in such a demanding industry. Somehow she made it look effortless to be a serious, accomplished journalist and a carefree human being at the same time. What a strange but beautiful contradiction she was.

Then, in that moment, watching Genesis throw her head back in laughter and lightheartedness, Melanie remembered something Genesis had said just an hour earlier: *You could use some fun.* And she had to admit, it would be really fun to see her grandmother again.

She'd have to be in Bogotá by Monday, but would it really hurt her to spend a few days visiting her grandmother? There would probably never come a time again when she would be so close to her grandmother's home. Something told her she'd regret passing on this opportunity.

Just this once, it would be okay to spend a little downtime visiting her ailing grandmother. And it felt good to finally give her mother a yes.

"Okay, Mom. But I have to be in Bogotá no later than Monday morning. This story in Bogotá is super important for my career. I cannot mess this up." Melanie sat down with her piping hot cup of coffee. She'd have to update all the travel she'd just booked before leaving the office for the day.

"*¡Que bueno, mija!* Let me know what flight you get on so we can meet at the airport in Cali. *Bueno pues,* I'll call you tomorrow."

Melanie hung up and placed her phone facedown on her desk. "How does she always end up getting what she wants?"

"Who, your mom?" Genesis smiled. "Hispanic moms have a way of doing that."

"Somehow she got me to agree to go with her to Cali before I go to Bogotá. I mean, I'm excited to see my grandmother— I haven't seen her since I was fifteen. But I also feel like maybe I should get to Bogotá tomorrow to scope things out before the president's address. It's not like I can just fly back to Bogotá if I forget something. I have to be on top of my game." Melanie took a sip from her mug before spitting it back out. "Ouch."

"That's amazing! You've never been to your motherland before, and you finally get to go on the *Herald*'s dime. It could be really fun. You'll get to meet all the extended family members you've never met. You don't know what I would give to meet all the cousins I have in Cuba."

Melanie gave an empathetic smile. "You're right. It will be nice. I just wish it was happening on a different weekend. Not the weekend I should be getting ready for this story."

"There's no reason you can't write an excellent story while also visiting your family. You're going to burn out if you don't learn how to have a little fun sometime soon." Genesis stood, grabbed two sheets of paper, and walked toward the copy editor's desk.

It was good timing because Melanie didn't have any more time to waste. She dialed the travel planner's extension to have her update her itinerary—it would be faster than email. Once Genesis was back, they could start combing through research, planning her interviews, and outlining her article.

She had only the evening before she'd be on a flight headed to Colombia. The clock was ticking—faster it seemed—and every single minute was an opportunity to get closer and closer to proving Ignacio wrong. To saving her job. To getting back on her perfectly polished ten-year plan. There would be no more detours—not even one.

PART 2

CHAPTER 6

CALI, COLOMBIA

MELANIE

How could one small woman carry that many oversized suitcases?

Melanie and Anita stood at baggage claim in Alfonso Bonilla Aragón International Airport in Cali, Colombia, for twenty minutes waiting for the extra luggage Anita had checked. It had probably taken three large men to get those giant suitcases full of clothes, shoes, and even small household appliances onto the conveyor belt. Not even Santa Claus brought this many gifts to Cali.

A slight moan escaped Melanie when they walked outside into the muggy air, arms aching because her mother refused to pay for a luggage cart. It wasn't long before Anita spotted her older brother, Juan Carlos, who stood outside the passenger door of his yellow taxi. Melanie had seen photos here and there of her uncle, but had she been alone, there's no way she would have been able to pick him out in a crowd.

Anita yelled his name and started toward him.

"Is all of this even going to fit in there?" Melanie asked as they power walked to Juan Carlos's four-door sedan. Either there had been miscommunication about how much luggage Anita would have or Juan Carlos planned to make multiple trips.

"Definitely," Anita responded, the widest smile on her face.

While Melanie could appreciate anybody who lived with a sense of determination, her mother's version had a tendency to inconvenience her. She would force things to fit by any means possible. Which, in this scenario, meant Melanie would have to ride to her grandmother's home squished between bulky suitcases.

Juan Carlos greeted his sister with a big kiss on the cheek and a warm embrace that lifted Anita off her feet. He was much taller than Melanie had expected him to be—almost six feet. He wore faded jeans with a loose-fitting T-shirt tucked in and a brown leather belt that cinched the two together at his waist. His eyes were small and narrow, and his wide shoulders could match any linebacker's.

Droplets of sweat gathered on Melanie's lower back as she watched two siblings who, it was clear, longed to live closer than a continent apart. Juan Carlos's eyes were squeezed shut as if nothing else in the world mattered right now except taking in every second of this embrace.

"This is why everyone calls him *Oso*. Bear," Anita said as Juan Carlos lowered her to the ground. "His hugs are famous in Cali."

Melanie smiled and clutched the handle of her carry-on bag. She reached out her free hand for a handshake, but the gesture must have been foreign to him. Before she could think of what to say, he lifted her up in an embrace as if he'd been waiting for this moment his entire life.

"*¡Por fin! ¡Que gusto en conocerte, Melanie!*" he said in Spanish. "Finally! It's so nice to meet you, Melanie!"

"Whoa!" Melanie shrieked. Her legs and arms went stiff as

they hung in the air. Something about being near her uncle took her back to her childhood—not the childhood when she'd often clashed with her mother, but the childhood she'd almost forgotten. In a brief moment of vulnerability, she released the weight she'd been carrying on the five-hour flight and wrapped her arms around her uncle's neck.

"It's so good to finally meet you too, *Tio*." When Juan Carlos placed Melanie back on her two feet, she caught a close glimpse of his face. There was something about his eyes that gave her the freedom to take a deep breath.

Like the sound of a leaky faucet, the fear of losing her job had kept her on edge until this very moment. And not only that, but the real fear of traveling to Colombia.

And who could blame her? What with all the stories and comments she'd heard growing up from adults around her, anyone would be afraid to visit this country.

When Melanie was a child in New York, her home was often filled to the brim with her parents' friends, most of whom were immigrants as well. Their conversations almost always reverted to each person's home country. With boisterous voices, they'd talk about what they missed, the current political climate in each place, a new expat they'd met, and so on.

Whenever her parents brought up their beloved country, someone in the room would undoubtedly laugh, scoff, and even, at times, grow angry at the positive things they had to say. They'd counter her parents' fond memories with criticisms of the Colombian government and horror stories of kidnappings and child soldiers. Melanie even remembered rare moments when tears would emerge when people spoke of a man named Pablo Escobar—she came to understand the meaning behind the man's name only when she was much older.

While the other kids in the home entertained themselves

with cartoons or games, Melanie listened intently to the adult conversations. No part of her wanted to believe what these people had to say about her parents' country. She wanted to believe all the beautiful things her parents, especially her mother, bragged about. But when Melanie noticed that her mother never packed jewelry or clothes with obvious brand names for her trips to Colombia and that she always hid a thin fanny pack underneath her shirt to carry her money, she began to wonder whether perhaps, deep down, her mother knew these comments to be true.

The safety she'd felt in Juan Carlos's hug lasted only a brief period of time before all the memories came flooding back.

"How long is the drive to your house, Juan Carlos?" Melanie tried not to sound worried. But she'd be lying if she didn't admit she was anxious to get to a safe place where she didn't feel so . . . exposed.

"Only fifteen minutes. Your *abuela* cannot wait to see you. I bet she'll be waiting right out front for us." Juan Carlos still lived with his mother, Melanie's grandmother. He was in his late fifties now, but he'd never moved out. She'd never wondered why until this moment.

He tied suitcases to the roof of the car, stuffed two of them in the trunk, and placed the rest in the back seat, leaving just a few inches of space for Melanie. Once they were on their way to her grandmother's house, Melanie pulled out her phone and attempted to activate the international plan she'd purchased at the Miami airport. Spending the weekend in Cali didn't mean she could disconnect from work.

"Look, *mija*. Look around. This is my city," Anita said, staring out the window of the passenger seat.

Melanie lifted her eyes momentarily. The road was surrounded by big, lush trees on either side, and every few minutes, they'd pass a structure that looked like it'd seen better days.

When the car slowed and turned off the two-lane freeway, Melanie looked up from her phone. She'd had no luck accessing her email.

The homes and businesses were getting closer and closer together, and she noticed decrepit structures made of brick that looked abandoned.

They turned right at the next intersection, and there, on the corner, was another simple structure made of brick and cement. But this time, she saw a familiar sight: Her grandmother pushed herself up from a white plastic chair and walked toward the sidewalk.

Her entire life, whenever her mother spoke about her neighborhood, Melanie always imagined a dusty desert with shanty homes. She had no idea why she pictured her mother's hometown as a desert, but she'd been dead wrong. There weren't expansive lands of dust or sand but endless rows of concrete sidewalks with a few trees scattered about. It reminded her of Brooklyn, not the Wild West.

Desert or not, the neighborhood worried Melanie. She'd be sleeping here a couple of nights, and it felt anything but safe.

When Juan Carlos opened Melanie's door to let her out, she nearly fell onto the sidewalk. She gathered herself, shook out her legs, and looked up at the home.

The white cement box was surrounded by a retaining wall made of bricks about hip height. Black steel bars enclosed the rest of the home for extra protection, and an aluminum roof provided the front patio with a shady place to sit. There was a black metal gate in the front center, and that's where Melanie met her grandmother, Alba, after almost ten years of being apart.

"*Ay, mija, que gusto en verte. Me has hecho tanta flata.*" Melanie didn't hear anything her grandmother said. She buried herself in the smell of *arroz con leche.* Her grandmother always smelled of that sweet, lumpy dessert.

She pulled away from her grandmother to get a look at her face. The wrinkles around her eyes and mouth had gotten deeper, and her hair was shorter and whiter than she remembered. But her chocolate-brown eyes were exactly the same—warm, inviting, and on the mysterious side. "Hi, *Abuela.* It's so good to see you. I've missed you too."

Melanie brought her close for another hug; she wanted to breathe in that sweet treat one more time. When she stood back, she attempted to walk back to the car to get her bags, but her grandmother grabbed her wrist and redirected her. "Come, come inside. I made *arepas.*"

It was so like her grandmother to offer food right away, as if they needed nothing more than a warm cheesy corn cake to reconnect after almost a decade apart.

"Is that your *tiendita?*" Melanie asked her grandmother when they crossed the threshold of her home and into a room that resembled the *bodegas* she remembered from her childhood in New York City.

"*Sí, mi amor,* it's still going strong after all these years," Alba said.

The little store her grandmother had set up in her home when her children were young had a large window directly across the room. Alba used it as a walk-up window to sell her goods so that customers didn't have to come inside her home. Short shelves lined the walls and were stocked with small treats, drinks, household items, and even a few dresses with intricate details. Even from afar, Melanie could tell they were beautiful dresses that must have taken her grandmother days to make.

On the opposite side of the store was a small living room with worn furniture you could tell, though old, had been well taken care of. A few family photos sat scattered around the room in chipped frames, and others lined the walls of the hallway that led to the kitchen. When they walked into the kitchen, Alba took Melanie's satchel off her shoulder and pointed at a chair that was tucked beneath her round wooden table.

Melanie took a seat, and her mouth instantly salivated at the tall stack of *arepas* at the center of the table—although uncovered, they still looked warm and cheesy. Anita and Juan Carlos walked into the kitchen just a few moments later. They each sat down while Melanie's grandmother placed small plates and mugs in front of them. Then she moved over to the stove to prepare fresh *café con leche*.

Melanie had grown up eating *arepas* with *café con leche* in her own home. But there was something special about having them made by her *abuela* in the country where they originated.

Without even asking whether anybody would like some, Alba filled each of their mugs. The sweet smell and luscious golden-brown color intoxicated Melanie. She slurped her coffee between big bites of the tender corn cakes. She could eat this all day.

After consuming two *arepas* and a second cup of coffee, Melanie pushed her plate away to force herself to stop. Not even the Colombian bakeries she grew up driving to with her family could stand up against her *abuela*'s cooking. It was as if everything Alba touched, no matter how simple, turned into a delicacy.

"Aren't you going to have some, *Abuela*?" Melanie said. Alba had taken a seat at the table and slowly sipped her coffee while watching her family eat.

"I'm too busy enjoying the view," Alba said. "I never thought I'd have you here eating at my dining table. I'm soaking it in."

"Mmm, *Abuela,* there's something different about your *arepas,*" Melanie said.

"*Abuelas* have a special superpower," Anita said.

Alba smiled and nodded. "She's right. God gives our hands a special ability to lure our kids and grandkids into visiting us." They all laughed and finished off the stack of *arepas* on the table.

"Well, I'd better get settled and check my email before I eat another ten pounds' worth," Melanie said as she scooted her chair back from beneath the table.

Her grandmother also stood. "Come, I'll show you your room. I hope it's okay that you're sharing with your mom. I didn't want to ask Juan Carlos to sleep on the couch."

"My back thanks you, Melanie," Juan Carlos said with a mouthful of food.

Melanie smiled. "It's no problem at all." It had been many years since she'd shared a bed with her mother, but she'd do it for her grandmother.

Her room was the one at the far end of the hallway. It wasn't very impressive, but it contained everything she needed for her short stay. There was a small window on the opposite end of the room. Beneath the window was a queen-size bed and small end table, and a wooden chair stood by the closet.

"This was your mother's bedroom growing up, did you know? I guess it was also your *tias* Diana and Carolina's room as well. All three of them shared this room and slept on that bed together," Alba said as she watched Melanie look around the room and drop her satchel onto the bed.

"All three of them in here?" she responded. She walked over to the closet and peeked inside, only to confirm it was much too small for three young girls to share.

"Mm-hmm. I'll let you get settled. We'll be in the kitchen,

but you rest as much as you need. I know you had a long trip here."

Melanie let out a sigh of relief when her grandmother closed the door behind her. Relieved she'd made it to her grandmother's home safely and relieved she now had a few hours alone to get her email up and running and catch up on work before her grandmother's birthday celebration that evening. This might be her only opportunity today to get some work done. She had to make the most of it. There was too much on the line to take even one full day off.

CHAPTER 7

She wouldn't feel settled until her suitcase was emptied and her clothes neatly stored away. Packing for her time in Cali had been more of a challenge than Melanie expected.

Considering how often her mother talked about what her living conditions were like when she was a child, Melanie wanted to be thoughtful about the kind of attire she packed. She'd been raised hearing the stories of outgrown shoes patched with rubber from old tires and having meat on the table once or twice a week. While Melanie never thought her family had much in the United States compared to her peers, Anita always made it clear they were immensely wealthy compared to her family back in Colombia.

Considering she was a rookie journalist with hefty student debt, it wasn't hard to find clothes to pack that would help her blend in—nothing flashy that would draw attention. She grabbed all the white and blue T-shirts she owned and packed her rubber flip-flops rather than branded slides or sneakers. In Bogotá—the big city—she could get away with wearing a few nicer pieces for the interviews she had lined up, but in Cali, she wanted to blend into the background.

Once her clothes hung neatly in the bare closet and her empty suitcase was tucked away, she walked over to the bed, scooted back against the headboard, and pulled her laptop out of her satchel. It was time to get to work.

Scrolling through headlines of Colombian publications made it clear why impartiality was a constant battle in journalism. No matter how hard a person tried, personal life experience often colored how someone perceived a story or event. Just a quick scan of the headlines showed a widely different perspective on the drug trafficking issue than appeared in U.S. publications.

Bogotá insisted they were moving in the direction of peace with the largest group of rebels, resulting in an obvious decline in drug trafficking and all the violence that comes with it. Miami claimed the exact opposite. They reported that Colombian officials still hadn't done enough to control the drug trade, evidenced by the continued rise in deaths and gang violence. According to Miami, peace with the rebels wasn't nearly enough to make a significant impact.

Melanie considered what felt like two opposing views.

Miami had to be the voice of truth, right? They were the ones experiencing the real impact of Colombia's supposed leniency. Plus, why would Colombia admit any wrongdoing? Of course they would advocate for their own innocence.

Her lips curled inward, and she turned her gaze away from her computer screen. She'd need to do more digging before deciding what to share and what not to share in her article.

Maybe my abuela or mom will have some advice. . . . No, I can't ask them. They'll say the same things these Bogotá papers say.

She slouched and rubbed the back of her neck, her eyes feeling heavy and dry. Maybe a catnap would help. The night before, she'd slept only two hours. And she'd been too anxious on the flight to get any shut-eye. To say she was exhausted would be an understatement. Genesis's warning from the day before about burning out tickled her ear.

As much as she didn't want to, she had to heed her advice right now. Hopefully, a short nap would clear her mind enough to comb through the abundance of information later.

She closed her laptop, probably more forcefully than she should have, and leaned over to the end table by the bed to store the computer out of sight. But when she opened the drawer, something caught her eye.

Inside the drawer was a worn leather journal. Melanie had an affinity for notebooks. Back at her mother's home, she had multiple plastic bins that were bursting at the seams with pages she filled with stories of her life, both true and exaggerated. It must have been years since she journaled—what a shame. College and now work occupied every moment of her life.

This one was beautiful—she had to get a closer look. She picked it up and replaced it with her computer. Before she opened the journal, she lifted it to her nose: *Mmm, real leather.* She brought it down to her lap and stroked the front and back, secretly hoping it hadn't been used so she could take it home and add it to her collection. Maybe journaling would help her relax.

The notebook was bound with a leather string. Without thinking too much about it, she began unwinding it slowly. Like opening a gift, every go-around of string elevated her pulse, and she held on to hope that she'd just discovered an antique she could keep.

To her disappointment, the journal was covered in cursive writing from front to back. It made Melanie want to pick up the old-fashioned way of penmanship—how beautiful it looked inside a worn leather journal. She leafed through the pages. She admired how the worn edges gave the notebook a charming antique look and how the writer hadn't allowed even an inch of each page to go unused.

Who could this journal belong to?

Curiosity kicked in and Melanie read the first page without giving confidentiality a second thought:

February 7, 1987

My father had another one of his festivities of drunkenness yesterday, but this time, he went too far. . . .

CHAPTER 8

FEBRUARY 7, 1987
CALI, COLOMBIA

ANITA

"**W**hat do you mean you left home?" The first thing Anita did when she moved out of her childhood home was call her sister Carolina, who'd been living in America for three years.

"Exactly as it sounds, and I'm not going back," Anita said.

"But did something happen? I know *Papi* comes home drunk most Friday nights, but did something else happen?"

Anita pressed the phone to her ear using her shoulder for support. Every shirt she placed in the wooden chest of drawers in her new—temporary—room felt like another callus forming on her heart. What would happen when it became completely hardened?

"I should have known better than to invite Armando over on a Friday night. Three years of dating and he's never seen *Papi* like he did last night. How could I have let my guard down like that? It was so stupid of me!"

"Anita, *que paso?* What happened?"

Anita pictured her sister shaking her hand in the air—the way she always did when she became exasperated.

"*Papi* pulled out his gun."

Carolina gasped. "What? You're kidding."

"I wish I was, Carolina. He pointed it at me . . . well, at the sky, but it was meant to scare me."

"But why?"

"How am I supposed to know? I'm not even sure why I'm so surprised, what with the madness he brings upon our home every weekend. I guess it was time to take things to the next level. He must have been getting bored with the usual music blaring and him yelling like a maniac to wake everybody up." Anita paused and looked up, trying to keep her eyes from watering.

"Poor Manny," Anita continued. "I shouldn't have left him. I need to get him out of there."

"What did he do to Manny?"

"It's my fault, Carolina. I wasn't watching the clock like I should have been. I could have stopped the whole thing from happening . . . could have kept him from ever going into Manny's room. I could have locked his bedroom door, guarded it before he could reach it.

"But I was distracted. The one night I think it's okay to have company, *Papi* comes home early. When I heard the metal gate out front slam shut, my entire body tensed up. I think Armando could tell. But it was too late to get Armando out, so I just said a prayer in my head that maybe *Papi*'s early arrival meant he hadn't drunk as much as usual."

Anita sat down on the bed and hugged her knees to her chest.

"You could smell the *aguardiente* coming out of his pores from the moment he walked through the front door. He reeked. And he had that look on his face. I'm sure you remember. The face he gets whenever he drinks. The way his eyes turn darker and his brows never relax. I saw it immediately. My heart was racing so fast I thought I might have a heart attack from the pressure inside my chest."

"Anita, I'm so sorry." Her voice came through the receiver tender and soft. Carolina was a fighter—like all the Carvajal women—but she had the incredible ability to tame her fury from one moment to the next.

Anita cleared her throat and continued. "His eyes were so empty. Full of rage, but at the same time, it was like I was staring at a zombie. A tense body and blank eyes . . . nothing registering inside his brain. I'll never be able to get that image out of my head."

"I remember those eyes," Carolina said.

"It's all kind of a blur, but I do remember us locking eyes when he opened the front door. He just stood in the frame and stared me down like a lion who'd spotted its prey. For a second I thought he might act normal since I had a guest over, but I was only kidding myself.

"He was so out of it that he never acknowledged Armando, who was sitting right next to me on the sofa. In that instant, I felt it in my spirit that something really bad was about to happen— worse than anything he'd done to us before."

"Manny?"

"*Sí*. Poor baby. He'd been asleep for two or three hours by then. But the demon inside *Papi* didn't care. He went into the bedroom and picked Manny up by his underwear and started stomping toward the bathroom with his little limp body hanging from his grip. I heard him turn on the shower, and that's when Manny started screaming, so I ran to him."

"*Increíble*. Unbelievable," Carolina whispered.

"I was so furious he would do something like that to our baby brother. I was right in front of him; why didn't he just come after me? He probably knew hurting Manny would hurt me more than if he'd just come after me."

"*Por Dios*, how could he do something like that? *Papi*'s taken this too far," Carolina said. "We should report him."

"To who? His colleagues at the precinct? I wouldn't be surprised if they do the same thing to their families."

"Well, they're certainly not spending all their money on alcohol like *Papi* does. Their families live in the nice neighborhoods. I bet this stuff doesn't happen there."

Anita rolled her eyes, dismissing her sister's naïveté. "I grabbed Manny and tried to run away from *Papi*, but my long hair got in the way. He grabbed my hair with his fist and pulled me back toward him. Manny and I fell to the ground. And the next thing I remember, I was running out of the house. I had nowhere to go, but I just ran. I can't believe I left Manny. I didn't mean to."

"You weren't thinking straight, and it's understandable, Anita. Don't beat yourself up about it. Surely *Mamá* or Juan Carlos came to help soon after you left."

"Carolina . . ." Anita sniffled. "He followed me outside, aimed his gun at the sky, and shot into the air twice. It probably woke up the whole neighborhood. What kind of father does that?"

"A bad one."

"I don't even know why I ran. I wasn't really scared. I was more angry. Still am. Maybe I was hoping if I ran fast enough, I would run into a different life."

"When are you going to come here? To America, to live with me?"

Anita's voice turned from grief to anger. "Don't start with that, Carolina. I'm not coming to America."

"Then what are you going to do? Where are you going to live? You can't afford your own place."

"I'm staying at Carmen's house. She said I could stay as long as I need. It's so embarrassing, though. She knows how *Papi* can be."

"You can't stay with Armando? Even temporarily?"

Anita jumped up from the bed and paced around the room, the cord of the phone wrapping around her foot. "Pffft, he didn't even come looking for me. I don't know what he did during that debacle, but he disappeared. I still haven't heard from him. I could be dead and he wouldn't know . . . or care."

"Don't say that," Carolina said. "Maybe he came looking for you this morning but couldn't find you. Does *Mamá* know where you are?"

"Not yet. I'll go see her as soon as I know *Papi* has left for work. But I doubt Armando has come looking for me. He's a coward—like they all are. I'm not sure what's worse: a father who would aim his gun at you or a long-term boyfriend who disappears when he knows your father tried to kill you."

There was silence on both ends of the receiver before Anita spoke up once more.

"He can just forget about me because I'm not going to go looking for him, just so he can know where I am. And I already told Carmen to tell him I'm not here if he comes looking. I've had enough of him and his cowardice."

"Please consider coming. I could help you until you get on your feet. There's a lot of work here in New York for immigrants. You could start making money right away and maybe we could help *Mamá*, Manny, and Juan Carlos together that way."

"It's not happening, Carolina. I can help them better by staying here. I've come to terms with your and Diana's decision to leave, but I'm not doing the same thing. *Mamá* needs me here."

Carolina sighed. This wasn't the first time they'd had this conversation, but Anita hoped it would be the last.

"What are you going to do, then?" Carolina asked.

"I need to go make sure Manny is okay. But I'm cutting my hair first. I won't allow my long hair to make me powerless again."

"I've always thought you'd look good in a pixie cut."

"Well, I hope Armando hates it. I hope he thinks I'm ugly now and never speaks to me again. Better yet, I hope I never see him again."

"Don't be so quick to shut him out. Maybe there's a good reason he disappeared. Talk to him first, Anita."

"I don't need him. I don't need anyone."

CHAPTER 9

2018
CALI, COLOMBIA

MELANIE

Whoa. *Should I be reading this right now?*

What a sad story. Depressing even. But something about the writer excited Melanie. She was a boss for going up against her dad that way and then chopping off her own hair.

Who could this person be? Logically, it had to belong to her mother—all of her aunts and uncles were mentioned by name. The only one *not* mentioned by name was her mother, Anita.

It just felt so at odds with the woman she knew. To begin with, her mother wasn't much of a writer, and the words she'd read in that first journal entry were poetic with a distinct voice. They were in Spanish, and, sure, they were desperately tragic, but Melanie could recognize good writing from a mile away.

She flipped through the journal again, her eyebrows slowly coming together. On the back cover of the journal was the confirmation she was looking for. A miniscule imprint with a name: Anita Carvajal.

How could it be?

Her mother was the last person Melanie would have guessed after reading this journal entry. If she had to guess how her own mother would have reacted in a situation like the one she'd just read, Melanie would say her mother would have cowered under her father's authority and perhaps even hid in her room until it ended.

Because that was how her mother handled most things.

When Melanie's father filed for divorce when she was sixteen years old, her mom simply shrugged, quietly packed her things, and moved her kids to a new state for a "fresh start."

When Anita was fired from the daycare where she worked for more than ten years over a false accusation, she didn't fight back or try to clear her name. She hugged the children there tight and looked for another job.

When Anita's youngest brother, Melanie's uncle Manny, was on the brink of hanging out with the wrong crowds back in Colombia, she didn't ask any of her siblings to help her with the financial burden of bringing him to the United States. She borrowed money and raised him as her own son.

Anita was like a doormat; she quietly tolerated every shoe that smeared its grime on her.

Anytime Melanie urged her to stand up for herself, to speak her mind, to ask for whatever she needed, her mother dismissed her comments with a creased forehead and an exasperated sigh. It drove Melanie crazy. How could she be so weak? And how was Melanie supposed to respect her mother when she had such a submissive attitude toward the world? When she simply let life happen to her instead of taking it by the reins like Melanie had always done?

The woman in this journal was the complete opposite of the woman she'd lived with for eighteen years. Anita's name engraved on the inside may have confirmed she was the author, but there had to be some kind of explanation for the transformation she'd obviously gone through. Her mother didn't even seem like the journaling type.

Reading another entry might help clear things up.

Going back to where she left off, Melanie turned the page to the next entry. But she read only the first two lines before she heard footsteps coming toward the bedroom.

Her heart began to race as she tossed the journal back in the drawer and grabbed her laptop. Then she threw her body back onto the pillows and pretended to type. While one part of her knew she shouldn't be reading through someone else's journal, the other part of her wondered what harm could come from reading a few of the pages. They were entries from decades ago; surely none of it was secret anymore.

Even still, she did her best to act casual as the doorknob wiggled and her mother popped her head in.

"I have to run to the *panaderia* to pick up the cake for the party tonight. Do you want to come?" Anita asked.

Melanie didn't think before nodding and jumping out of the bed. "Will this take long?" she asked while slipping on her flip-flops.

"Why? Do you have somewhere else to be?"

She didn't respond. She only gave the end table a wistful gaze before following her mother out the bedroom door.

CHAPTER 10

As they walked the narrow concrete road to the bakery, Melanie struggled to keep her eyes off the ground.

The road was littered with potholes and uneven asphalt— she worried she might trip and break a toe in her rubber flip-flops. And she had to be careful of any injuries because the last thing she wanted was to visit a hospital in a country she didn't know.

The farther they walked, the more crowded the road became with street vendors selling fresh fruit and homemade juices. Melanie even spotted a beautiful dark-skinned woman balancing a shallow basket on her head. With every few steps she took, the woman yelled, *"¡Chontaduro!"*

"That's a woman from the coast. Many of them travel here to sell that delicious fruit," Anita said when she noticed her daughter staring.

"How far is the coast?" Melanie asked.

"Not far. About three hours."

Travel three hours just to sell fruit? It must be worth the trip financially, but could they possibly make enough selling fruit?

Melanie's attention shifted to her mother. Her arms were flailing in the air as she ran toward a woman with a cart carrying a mountain of bagged fruit on top.

Anita enveloped the woman in a tight hug before pointing at Melanie. She couldn't hear what her mother said to the woman, but before she could find out, the woman walked toward her and leaned in for a hug and a kiss on the cheek.

She had a sweet smell about her and looked to be about her mother's age. Her auburn hair glistened in the morning sunlight and defied the laws of humidity. Melanie still hadn't learned how to keep her hair flat and manageable in the moisture-rich air Colombia and Miami seemed to share.

Her mother and the fruit lady spoke so quickly that Melanie had a hard time keeping up. Rather than attempt to join them, she stood back and kept her distance until they finished their conversation.

It looked like the woman wasn't going to allow Anita to walk away without her hands full of small baggies of fruit she must have sliced at home. The woman then turned to face Melanie and attempted to fill her hands with bags of fruit as well. Melanie shook her head and smiled, trying her best to politely decline this woman's gift. She was doing everything in her power to be careful of what she ate and drank—she had to watch out for foreign bacteria invading her insides.

"Please, I insist," the woman said to her.

"It's okay. I'm very full. Thank you, though," Melanie said. The woman smiled and placed the baggies back on her cart. Then she pulled Anita in for one more hug before Melanie and her mother continued on to the bakery. The interaction reminded Melanie of all the Sundays she spent waiting on her mother once the church service had ended because she couldn't help but visit with what felt like every single person in the congregation. Melanie would leave church with her stomach growling from the hunger pains. It hadn't crossed her mind that being in Colombia would offer a similar experience since her mother saw these friends only once a year.

"Mmm, Melanie, you're missing out. This is the juiciest fruit you'll ever eat. Way more flavorful than anything you get in America, that's for sure," Anita said as some of the juice from the soft papaya slid down her chin.

"Mom, you should really be more careful. You could get sick eating from street vendors."

"*Ay*, I grew up eating this! Yes, you need to be careful about the water, but the food is safe."

Melanie grimaced. *Is she for real?*

Before Melanie could say anything else, Anita shared about the woman they'd just met at the fruit stand.

"That was Ximena. She grew up in this neighborhood with me. That used to be her mother's fruit cart, and now she's taken over."

Melanie skipped over a chunk of uneven asphalt and moved her satchel from sitting on her lower back to her hip, where she could better grip the strap with both hands.

"Mom, how much longer until we get to the bakery?"

Anita pointed a few feet ahead. "It's right there."

So that was the familiar aroma she'd breathed in a few moments earlier. The smell of warm *buñuelos, pandebonos,* and *empanadas* was unmistakable. How amazing that one whiff of food could take you decades back to your childhood. Melanie remembered being a young girl and walking hand in hand with her mother to the Colombian bakery near their apartment in Queens. It was one of her favorite memories from the time they lived in New York.

The *panadería* here in Cali even resembled the one she remembered from Queens. It sat on the first floor of a white three-story building. It was open-air, as if the bakery never closed—no doors, windows, or anything. Just two large glass counters lined with a variety of pastries—both savory and sweet—and elaborately designed cakes.

There were several aluminum picnic tables out front where couples and families sat enjoying an outdoor lunch. Stacked on top of the bakery were apartments with Juliet balconies covering the side. The modern architecture and design surprised Melanie, as well as the long line that snaked around the tables. It wasn't an organized line by any means, but she guessed they must all be in on some insider knowledge because everyone knew exactly what to do and who was next to order.

Melanie and her mother joined the patrons at the end of the queue and waited patiently as the line crept forward under the warmth that grew more intense with each passing minute. From the moment she'd stepped out of her grandmother's home, sweat had begun to gather on her back and stomach.

The line moved quickly as groups of two and three walked out with white paper bags covered in grease stains. When Anita made it to the counter, she pointed at an oversized *tres leches* cake topped with fresh berries. The woman behind the counter packaged the cake in a window box and slid it across the countertop to Anita.

Melanie watched as her mother spun around and showed off the dessert like an Olympic gold medalist showing off their trophy, as if she'd made the cake with her own two hands.

"This is the best *tres leches* cake in the whole city," Anita said.

Melanie had never tried the traditional dessert made with three kinds of milk before, but the sweet aroma comforted her. She noticed that everyone in the bakery and behind the counter was smiling, made eye contact with her, and even said hello when passing by. They had kind eyes and seemed ... normal.

Why is that so surprising?

"Did you ever feel unsafe growing up here?" Melanie asked her mother as they walked out onto the sidewalk. "I remember so many stories from you, Pa, and your friends, but the people here seem nice."

"Of course they're nice. They're Colombian. They greet you and welcome you in. That was one of the hardest things to get used to in America. People can be so cold when you don't speak their language. They don't even look you in the eye in a big city like New York. When you walk by them, they look down at their shoes or their phone."

"So why do I only remember stories about people getting robbed and kidnapped and other scary stuff?"

Anita chuckled. "Well, it's true, those things happen. Although I know I told you other stories too! *Gringos* especially have to be careful in certain areas, but that doesn't mean the majority of people are dangerous. So, to answer your question, growing up, I tried to be wise, you know, stay away from sketchy places, but overall, I never really felt unsafe. It's like any city you visit in America or anywhere else in the world."

Anita handed Melanie the cake so she could finish her fruit. She did her best to balance the box in her hands while still keeping an eye on the ground and her purse.

The noises around her became increasingly distracting: more and more motorcycles zipping by (no doubt there were more motorcycles than cars); people standing outside small stores, laughing and chitchatting; and others sipping coffee while seated in plastic chairs outside their homes.

While this city certainly struggled with litter, uneven roads, and homes that looked structurally unsafe, it wasn't the Colombia that Melanie had pictured all her life. Maybe she wouldn't let her guard down, but in a better pair of shoes, she could lift her chin and take in more of her surroundings with less fear.

"What did you do around here for fun?" Melanie asked.

"You know, I really tried to stay out of trouble . . . like you as a child, actually. I had a great group of friends, and we'd get together every weekend to bike around the city or up the mountain to Dapa. Sometimes we'd take the bus to Rio Ponce or the beach. We played basketball and anything else we could find outside. No matter what we did, time with my friends was like a rest for my soul . . . and from my home."

From her home?

Melanie thought back to the journal entry she'd read earlier. The woman in the journal definitely wanted to escape her family. But why had she never heard about her mother's experience growing up?

"Not your grandmother—don't get me wrong. My mother is the most incredible mother in the world. I hate that we live so far from each other, but my dad was tough, *mija*. I know you never got to meet him, but sometimes I'm glad. He had his days when he was kind and even generous with us, but it's hard to forget all the terror he put us through. Things I wouldn't even want you to know about, truthfully. God rest his soul."

Melanie gulped down an uneasy feeling. How could she keep reading now? Clearly her mother didn't want to discuss this topic, let alone open her journal for anyone to read.

Unless this journal could provide insights, stories, memories she needed to understand her own identity. Maybe it could even make a difference in the article she'd be writing for the *Herald*. She didn't know much about her family in Colombia. Reading just one entry had opened a door of curiosity—there's no way she could close the door now and walk away. Especially if it could be the reason she wrote an article that saved her job.

If her mother knew the stories in this journal could help Melanie achieve success in her job, she was sure she'd let her read it. It was settled—she would tell her mom the truth about stumbling upon her journal and reading the first entry.

"Hey, Mom—"

"Are you ready?" Anita asked.

"Huh?"

"You go straight to the fridge while I distract *Abuela*, okay?"

Melanie had been so lost in thought she hadn't realized they'd made it back to her grandmother's house already.

"Oh . . . yeah, sure." The request would have to wait.

Anita walked to the doorway and yelled, "*¡Mamá, cúbrete los ojos!*" ("Mom, cover your eyes!")

When Melanie was satisfied with the number of milk and juice cartons hiding the cake, she whispered to her mother, "I'll be right back." She knew she had to get permission before reading another page, but being back in her grandmother's kitchen didn't feel like the right place to convince her mom to let her read more. The best thing to do would be to wait until she was alone with her mother again, perhaps when they went to bed that night.

She walked back to her room chewing on her nails.

I should probably wait until tonight . . . a journal is very private.

But tonight is a long time from now. And what if she's up late because of the party? I might not even be able to ask her until tomorrow . . .

Surely, she's going to give me her blessing . . . so is there really any harm in getting a little head start?

When she crossed the threshold of her mother's old bedroom, she placed one hand on the doorknob and the other against the frame, clicking it closed. It felt like any amount of noise might attract someone. And right now, she wanted to be alone. Even when her own thoughts continued to try and talk her out of reading more, she forced them away and replaced them with thoughts about potentially finding that missing something in this journal—that elusive piece of heart her writing had lacked since she started at the *Herald*. If she found the key in this journal, it would be worth the invasion of privacy.

She opened the drawer in the nightstand, the creaking sound of the worn wood making her feel like a mischievous teenager looking for her parents' stash of cash. Then she pulled out the journal, using the same care with which she handled a newspaper. She turned the pages past the first entry and read once more.

CHAPTER 11

FEBRUARY 27, 1987
CALI, COLOMBIA

ANITA

"I can't even believe I'm considering this right now, but what else am I supposed to do?"

"There's a reason so many people do it," Juan Carlos said.

They sat on the front porch of their family home, sipping warm, milky coffee and watching Manny kick a worn soccer ball against the door.

"But I love my country—*this* city. I adore these very streets. How can I live a life devoid of them? I don't know how people can just get up and leave without a guarantee that they can ever come back." Anita shook her head and took a sip of her coffee.

"I think you're the only person within a hundred miles who doesn't dream about moving to America."

Anita sucked her teeth. "It's disgusting, to be honest, the way people lust after that country. I want nothing to do with it. How hypocritical of me to even consider it right now—to entertain this idea. I've told Carolina again and again to stop bringing it up, but she takes any opportunity to remind me of what she thinks I'm missing."

"People just want a better life, sis."

"But why can't we make that better life here?"

"C'mon, Anita. You know it's not that simple."

Anita cursed under her breath. "Well, I can't go because then I'd be a traitor. Everyone would say it."

"What are you talking about?" Juan Carlos almost laughed.

"Don't look at me like that. They've all heard the way I curse America when anyone mentions a friend or family member who's made the cross. They've seen the way I nod my head and move closer to the front when our teachers start raging about the Americans and their *patas de caucho pecuecudo*—their smelly feet in those horrifying rubber flip-flops they love to prance around in."

"Who are you even talking about?"

"They! Them!" Anita held out her arm and shook her hand as if pointing to an invisible crowd in front of her. "Everyone. Our neighbors, my classmates, our friends. They've all heard me talk about how the Americans steal from us. How they impoverish our beautiful country. First they steal the land they now live on from indigenous people, and then they cross more oceans to continue their plundering . . . leaving people like us with nothing."

"But—"

"Why would I go live there, eh? They're the reason our country is so poor. It's like *Señora* Enriquez always says: Colombia is the number one exporter of emeralds. Foreign investments pour into our mining industry. And our expansive lands for cattle raising, flowers, and coffee are endless and yet we live like we have nothing. Like our country is empty, lacking, and good for nothing. They fight for our resources because they can't stand to see another country flourishing where they cannot. It's disgusting. Do you know what—"

"Anita! Let me get a word in. I don't want you to be so naïve.

Our own government brings us plenty of trouble. They've never been bold enough to stand up for their own country. They gladly sell off much of what makes Colombia rich for pennies on the dollar, thinking it's a good deal for us. And they give in to the threats of cartels and guerrillas. This is not a one-sided battle."

"I know that, but at the end of the day, it's America's fault. If it wasn't for them bribing and even stealing so much from us, from desperate people, then our country wouldn't be so poor."

"You sound like a *revolucionista*. A revolutionist," Juan Carlos said with a slight roll of his eyes. He leaned forward and gave the ball a gentle push back toward Manny.

"Let me ask you something: Do you know anyone who's gone to America and is now rich?" Anita said.

"I don't. But they're certainly better off than they were here."

"Those Americans, they don't care what kind of education you got here. As soon as you get there and they know you're an immigrant who can hardly speak their language, they label you a foreigner who is only good for domestic work. People leave this country to become servants over there." Anita moved to the edge of her seat and turned her torso to face her brother.

"Is that what you want for me? You want me to end up watching spoiled children or scrubbing floors the rest of my life? I'm supposed to go on a dangerous journey to a foreign country just so I can work like a dog for very little money and then send half those measly earnings back here? You're the one being naïve, Juan Carlos. Wealth is the same fantasy in America for people like us as it is for us here."

Juan Carlos continued kicking the ball back and forth with Manny, allowing Anita to continue her tirade.

"Because even here, I'll never have a decent-paying job—those are reserved for wealthy people and their families. The poor stay poor and the rich get richer. But I'm still better off here than there. I have zero interest in materialistic ambitions. That's the real reason everyone goes over there. I don't daydream about a two-story house or owning my own car. Those kinds of things are not important to me, so why would I go to America?"

Juan Carlos sat up to respond. "No one is forcing you to go. You know I would rather have you here. *Te quiero*, Anita. I love you, and I don't want to lose my last sister to America. I just want you to keep an open heart and an open mind to what the future may hold for you. It may not be as ugly as you imagine. But if I'm being honest, I have to admit it would make me feel a lot better knowing you're nowhere near *Papi* anymore. One less sibling to worry about."

Anita scooted back in her chair and hugged her mug to her chest. Her brother's gentle words steadied her fast-beating heart for a moment, allowing her voice to come down as well.

"Can you imagine raising children somewhere else like Carolina is doing? I don't picture myself ever having kids, but if somehow it happened, I'd want them to grow up here. I want them to be proud Colombians, not American.

"Who knows what will become of our niece, Rosa. She'll grow up speaking English, spoiled, without the slightest idea of how the rest of the world lives. Will she ever even know who we are? Why would she visit if she has everything she needs in America? She'll never know Colombia, and I wouldn't want that for my children."

Juan Carlos was silent for a moment. Then, with furrowed brows, he asked, "Why do you say that?"

"Say what?"

"You don't picture yourself having kids."

"Because I don't."

"But why?"

"I don't know . . . alcohol, I guess. It runs in the blood."

"So you're going to let that one fear keep you from becoming a mother?"

"It's not a fear, Juan Carlos; it's reality."

"I think it's fear. Everything you're saying is fear. You're afraid of something different."

"I'm afraid to leave our mother—that's it. I can't leave while *Papi* is still around. He will take advantage of having fewer people to abuse and direct his abundance of anger onto her and you and Manny." Anita pulled Manny in and tousled his messy hair, sucking in breaths to keep from crying.

"I can take care of them."

"I can't let you shoulder that burden alone." She released Manny but kept her eyes glued on him, unable to look at her older brother.

"Anita . . ." Juan Carlos reached out his hand and placed it over hers. "I want you to be free. I want you to go where your heart leads. Don't let this home become a prison for you. I will take care of *Mamá;* it's my job as the eldest brother. I promise I will never leave her side. Don't spew out these revolutionary words to try to convince yourself to stay. Go and find greener pastures. We'll be right here with open arms whenever you want to come back."

"Come back where?" Juan Carlos and Anita turned around and sat up straight at the sight of their mother. She dried her hands on her signature dusty-blue apron, which was covered in a medley of colorful stains.

"Um, nowhere, *Mamá*. It smells like the soup is ready," Anita said, smiling despite the tenseness in her stomach.

"*Sí,* come inside before it gets cold." Alba grabbed Manny's hand and walked inside.

Anita stood first and Juan Carlos followed close behind. He reached out his arm and gave her shoulder a gentle squeeze.

What had her life come to? How could she consider a move even a moment longer?

If she left, her mother wouldn't be the only person she'd risk losing to distance. She couldn't bear the thought of being apart from her brother, the only man who'd never broken her heart.

CHAPTER 12

2018
CALI, COLOMBIA

MELANIE

Every doubt had long washed away, but the question still remained: *How could this be my mother?*

Not only was the vocabulary and word usage so unlike Anita, but the sentiment was too.

Melanie knew her mother loved and missed her home country, but she also loved America. She vividly remembered listening as she, time and time again, defended the land of the free and talked poorly about the communist teachings the schools in Colombia were prone to share. Whenever Melanie or either of her siblings complained about pretty much anything, Anita would always nullify their grievances with a story of how truly blessed they were compared to what she and her family endured in Colombia.

They didn't want leftovers for dinner? Anita would tell them about the rice and beans they ate almost every day, even for breakfast.

They wanted a fresh wardrobe for the new school year? Anita would share about how lucky she felt to own a piece of clothing her mother hadn't made with her own hands.

They didn't want to spend three hours at the laundromat

with her every weekend? They'd hear about the luxury of having access to a washing machine so that you didn't have to clean every piece of clothing and linen by hand.

Anita had a quip for each one of her children's verbal acts of discontentment toward their lives in America.

So how could this writer, someone who clearly had disdain for the United States, be her mother? If it was, she'd flip-flopped significantly.

On top of all that, Anita simply did not have this kind of intense and fiery spirit to her. She was the exact opposite, actually. The woman Melanie read about in this journal sounded more like herself than her mother.

Anita was patient, almost to a fault, and she was as meek and passive as a squeaky little mouse. She didn't fight about anything; instead, she floated along whatever current she fell into. Never did she plant her feet to the ground and change direction if she didn't like her destination. Melanie felt her mother never advanced in a real career or made headway on her finances because of her passive nature. Which, to an extent, frustrated Melanie because she felt she never had a parent who could help her in her own career.

If this was who her mother was as a young adult, what had changed her personality so drastically? It had to be more than just a move to another country.

The journalistic instinct in her fired off in all directions. She tapped the corner of her laptop incessantly and eyed every corner of the room.

Like a good investigative journalist, she would keep looking, but she would have to be cautious and discreet. Learning more would require reading a few additional entries to find other clues about what had happened to change her mother so much. If she straight-out asked her, she might not be totally honest, trying to

protect Melanie from a painful past. Melanie wanted the unfil-
tered truth, so she would continue reading in secret—just for a
little while longer—and then, she swore to herself, she would
talk to her mom. For now, she wanted nothing to deter her from
discovering what had happened.

Before she returned the journal to the still-open drawer, her
eyes drifted to a line on the open page she had just read that had
felt like a dagger to her heart: *Will she ever even know who we are?
Why would she visit if she has everything she needs in America?*

Butterflies filled her stomach. How disappointed her mother
must feel to know her fears about her niece—and her own
children—had come true. To have a daughter who never once
asked to visit her ancestors' land or even cared to ask what it was
like. Melanie wondered whether her mother lived with disappointment in the children she raised in a foreign land. Did she
regret not raising them here? In this home, this neighborhood?

She hid the journal underneath her laptop. Then she shut the
drawer and stood up to head back into the kitchen—her family
would be missing her by now.

As she aimlessly slipped her feet into her flip-flops, she pro-
cessed once more everything she'd read. When she reached for
the doorknob, she paused and looked down at her feet. Had her
mother ever owned flip-flops? She couldn't remember. How
ironic that she was the only person in the home who'd been born
in America . . . and the only one in rubber flip-flops. Were they
all laughing at her right now?

Melanie turned around and walked back to the closet, where
she had emptied her suitcase. There she found the white pair of
sneakers she'd thrown in her suitcase for her time in Bogotá and
exchanged them with her flip-flops. Maybe no one had noticed . . . and maybe she could figure out a way to bring her two
worlds together.

CHAPTER 13

"Juan Carlos, turn the music down," Anita said. "*Mamá* is moving too much, and her ankles are swelling!"

"*Ay, mija,* the swelling is not from my dancing. I wish you'd stop worrying so much about my health. I'm about as healthy as a ninety-year-old woman can be. Plus, we can't prepare this feast without a little Carlos Vives in the background," Alba said, shaking the wooden spoon in her hand, which sent a splatter of oil to the other side of the room.

Melanie found a rag and wiped at the stain on the beige-colored wall. When she stood, she paused to take in the view she'd walked into.

Anita stood at the counter by the small black stove, chopping yucca into thick strips and slowly stirring the contents of the largest pot Melanie had ever seen.

As the broth simmered, the small space in the kitchen filled with the aroma of garlic as Alba threw a mountain of it into a black frying pan whose bottom was covered with oil. The small window above the sink was cracked open to allow the breeze to blow through and provide relief from the heat, though the aroma was too thick to blow away with it.

When her grandmother added a pile of tomatoes and green onions to the pan filled with garlic, the pungent smell shifted to include the scent of sweet ripe tomatoes blending with the kick of an onion. It was a glorious dance of flavors twirling through the air. Melanie closed her eyes and drank it in. It must have been years since she sat in a fog of fragrance this heavenly.

She allowed herself to be completely present in the moment— to slow her breathing, her thoughts, and her heart rate. To savor the smells and the view. To allow the fog to take her back to her mother's home and the oversized meals she served whenever family came to visit. Much of her upbringing may have brought Melanie pain and frustration, but one thing was undeniable: The food made up for a lot of the ache.

Her jaw softened and her limbs felt loose. She pulled out a chair from the dining table and took a seat. There was something serene about watching her mother and grandmother move comfortably around a kitchen and create magic with simple vegetables. Most of her meals were microwavable and squeezed in between whatever story she was working on. She couldn't remember the last time she put anything more than an egg in a frying pan.

If only she could carry this fragrance and this image of her matriarchs everywhere she went—it was more effective at calming her nerves than any prescription. Who would have thought?

While she wanted nothing to stifle the sizzling sounds coming from the stove, she parted her lips to speak. "Can I help?" Anything to get even closer to the smells and sounds of her pain reliever.

"The more hands the better. We have many mouths to feed tonight. Here, start with this," Alba said, handing her a brown paper bag filled with corn that needed shucking.

Melanie took her time stripping the corn. The movement took her back to her childhood, when all she wanted was to help her mother prep for dinner in the kitchen. Anita would pull up a stool to the counter or seat her at the dining table with a vegetable and a butter knife.

It wasn't until someone in her school asked about the apparent foul smell coming from the cubbies that she became aware that the food she ate at home was very different from that of her peers. When the young girl sniffed every lunch box and declared Melanie's the culprit, Melanie threw the storage container away and spent her lunch hour in the library instead. That night, she begged her mother to stop packing her a lunch and to let her buy her lunch at school like everyone else in her class.

Even after her mother relented and gave her lunch money every morning, Melanie never again accepted her mother's invitation to help her prep dinner, claiming her homework had piled up. She lived in fear that the scent of her mother's foreign food would seep into the pores of her hands, clothes, and hair.

Those early years helping her mother in the kitchen didn't stick with Melanie enough to prepare her for adulthood. Maybe if she would have kept at it, she would be able to tell a zucchini from a cucumber.

Alba turned away from the stove for a moment to look toward Melanie. "*Mija*, tell me about how your writing is going. We are so proud of you. And to be doing a story here in Colombia . . . how marvelous."

Melanie wished for just a few more moments in this kitchen without a thought about her work. It was as if the outside world didn't exist when her hands were occupied in the kitchen. There was no pressure to improve her writing. No impossible boss to please. No article to revise until her carpal tunnel flared up.

She'd become so engrossed in the journal she'd found that she'd even forgotten to check her email since this morning.

Maybe that's why I'm feeling more relaxed.

Her grandmother's praise brought her work back to the front of her mind. While she had convinced herself that the journal could help her write a better article, she couldn't let it take up *all* her time right now. There was still a lot of research and prep to finish. The number one priority was still to write an article that would make Ignacio believe in her writing again. She couldn't keep getting distracted like this or she might not have a job to return to.

She attempted to answer her grandmother's inquiry without giving any clues into how she really felt because it wasn't a topic she wanted to camp on.

"It's fine, *Abuela*. Definitely a lot harder than I imagined, but I'm working at it and, you know . . . staying busy." She looked up and smiled at her grandmother, hoping her words were convincing.

"I'm sure you are. You've always written beautifully. I'll never forget the poems your mother sent me that you wrote for that competition a few years ago. They were published, weren't they?" She looked at Anita, who nodded with glistening eyes. "You must have gotten your gift from your mother. She's always been a wonderful writer as well."

Melanie froze with her hands in the middle of yanking another strand of the corn's husk. She looked up at her mother, who still faced the stove. When her mother didn't turn around, Melanie said, "What? Since when are you a writer? You never told me that."

This would explain the skilled writing in the journal. But how could that be? Never in her life had Melanie heard her mother mention anything about an affinity for writing. She always encouraged Melanie's choice to pursue journalism and, when Melanie was young, praised her anytime she won another award in creative writing. But not once had she ever mentioned that she, too, loved to write. It would have been nice to know, as it could have been something that brought them together—connected them. Instead, Melanie thought she had absolutely nothing in common with her mother; they didn't even look alike.

"*Mamá*, I've never been a writer. Melanie is the real writer," Anita said.

"Just because you never published anything doesn't mean you're not a writer," Alba said. "I've read your poems, and let me assure you, you are a wonderful writer."

Anita's eyes grew twice their size as she looked at her mother in shock. "You read my journals? *¡Mamá!*" You never got too old to bicker with your mother.

"Just the ones with the poems . . . and the one you left in the nightstand. I found it when I was cleaning one day. What did you expect? For me to just ignore it?" Alba sent tomato juice flying through the air as she waved her wooden spoon once more in her defense. "It was the only piece of you I had here. You used to show me your poems when you were young. I didn't think you'd mind. Plus, there's nothing in there I didn't already know about."

Melanie looked back down at the corn she held, hoping to avoid eye contact. This was not the time for Anita to find out she had also read the journal from the nightstand. Although it was still hard to believe it belonged to her mother, this conversation was all the proof she needed. She still wanted to investigate further, though. There had to be a reason—perhaps an event—that transformed Anita into the person Melanie knew today.

"I brought them back here because I didn't know what else to do with them when we moved into that tiny apartment in Maryland. I definitely didn't leave them here so you could read through them, *Mamá*. It's personal stuff . . ." It was obvious Anita couldn't stay mad at her mother. Her love for her was evident from miles away—no matter what, Alba could do no wrong in her eyes. Before she even took another breath, Anita smiled and gave her a playful nudge. "Anywayyy, *Mamá*, writing in journals doesn't make you a writer. But my daughter? Now, she's a *real* writer. An excellent one."

Melanie gave her mother a half smile. Everyone seemed so sure Melanie was a great writer, yet nobody knew the truth: She was failing miserably at her first real writing job. She held on to hope that she could salvage it before anyone had to find out.

"Mom, what kind of poetry did you write?" Melanie asked. "I can't believe you never told me, especially when I was learning about poetry and essays. You could have helped me. Poetry was always hard for me."

"I couldn't have helped you. You were in an American school. I don't know anything about American poetry. Plus, my poetry wasn't real poetry." She paused. "It was more like a broken heart poured out in ink." She stared ahead for a moment before getting back to the simmering soup.

"I think poetry is the same no matter what language you write it in," Alba said. "That's the beauty of the written word. It's like math—it's the same no matter where you do it."

"Now you sound like the poet," Anita said. "Like I said, my writing was for notebooks. I never felt like I had any real talent—certainly no Gabriel García Márquez or anything."

"Márquez . . . I've heard that name before. Maybe in college English class or something. He's Colombian?"

Melanie raised her eyes from the corn in her hands in time to see Anita and Alba turn sharply toward her.

"*Mi amor,* how could you ask that question? We are so proud to call Gabo ours. He gives our country a good name," Anita said.

"Mm-hmm. Not all Colombians do that, so we hold on tight to those who do," Alba said.

"Then I'll have to check out his stuff," Melanie said.

"I have a copy of *Love in the Time of Cholera* on my bedside table. Take it. My gift to you. But it's in Spanish. Can you read in Spanish?" Alba asked.

A flush crept across Melanie's cheek. "Of course I can."

She wasn't lying. She *could* read in Spanish. Complicated topics might just take her twice as long to get through.

When she had emptied the brown bag of corn and peeled and chopped a few green plantains, Melanie asked her grandmother for permission to spend an hour or two working before the guests arrived for the party. The last thing she wanted to do was lock herself in the bedroom some more when she should be relishing quality time with her grandmother. But if she didn't check her inbox soon and confirm some last-minute interviews, she'd be job searching the minute she got back to Miami.

It'd also be prudent to put the journal out of her mind for the time being. While it felt like an intense magnetic force pulling her in, it was yet another distraction keeping her from what should be her priority right now.

"*Sí, mi amor,* but promise me you're going to put all the work away for the party. I don't want you to just meet your family; I want you to connect with them, bond with them, so you can stay in touch when you go back home. I want you to know these people, and they want to know you. Okay? There's nothing more important than family, even if you live a world away."

"Of course, *Abuela.* I promise."

Back in her bedroom, Melanie pulled out her laptop from the

nightstand. She spotted the journal but shut the drawer before she could scoop it up.

Her inbox was flooded. How could she have gotten this many new emails in less than twenty-four hours? Immediately, her shoulders became tense with stress.

Some of the emails were from Genesis—she'd sent a few articles she'd stumbled upon that could help speak into Melanie's piece. And the copy editor had sent an email asking when she could expect Melanie's article—she'd been told to make it top priority for the Monday after next. There was also an email from Ignacio. It contained a link and a short message:

The *Times* published this article today. Read it. It's good.
They chose the right subject to build their story.
How do the people you're interviewing compare?
Send me a draft as soon as you have it.

Her posture collapsed forward and she cradled her face in her hands. This was too much to bear. Was it too late to get back to the kitchen, where this world didn't exist?

She looked at the closed door of her bedroom, then back at her computer screen, longing to be just a few feet away from here.

Another email came in. That settled it. No more distractions. It was time to face the looming article.

She clicked on the link Ignacio sent and a few from Genesis and read each one. More and more of the same views on the issue—the Miami view. What was the point of sending Melanie to Colombia if Ignacio expected her to write an article like the ones he'd sent? Just recently, he had told her to stop writing like everyone else, yet here he was flooding her inbox with articles of the very same kind.

This was only making her job harder. Each day, she felt more and more confused. Lost. Like searching for an unknown object in a pitch-dark room.

If Ignacio wouldn't pinpoint what she should do differently, Melanie would have to spend the time finding it herself. She pushed her laptop to the other side of the bed and reached for the journal. It was the exact opposite of what she'd promised herself she would do, but something nagged at her, insisting this journal was where she'd find the answer to many of the mysteries she grappled with.

CHAPTER 14

FEBRUARY 28, 1987
CALI, COLOMBIA

ANITA

Anita looked up from her bed, where she'd been writing in her journal. A tear fell from her cheek, smearing the fresh ink on the page. There was a knock at her bedroom door. She wiped her cheeks with the backs of her hands before inviting Carmen in.

"Carolina is on the phone for you," Carmen said from the doorway.

One of the bright spots of living at Carmen's house was getting to speak with her sisters more often. She'd never had a phone in her own home, but Carmen had been one of the first—and few—in the neighborhood to afford one.

"*Gracias.* I'll pick it up here."

When Carmen retreated, Anita leaned over to the bedside table and lifted the receiver.

"I finally have enough to get *Mamá* here," Carolina said.

"But *Mamá* doesn't want to go there. You know what she always says: 'What's an old lady who doesn't speak English going to do in America?'"

"I was hoping you could help me convince her. That's why I called."

"You'll have better luck trying to change *my* mind. . . . You may not have to try very hard anymore, actually."

"What do you mean? Are you seriously considering coming? I never thought I'd live to see the day. I guess my persistence paid off."

Anita drew her limbs close to her body and sniffled.

"Is everything okay?" Carolina asked.

"I met up with Armando last night."

"So, he found your hiding place?"

"I forgot to tell Juan Carlos to keep my whereabouts from him. He stopped by and asked if we could walk to Don Pedro's bar to talk. The only reason I agreed was so that I could break up with him. Tell him how terrible he is. But first I wanted to see how he would respond to me leaving . . . somewhere far away.

"I told him I was thinking about going to America to be with you and Diana. I wasn't actually considering it then, but I think part of me just wanted to know what he would say to the idea. Or if that comment would push him to think about our future to-gether at all. Would he try to make me stay? Beg me? Or maybe he'd ask if he could come too. Offer to run away together."

"What did he say?"

"He told me it was a great idea. That I should go there and work for a while and save up money, then come back here. He said it so casually. Not seeing me for a year, or potentially more, was no big deal to him. Not to mention the danger the journey across the border poses for a young woman traveling alone. I think he would have packed my bags for me if I'd asked. I'm not sure why I'm surprised at his response. I guess no matter how much someone in your life disappoints you, you still hope they care about you."

"Forget about him. Even more reason to come here—a fresh start."

"I'm so mad at myself for even being upset about it. Why did

I think he would sacrifice anything for me? He's yet to sacrifice so much as a dinner for me.

"But still, it hurts. I can't lie: My heart was broken. The one person I thought cared about me, loved me, had chosen to be with me had no problem living without me. In fact, he encouraged it. He wants me to go. You know the worst part about it?"

"What?"

"When I told him Carmen had taken me in because I couldn't go back home, he never offered to help. We've been dating three years—it's not like we're in high school anymore. Part of me hoped he'd take this as an opportunity to settle down, get a place of our own, get married . . . but he mentioned none of it. He never even brought up what happened at our house with *Papi*. It made me wonder if I had imagined it all and maybe he hadn't been there that night."

"Well, from what I know of him, he's never been Prince Charming," Carolina said.

"I know, but I still expected some kind of offer of help, of support. Anything would have meant the world to me right now when I feel so alone. Like no one cares about where I end up. How could he not know that?"

"I care, Anita. All of your family cares. Why do you think I've been trying so hard to get you here? To get *Mamá* here? But if *Mamá* won't come, you can help me help her. If we can send her enough money, she won't need *Papi* anymore. She can be free."

Maybe I can be free too.

"I talked to Juan Carlos this morning," Carolina continued. "He said you showed up at the house the other night around eleven and asked if he would take a walk with you. He told me he's worried about you—that you didn't seem like yourself or even look like yourself. He said you looked like a zombie."

The memory was blurry, but Anita knew it was true. "That's

exactly how I feel sometimes. Sleepwalking through life because it's too hard to be awake. I'm doing everything I can to stay here, but none of it seems to be working out."

Anita considered the job she'd recently started as a receptionist at a local mechanic shop. She had to be honest with herself. The job she had—or any job she could have here—would never pay enough to support herself, her mother, and her two brothers. At least the money in America—even as little as she might make as an undocumented immigrant—would go a lot further here.

Even sending a hundred dollars back to her mom every month would improve their lives dramatically.

I'll do this for my mother. For my brothers. Maybe a different life is what we all need—a fresh start, a new beginning.

And maybe there's something in it for me too. Maybe in a foreign place, I can become someone new. I can create a different life where I can actually experience some happiness.

If happiness is not here, maybe it's there.

"I guess I have no other choice," Anita finally said.

"I'll start working on the details of the trip. Don't worry, I'll take care of everything. You won't have to go through the desert like I did. I helped Diana get here through a completely different route—so much safer—and it worked beautifully. I promise, it will be . . ."

Carolina's voice faded into the background as Anita watched the future she had always imagined for herself fade with it. A simple life here in her country with her people—gone.

After a few more words of encouragement from her sister, Anita heard the dial tone. She returned the phone to its receiver and rolled onto her side, bringing her knees to her chest.

Where are you, God?

CHAPTER 15

MARCH 25, 1987

"Getting to America is going to be a challenge. This is probably the worst timing to try to cross the border."

It was busy at the *Plaza de Mercardo,* but it was Juan Carlos's favorite time to shop. He always told Anita the energy from the crowds of people was half the fun of shopping for groceries.

"Is there ever a good time to sneak into a country?" Juan Carlos said as he gently pressed into a mango.

"Not when you're Colombian, I guess."

Juan Carlos sniffed the mango before biting into it.

"Are you allowed to do that?" Anita asked.

"They know me here. It's okay. But you're right. It's going to be a challenge no matter when you go. It's a hard time to be Colombian."

"I just don't get it, though. I mean, I do, but the world really hates us without having the slightest clue what we—the actual citizens—endure here."

Juan Carlos whispered to the fruit vendor, "Here comes her sermon."

Anita placed a few limes in a plastic bag. "They blame us for all the drug trafficking, assassinations, and the rise of cartel violence. They blame a whole country as if people like me—like us—fund their chaos."

Juan Carlos looked at Anita, nodded, and then winked at the vendor.

"It'll be a miracle if I make it there alive," Anita said.

"I know it's a challenge, but Carolina and Diana made it there fine. They wouldn't be so persistent about you coming if they were worried you wouldn't make it alive."

As if Anita hadn't heard a word her brother said, she pulled out a few coins to pay the woman behind the cash register and continued on a tirade about Pablo Escobar and his friends littering her country—and its reputation—with drugs and political unrest. There was momentary relief across Colombia when the government finally captured and extradited Carlos Lehder, the cofounder of the Medellín Cartel. But her country was soon back to feeling the ripple effects of angry cartels set on getting payback.

"Even other Latin American countries are afraid of us," she added. "Isn't that ridiculous? As if they don't have their own cartels to contend with."

"There's no sense in getting all worked up about it, Anita. It's out of our control. We just have to do what we can to make our own lives better. And that's what you're doing."

Anita scoffed and rolled her eyes. "Reluctantly. I'm in too deep now to turn back. All the money I've spent, loans I've taken out, and time I've invested in getting everything done . . . I have no choice but to go, despite how much I keep rethinking it."

"When do you think everything will be ready for you to actually go?" They walked over to another vendor, who had large bins of spices. Juan Carlos pointed at the cumin and watched as a young girl—likely the vendor's daughter—bagged a small portion of the spice.

"Probably by the end of next week. I thought it would take longer, but Carolina is a pro."

"Well, she's done it twice already. You're blessed to have her doing so much of the work for you. Many people who cross the border have to figure it out on their own."

"Shh, keep your voice down," Anita said. "I don't need more people knowing I'm leaving. Enough people know I'm a traitor."

Juan Carlos put the spice in his tote, and Anita followed him to an open-air restaurant inside the market.

"I'm starving. Let's get some lunch," he suggested before asking about her first stop on the trip.

"Mexico. Carmen keeps telling me to be careful in Mexico because, surprise, surprise, they're not too keen on us. I guess they've had enough of Colombians bringing drugs into their country and using their border to smuggle them into America. But again, their country is also littered with their own kind of cartel violence and drug smuggling."

"Everyone's got their own devil to fight, but I guess no one has such a notorious devil as us," Juan Carlos said.

"That Escobar—it's all his fault. Because of him, every Colombian is labeled a potential drug smuggler. . . . The media doesn't help either."

The pair ordered two large plates of *arroz con pollo* before sitting down at a white plastic table with matching chairs. There was a red tablecloth draped across the table and a plastic protective layer on top.

"Are you going to pretend to be a student too? Like Carolina did?" he asked.

Anita laughed and nodded.

"Apparently, I'm a college student studying in Mexico and living with my aunt, who married a Mexican citizen. There's this whole story I have to memorize and a fake address too. I've been in touch with the guy who creates all the fake documents I need to prove I'm a student—I think he's from around here."

"Who would have known there was a whole industry dedicated to getting people like you across the border? I wonder who introduced Carolina to all these people," Juan Carlos said.

"I wouldn't be surprised if she figured it out on her own. She's always been *una verraca*."

A woman in a blue T-shirt and bell-bottom jeans dropped off two steaming bowls of yellow rice mixed with chicken and vegetables. She also placed a small plate of fried plantains at the center of the table.

"*Buen provecho,*" Juan Carlos said before digging in.

"Can you believe I have my own coyote? Well, I've been referring to him as a tour guide in my head. It sounds better than human smuggler."

"I guess a tour guide sounds more trustworthy than a coyote. Do you want to share a Coke?"

"Sure. But nothing else; I'm out of money, Juan Carlos. We thought what Carolina had saved up would be enough, but it wasn't. Prices have gone up."

"Is that what you came to talk with *Papi* about that one day?"

Anita nodded, looking down at her rice. "I hate that I had to talk to him, but what else was I supposed to do? People don't really give out loans to poor single women. He was my only option. Either he's excited to get rid of me or he hopes I'll send him back envelopes full of American dollars. Whatever it is, he helped me without giving it a second thought. I don't get him. Sometimes he can act like the best dad around and the next day he's pointing his gun at you."

Juan Carlos shook his head as if trying to erase a memory.

"I hope it's worth all it's cost me," Anita said. "I hope I can earn enough once I get there to pay all the money back. The last thing I need is debt collectors showing up at our mother's door. I'm trying to make her life easier, not more difficult."

"Everything will be fine, Anita. Just follow Carolina's directions to a T, and you'll be okay."

When Anita looked away over her shoulder, Juan Carlos probed for more. "¿Que te pasa? What's the matter?"

She turned to look at him. "It's just really starting to hit me. I could be leaving as early as next Friday. I think the hardest part is that everyone has been very encouraging about my decision to leave. Most of them wish it were them leaving . . . and so do I. I wish I could send them to find a new life for me.

"Here I am, the only person around who hates that country, and yet I'm the one going over. I'm such a hypocrite. I should be grateful for this opportunity, but all I can do is wish it weren't me."

Juan Carlos put his spoon down and placed his hands on his lap.

"Colombia has disappointed me." Anita's voice became shaky. "I expected it to love me the way I love it. To embrace me and provide what I need to make a life here. And yet I feel it gently pushing me toward America too . . . like it wants me to leave because it has no place to offer me here."

"Maybe it's not Colombia pushing you there. Maybe it's the Divine. There could be a lot of good waiting for you there, *hermana*. Try to think positively."

"The only positive thought I have is Colombia taking me back one day."

"This will always be your home, no doubt about it. If things don't work out, we'll be right here waiting for you with open arms."

CHAPTER 16

2018
CALI, COLOMBIA

MELANIE

Melanie gently rubbed her thumb across what looked to be smeared ink. The pages were wrinkled where the ink stretched. Anita must have been in tears when she penned the last two entries.

She closed the journal and stared straight ahead at the wall in front of her.

With each entry, the journal became more and more difficult to read. The words were getting darker with every turn of the page. While every line felt like a dagger in her side, the writing, and the writer, captivated her. This woman was a complex character filled with deep emotions and dilemmas that no one should have to endure at her age.

A bright light from the top of her nightstand caught her attention. She grabbed her phone to find a text from her younger sister, Naomi.

> How's Colombia so far? Daniel wishes he was there with you.

Naomi's message came through with a photo of her infant's gummy smile. He was propped up on his forearms under a colorful mobile. She smiled at the photo and felt a pang of guilt in her stomach that she'd yet to meet the adorable baby in person.

> He's getting so big! And cuter by the minute.
> Colombia is great . . . learning so much, actually. Did you ever know anything about Mom's upbringing? Like her childhood? Ever ask her about what her homelife was like?

She bit down on her bottom lip, hoping for a specific response from her sister. Had she been the only one of her siblings who never asked their mother about her life in Colombia? Perhaps her sister, Naomi, or her brother, Alex, had been just as clueless.

Three dots appeared on her screen.

> A little. I wrote a report about her life as an immigrant for a high school paper, but that's about it. Why?

Her stomach churned again. Never once as a student had she considered writing about her mother's immigrant experience. Thinking back, there had been plenty of opportunities to write about it, but had it ever even crossed her mind?

A memory came to her.

It was early in her senior year of high school. The days when writing essays for college applications felt like a full-time job. Northwestern was her dream, so when it came time for the essay portion for that particular application, Melanie recruited her English teacher's help.

Most essay prompts were some version of "Write about how you overcame something difficult in your life." That was easy. For every essay, Melanie wrote about becoming the editor in chief of her school's paper as a junior—a position normally reserved for a senior who had paid their dues.

When Mrs. Shirer reviewed Melanie's application from start to finish, the only qualm she had was with the essay. "Melanie, this is a great story and it's very well written, but don't you think the story of your family life would be more interesting? I've met your mom, and I just think it's amazing how she came to this country and all that she's accomplished since. I mean, look at you!" she'd said to Melanie.

But Melanie told her she didn't want to write about her family. That the story she referred to was about her mother, not about herself. Integrating her family's story into her college application process also didn't sit right with Melanie. The last thing she wanted was special treatment for a part of her life she felt no connection with—a part of her life that had caused more frustration than joy. "I think *this* is a better reflection of who I am and what I'm capable of," she responded, pointing to the printed essay on Mrs. Shirer's desk.

Mrs. Shirer tucked her lips in and returned her eyes to the essay on her desk to skim it one more time.

"It's great, Melanie. Any college would be lucky to have you."

Melanie sighed in relief, thanked her teacher, and picked up her essay before turning to leave the classroom.

The original plan had been to submit the application as soon as she had confirmation from Mrs. Shirer that her essay was the best it could be. But on her way to the school library that afternoon, because Mrs. Shirer had put unnecessary doubt in her head, she got the sudden urge to have one more trusted person review it. It would be the most prudent thing to do.

When her journalism teacher offered a similar comment as her English teacher, Melanie regretted having asked. Like Mrs. Shirer, Mrs. Thomas praised her writing but encouraged her to consider her family's story as the essay topic instead, seeing as it was unique and would stand out among a pile of other similar accomplishments students might write about.

Northwestern was on the line, so Melanie considered their advice.

Back in the school library, she sat on one of the rolling chairs with her legs crisscrossed in front of a desktop. The blinking cursor on her screen taunted her.

What's it going to be, Melanie?

She threw her head back and groaned before moving her hands to the keyboard.

Two hours later, she'd written a three-page essay about the day her mother moved Melanie and her siblings from New York to Maryland. Melanie explained that her parents had emigrated from Colombia to New York with nothing to their name. When her parents divorced, Anita followed friends to Maryland, where the cost of living was lower and a job at a daycare already awaited her.

When they arrived in Maryland, Melanie had to figure out how to get herself and her siblings enrolled in school. Because Anita still hadn't mastered the English language, it would have taken her hours to fill out paperwork that Melanie could complete in thirty minutes.

Being the eldest, she'd grown competent at completing official paperwork on behalf of her mother. She could even recite from memory things most children don't know about their parents, like the year they were born and medical history.

She huffed and obliged—and later regretted it when the bus didn't show up to their home on the first day of school. Melanie had made a mistake with their address on the school's intake forms, leaving them stranded and forcing Anita to be late for work on her first day. She and Melanie grumbled the whole way to school. Melanie recalled telling her mother she should have never been in charge of that paperwork to begin with—but she left that part out of the essay.

Melanie wrote about that experience in detail, along with two others that highlighted the struggles of growing up as a cross-cultural kid and navigating roles normally reserved for parents who spoke the country's native tongue.

She knew this essay would bode well with the admission staff, but it didn't make submitting the application any easier. Reliving those events had been one of the hardest things for Melanie to do. It was as if she'd been forced to look in a mirror and accept that this part of her life would always follow her. That no matter how much she achieved, the world would see *this* part of her before anything else—a part of her that, if she were being really honest, she wished wasn't real.

From the weird lunches to the embarrassing vehicles and the endless responsibilities that she felt forced her to mature more quickly than her peers, Melanie grew resentful of what she felt was her mother's heritage, not hers. It often left her fantasizing about what it would be like to have American parents and not constantly feel so different from both her parents and her peers.

That was the first and the last time Melanie wrote about her family.

I'll explain soon . . . I think.

When Melanie finally responded to her sister's message, she included a few pictures she'd taken with her grandmother.

> *Abuela* looks so sweet. I'm jealous you get to be with her!

The phone went back to the nightstand. Melanie picked up the journal again. She didn't open it but just held it in her hands, staring at the cover.

How could I have been so clueless about all the pain my mother has carried? Probably still carries.

Part of her didn't want to accept that her mother had lived such a tortured and sorrowful youth. If she had, it would explain so much about who her mother was today. And the explanation—one Melanie had never considered—would fill her with regret for all the years she spent viewing her mother as a submissive woman who'd let the world chew her up and spit her out without so much as a protest. If there was more to her mother's story, Melanie would have to learn to love a different woman.

Did she have any other choice but to accept it? Denying her own story hadn't done her any good. Maybe if she would have learned to accept her family, her heritage ... herself, she wouldn't feel so lost right now.

She thumbed through the pages of the journal and found where she left off. . . .

ANITA

Carolina had warned Anita to prepare to be with customs at the airport in Mexico City for a while, but she never expected a four-hour ordeal. No amount of warning could have prepared her for what happened.

She arrived at the airport at about one in the afternoon. Everything in Colombia had gone smoothly, so she expected nothing less in Mexico City.

The large, bustling airport soon became quiet when Anita noticed immigration officers separating groups of travelers from everyone else. The *República de Colombia* etching on the covers of their passports was unmistakable—she could see it from afar.

Anita could feel her heart beating faster with every step she took toward the officers.

What if I just run?

They're going to figure me out and send me back to Colombia.

Will they put me in prison?

Regret flooded her.

There were only two people in front of her now.

Not Colombians—they don't know how lucky they are right now.

Anyone without a Colombian passport was allowed to continue through customs with the normal checks and questions, which didn't take more than two minutes at most.

When the officer got a glimpse of Anita's passport, he pointed to a female officer across the room. "Go see her. Take all your belongings," he said.

She gulped and followed his directions.

With her index finger, the female officer pointed at a small, secluded room just a few steps down a dark hallway.

This must be where they interrogate, or hold, criminals.

The officer followed Anita into the room and shut the door behind her. It was a windowless room wrapped in gray cinder blocks—the perfect place to scare someone into submission.

Anita didn't speak; she only gulped once more.

"Why are you traveling to Mexico?" the officer asked.

Anita recited the story she'd practiced and memorized in her head the entire flight over. She was careful not to forget a single detail: the name of the aunt she would be living with in Mexico, the name of the school she was attending, the address where she'd be living, even the degree she sought.

The cold, dark room made her nerves skyrocket, putting her in danger of getting caught.

After what felt like an endless slew of questions, the officer told Anita to remove every piece of clothing—including underwear—so she could be searched.

"*¿En serio?* Are you serious?" Anita knew the question alone could get her into trouble, but it slipped out without much forethought. The officer's blank stare was enough to communicate to Anita that she meant every word she said.

Cold and embarrassed, Anita was forced to squat and bend over so that every crevice could be checked. The officer asked her to do push-ups and jumping jacks—up and down like a crazed animal. "Nothing is going to fall out of me," Anita said, breathless, again not giving her words much thought. "Is this even legal?"

The officer ignored Anita's questions once more.

"You may get dressed," the officer said after more searching.

Anita sighed under her breath. The worst was over and she had survived.

"Line up outside by the Exit sign at the end of the hall."

"What? Why? I don't get to go—"

"No questions. Follow the orders."

When Anita was dressed, she peeked her head out and saw the line growing longer. Were those all Colombians?

She walked to the huddle of people and stood at the end of the line. There was a woman in front of her who looked to be about twenty years older. "Where are they taking us?" Anita asked.

"The hospital." The woman spoke as if she'd been through this process before.

"The hospital? But why?"

"More searches." This time the woman didn't turn her head to respond, and she whispered as if hoping the officers wouldn't see her speaking.

They were loaded into a white van with an emerald-green stripe down the middle. With a large pit in her stomach, Anita climbed into the van and found a seat by the woman who'd given her the little bit of information the officer had not.

About fifteen minutes later, an officer Anita recognized from the airport unloaded the group of Colombians and escorted them through a back door of the hospital. Once inside, they were placed in a large room with four beds. There was a nurse by each bedside, moving a wand across the stomach of each Colombian, one by one.

"It's just an ultrasound. They want to make sure we haven't

swallowed drugs," whispered the woman when the officer left the room to guard the door.

Anita turned to look at her. "They only do this to Colombians?"

The woman nodded.

It wasn't until four hours later that everyone in the group Anita had been placed with was back at the airport and given permission to leave. Four hours of questioning, searching, and prodding without detaining anyone.

She picked up her luggage from baggage claim and nearly ran out of the airport. Once outside, Anita took a deep breath. Never again would she take fresh air for granted.

She followed the crowd to the line for taxis. When she made it to the front of the line, she suppressed a wide smile. With her breakup still fresh on her heart, she wasn't ready to think about love—not even close. But she couldn't deny her luck in being randomly assigned the youngest and most handsome taxi driver in the queue. At least in a foreign country there was no chance of commitment.

Their conversation flowed seamlessly back and forth from the moment she scooted into the back seat. His name was Mario, and even the back of his head was nice to look at.

"How far is *Plaza Garibaldi*? I've seen it in many of the Mexican *telenovelas* I've watched with my mother. It looks so beautiful."

"It's no more than twenty minutes from your hotel. How about we stop by the hotel to leave your things and I take you there?"

She met his gaze from the rearview mirror. His stare hypnotized her. She nodded while still wondering whether this was a good idea. Gallivant around Mexico with a complete stranger?

But then again, this might be her last chance to experience a real adventure—one that was nothing but fun. Who knew what life would be like once she crossed the border? She would likely land in America and get straight to work. She should have some fun while she still could. And having a dreamy tour guide only made the offer more appealing.

Carolina's instructions had been clear: "Once you get to the airport hotel, call me immediately." But when Mario pulled up to the hotel, she hurried to leave her things and completely forgot.

Back in Mario's taxi, this time sitting up front by his side, she spotted *Plaza Garibaldi* only a few minutes later. It was lit up, bright as day, and flooded with crowds of people and mariachi bands. She and Mario strolled through the wide-open space, passing brightly colored buildings with balconies, endless places to eat, and tall palm trees that reminded her of home. It was exactly like she'd seen on TV.

"Follow me. This place has the best tamales." He stopped in front of a street vendor, ordered a couple of tamales, and guided her to a bench nearby.

"Wow, you weren't kidding. These are incredible," Anita said after just one bite. "They're different from how we make them in Colombia, but still delicious."

"Maybe then you'll believe me when I say that place over there has amazing margaritas."

Her face turned serious. "I don't drink," she said without further explanation.

He looked at her for a moment, then glanced out at the plaza, noticing a mariachi band walking toward them.

"Oh, here they come," he said with a wide smile.

A group of six men stood in front of them and, without waiting for an invitation, began to serenade the couple. Anita could feel her cheeks turning red. She silently thanked God they hadn't sat down beneath one of the bright light posts scattered around the plaza.

Smiling and clapping along to their music, she forgot she was in a foreign place traveling as a criminal. But the end of the song made her realize it was getting late and she still hadn't called her sister. Carolina would be worried sick.

She thanked the band and asked Mario to take her back to her hotel.

"Do you need a ride tomorrow morning . . . back to the airport?" Anita had shared her plans with Mario—the made-up plans, not her real plans.

"I need to be back at the airport at seven."

"I'll be here at six, then, to give you plenty of time."

Anita smiled, unable to believe how lucky she had been to meet Mario. Maybe they'd keep in touch.

Or maybe they wouldn't. . . .

When he dropped her off at the hotel, an elderly man stopped her before she could reach the elevator. With a sharp look in his eyes, he shook his finger at her and said, "You are very naïve."

"Excuse me?" Anita responded.

"I saw you get back in the car of that young man. Don't do that again. You don't know what these men are like. They prey on travelers like you."

"Nothing happened. I'm fine."

"You are very lucky. But if you do it again, you might not have the same luck twice."

"But I have to get to the airport in the morning," she said, beginning to panic.

"I will take you. I'll meet you right here in the morning. 6:30 A.M."

Anita didn't respond with words; she just nodded and continued toward the elevator. She pressed the call button and reluctantly looked back to see if the elderly man was still standing where she'd left him. He was—standing as still as a statue. Is that where he had watched her earlier?

In the elevator, Anita remembered the night before she left Colombia when her mother laid her hands on her and prayed that God would protect her from predators.

It didn't make sense to trust another stranger, but something in her gut told her she could trust this man.

Maybe that man was an angel warning me about a predator. . . .

In that moment, she decided not to meet Mario in the morning. Why risk her journey and her life, for a guy she'd never see again?

She called her sister as soon as she was safely inside her room.

"Where have you been? I've been trying to reach you for hours." Carolina sounded out of breath.

"I was out getting dinner."

"*¿Estas loca?* Are you crazy? Don't go running around Mexico City on your own, Anita. You have to lay low."

"I'm fine, Carolina. I'm safe in my room. Immigration was a nightmare, but I made it out alive. You never mentioned the trip to the hospital for the ultrasound."

"The what?"

"Never mind. I want to forget it."

"You have a taxi reserved for the ride back to the airport tomorrow?"

"Yes." Anita held back the story about the man she'd just met in the lobby. She didn't need to add to her worries.

"Good. This is the last part of the trip you'll do alone. Once you're in Cuidad Juárez, you'll meet your coyote. It won't be much longer after that."

Tenseness in her stomach again. *Not much longer already?*

"I remember. I have it all written down. Airport in the morning followed by a taxi to the train station, which will take me close to my hotel. I will call you once I'm there."

"Right. Then I'll contact the coyote." Carolina's voice was fast and authoritative. "I'll give him the number to your hotel room so he can get in touch with you and give you the last instructions."

"Yes, I know. I have it all written down, remember?"

"I just want to make sure you don't miss a single step, Anita. This is serious. They will leave you behind if you're not there on time."

"I know, I know. . . ."

"Try to get some rest. And take care of yourself, okay?"

Sleep never came. She was exhausted, but thinking about going back to the airport in the morning kept her wired. What if they subjected her to another search like the one she'd just endured? Or what if they somehow discovered the real reason she was traveling?

Before the sun even rose, Anita got up, eyes dry and heavy, and dressed in long black shorts, a loose-fitting T-shirt, and a baseball cap she'd taken from her brother's closet. Beneath her shirt, she tightened the strap of a fanny pack her mom had sewed together for the trip. It would be the best way to keep her cash secure, she'd told her.

When she'd zipped her luggage bag closed, she took a deep breath and walked out of the hotel. From afar, she could see Mario sitting in his cab. She pulled her cap lower, as close to her eyes as she could get, and followed the elderly man who'd warned her about Mario the night before. There was something about him that reminded her of her older brother.

Thankfully, getting through the airport this time around was fast and straightforward. No extra checks or strange looks. And just two hours later, she was walking out of the small airport in Cuidad Juárez, a border town her sister had told her to be extra cautious about. "Don't trust anyone there," she'd told her. "Lots of gangs and violence." So she took care not to look anyone in the eye or fall into conversation, not even with the taxi driver who drove her to the closest station of *los ferrocarriles nacionales,* their local transit system.

On the train, she curled up by a window seat, hugging her luggage close to her chest until she reached her hotel—the last place she'd sleep before crossing into America.

The journey was almost over, yet it was just beginning.

CHAPTER 18

2018
CALI, COLOMBIA

MELANIE

The journal was heavy to read. The fear, the danger, the loneliness. . . . How could her mother have gone through all that? The second half of this entry had also been kind of exhilarating. What her mother experienced was unlike anything Melanie had ever walked through. She thought back to her junior year at Northwestern when she considered applying for a study-abroad program in Europe. It ended up being too expensive for her to pursue, but even if she'd been able to, how would she have fared on her own in a foreign country?

Would she have been able to figure out how to get around? Find food? Ask for help in an emergency? From the stories she'd read, it was clear her mother was resourceful, gutsy, and could hold her own. She knew when to speak up and when to yield. Even when she was afraid or confused or even depressed, Anita seemed more than capable of finding the fortitude needed to survive.

She was a fighter.

What happened next? Melanie had to know. But as she turned the page to the next journal entry, she heard a group of unfamiliar voices coming from the front of the house.

The party guests must be arriving.

This was the worst timing possible. While part of her looked forward to meeting a lot of her extended family, the story was getting *really* good, and the last thing Melanie wanted was to stuff the journal back into the nightstand and spend the night thinking about what else she'd learn inside.

But she'd promised her grandmother her undivided attention during her birthday celebration. She'd spent enough time locked up in her mother's old bedroom. It was time to enjoy her family, even if it meant speaking more Spanish with strangers than she'd ever spoken in her entire life.

After putting the journal back in the drawer, Melanie changed into a floral tunic dress and brown leather sandals. She brushed out the knots in her hair and swiped on a thin coat of mascara. It had been a long day of travel and unearthing a history she'd been blind to her entire life, but she didn't want to look as tired as she felt.

She took a deep breath and reached for the doorknob. Before she could open the door, a thought stopped her in her tracks.

How long would I have lived without knowing these stories had I never come here? Would I have ever known?

Her eyes shut tight and she shook her head.

I can't think about that right now.

As the bedroom door swung open, the sound of laughter and loud, excited voices covered her. The party had started, and it made Melanie wonder what more she might learn about her family tonight.

CHAPTER 19

Countless unfamiliar faces crossed the threshold of her grand-mother's home. Melanie was friends on social media with some of her extended family members who lived in Colombia, but none of the guests looked familiar yet.

It wasn't long before Alba and Anita began to usher every guest over to Melanie. They were so excited to introduce every-one to their *Americana*. And everyone couldn't believe they were finally given the opportunity to meet Anita's eldest daughter.

She was pulled into hugs and kisses by guest after guest, whom she assumed had to be neighbors or friends from her grandmother's church. But with every new person she met, she learned of a new connection to her family tree. She hugged great-aunts and great-uncles and politely waved at second cous-ins. How could the branches extend this far? But Alba insisted they were all connected to the Carvajal lineage.

The guests spoke fast and with dramatic hand gestures. Mela-nie found herself asking many of them to repeat their questions. "*¿Como?*" she'd say.

They asked about her flight and her impressions of Cali so far. Some asked whether she'd tried this type of food or that type of drink. Another wondered what it was like to live in Miami—he'd wanted to visit all his life.

Melanie did her best to be cordial and show enthusiasm for the new acquaintances, but their native accents were becoming increasingly difficult to understand. She needed breaks in between each conversation—the more they asked, the more drained she felt. It was something she hadn't considered. In the United States, she had a safety net. If she didn't know a certain word or how to phrase in Spanish how she really felt, she could easily throw in English. Spanglish was another language people of Miami knew. But not here. It would be Spanish all the way or nothing. Who knew internal translation would take so much out of her?

She walked into the kitchen, hoping for a moment alone. After pouring herself a glass of a pulpy drink she found on one of the counters, she sat down at the table, which was conveniently hidden behind a wall that shielded the living room from the kitchen. It was the perfect place to catch her breath and recover.

A look at the clock on the stove told her it'd been only forty-five minutes since she came out of her room. The night would surely be long.

Thoughts about her mother's story stole her attention away from the party. She wanted to know more. Who was this woman?

When she heard her mother's voice growing louder on the other side of the wall, Melanie got up from the table and peeked her head out. There she was, standing at the far end of the living room. Anita held her stomach from laughing so hard and squealed every time she saw another familiar face walk into the home. If it hadn't been Alba's birthday, Anita would have been the most popular person in the room.

Melanie smiled. She'd never seen her mother so carefree,

lighthearted, and well received. It looked like she was cracking jokes or sharing hilarious stories, because no matter what came out of her mouth, everyone around her howled. This woman was enjoyable to watch from a distance. In fact, Melanie wanted to get closer.

Glass in hand, she crept into the living room and found a seat close to her mother. It was good timing because Anita was sharing stories about her youth. Ridiculous pranks she pulled, embarrassing moments in school, and stories that some refused to believe were even true.

Anita was a gifted storyteller. How unfortunate Melanie only now discovered it. Melanie listened and laughed, but nothing amused her more than watching how the others reacted to Anita's stories. They couldn't get enough of her, and neither could Melanie.

"All right, who's hungry?" Anita yelled into the crowd. "Start lining up at the kitchen. We've made enough for everyone to have seconds!"

"I'll take care of the music," said a middle-aged man in an olive polo shirt and round glasses. He went out to his car and returned with a tall black speaker that he set up in the room that usually functioned as Alba's *tiendita*. It had been cleared out to make room for a dance floor, with mismatched plastic chairs lined up against each wall.

Within seconds, salsa music roared as the sun set into the horizon. Melanie plugged her ears while they adjusted, but no one else seemed to mind.

"I don't need any of the chicken feet, Mom, thanks," Melanie said as she handed her mother an empty bowl.

The *sancocho* continued to simmer on the stove and was accompanied by a perfectly shaped mound of white rice, boiled yucca, fried sweet plantain, and a salad of shredded iceberg lettuce and tomatoes. Anita had also made *jugo de maracuya*—a drink Melanie recognized from her childhood when Anita would buy it premade, frozen and packaged in plastic bags at the grocery store.

The food was a hit. But the party really got started when the first person spun onto the dance floor and reeled in a partner. Eventually, even Alba danced freely in the middle of the dance floor. Most ninety-year-old women couldn't move their hips like her . . . but other ninety-year-old women weren't Alba.

"Come on, *Americana*, show me what you got!" shouted a man with gray hair who looked to be just a smidge younger than her grandmother.

Melanie shook her head and waved her hand. "I'm too full to dance. You look great, though."

This happened a few more times—maybe there was a bet on who could get her on the dance floor first—but Melanie hadn't learned how to dance salsa growing up and this wasn't the place to learn.

Rather than risk more invitations, Melanie found a dark corner of the room where she could watch the party guests move their feet faster than she could register. It was the perfect spot to be present but hidden.

It wasn't long before her brilliant plan of staying invisible failed. It's not that she didn't want to have more conversations with her extended family; she just worried they would laugh at her *gringo* accent. And she hadn't fully recovered from the earlier conversations yet.

Someone she swore must be a second or third cousin, because she was about her age, came up to her, attempting to be heard over the earsplitting music. "Are you liking Colombia so far?" she yelled in Spanish with a wide smile on her face.

Her name was Marcela, and, like Melanie, she'd gone to university. Marcela had been working as an administrative professional at her alma mater for three years, which clued Melanie in to the fact that Marcela was two or three years older than her. They went back and forth talking about where they lived and what they did for work and play. When the conversation stalled, they both turned and looked out onto the dance floor. The space was nearly full of people of every age and stage of life. Children twirled on the floor as if attempting to show off some break-dancing moves. Young couples held each other tight while dancing in perfect unison. And the rest seemed beyond content to move and sway to the rhythm of the music, taking turns with whoever lacked a partner.

Watching the crowd, Melanie felt as if someone were slowly removing bricks from a backpack she'd been carrying. With each new person she watched dance, she relaxed more and more into the wall she'd been leaning on. How much lighter would she feel if she got out there and joined them?

"Hey, a couple of us are going to hit up *La Topa* after the party. It's a salsa club. You should come with us! This is the salsa capital of the world, after all, and *La Topa* is the place to watch some real pros. Not that these guys aren't impressive," Marcela said as she looked back at the guests.

Melanie smiled at the invitation—Marcela was trying to be kind—but the idea of leaving her grandmother's house without her mother made her stand upright again. Could it be safe to gallivant around Cali with her cousins late at night? She wasn't sure.

"That sounds fun, but I don't think I can. I have a lot of work to get done before I head to Bogotá." Melanie did her best not to stumble on her words from the nerves that had fired off.

"Oh, come on. You can work on that tomorrow, no? It's Saturday night and you're in Colombia. You can't leave here without experiencing one of our epic salsa clubs." In that moment, Melanie remembered, once again, Genesis urging her to have a little fun exploring Colombia. But going out at night didn't feel like the right way to do that.

"Well, is it safe? You know, my Spanish is not perfect." She recognized this wasn't the best response to someone who lived in the city, but Melanie said the first thing that came to mind. Perhaps it would have been better to stay quiet. Her cousin's furrowed eyebrows made her wonder whether she'd just offended her. It was hard to tell.

"Of course it's safe. Plus, Nicholas, Christian, and a couple of their friends are coming." She pointed at two young men across the room. They were tall with buff arms nearly bursting out of their fitted T-shirts. Their eyebrows looked freshly waxed, and she could have sworn she could smell their cologne all the way from where she stood.

"No one's going to mess with us when we have them with us. Plus, you don't want to stay here. In about an hour or so, the music is going to die down and everyone is just going to sit around and drink coffee. Boring. That's why we go out to keep the party going."

It made her feel better that there would be men accompanying the group, but a bigger part of Melanie still didn't like the idea of going to the club without her mom or grandmother to advise her of the right things to say and do. Maybe if she asked her mother, she would insist she not go. Surely, after all the horror stories she'd heard growing up, there was no way her mother would let her go out without her supervision, especially this late at night.

"It sounds fun. Let me just make sure it's okay with my mom. She might need my help to clean up."

Her cousin shrieked in excitement and responded, "You're going to love it! We'll probably leave here in half an hour." She ran off, probably to tell everyone else her age the good news about their American cousin agreeing to go out with them.

Melanie found her mother serving *sancocho* to an elderly man who looked at her with twinkling eyes. He was enchanted with either Anita or the oversized chicken feet she'd just added to his bowl. Melanie tapped her mother's shoulder and whispered, "Mom, Marcela asked me to go to some salsa club with her in about half an hour. But I figured it would be too dangerous."

"*¿Que?* You would love that! You should go. I bet they're going to *La Topa*. Diana and Carolina dragged me there all the time. You know I'm not much of a dancer, but there's an energy in that place that can turn anyone pro." Anita's face lit up. Melanie wondered whether her mother ever wrote about some of those memories—the ones that made her look lively and young.

"Are you sure? Especially this late at night?"

"I don't see a problem as long as some of your *primos* are going. You should go and have some fun. Just stay together. It's not too far from here."

There was nothing else she could say or do to get out of the invitation—even her mom urged her to go. It was as if everyone was in on the goal of making Melanie have more fun. It wouldn't be unlike Genesis to have planned this—forcing her into uncomfortable situations from a world away.

She stared at her mother a moment longer, remembering all the stories she'd heard from adults back home of muggings and kidnappings. Another squeal from Anita at the sight of a new guest who'd just walked in brought Melanie back to the room.

Suddenly her fear was replaced with a desire to experience more of that light feeling she'd felt earlier when she watched the party guests on the dance floor.

She kissed her mother on the cheek and walked back toward Marcela. Being in Colombia brought out a different side of Anita—a side Melanie liked more and more. She wondered whether Colombia would bring out a different side of her as well.

CHAPTER 20

"**S**o, what do you think?" Marcela said as the group took their first steps into the club.

"We're not at *Abuela*'s house anymore," Melanie said.

The salsa club might have been bigger than her grandmother's home, but there was a lot less room to hide. When she walked in with four of her cousins and two of their friends, it was like the party had been going on for hours.

There was no telling how many people were in the club right now. The ones standing off to the sides were shoulder to shoulder, and those on the dance floor were mere centimeters from crashing into one another. The walls in the entire place were painted a deep red, and the only light illuminating the space was bright hues of blue coming from the stage.

Melanie's gaze turned up and she noticed smaller crowds on a second floor. They mostly sat around small round tables, munching on appetizers and drinking from clear plastic cups.

A large piece of artwork caught her eye as they moved deeper into the club. It was a re-creation of da Vinci's *The Last Supper*, but instead of Jesus and his disciples, there was a group of Afro Latino artists and their instruments—maracas, guitars, congas, you name it. The painting spanned the entire length of the bar and looked strikingly similar to the live band playing onstage just a few steps away.

The men and women who filled the dance floor spun and swayed like seasoned veterans who'd been dancing salsa their entire lives. When she noticed that just about every woman was wearing heels, Melanie looked down at her sandals and pulled her feet together. Once again, she'd chosen the wrong footwear.

She looked down at her feet every few seconds, hoping to avoid being invited to dance. Having never learned any of the steps, she knew she would look foolish and very *American*— especially in these shoes.

Nevertheless, being in this crowded space started to change something in her. She'd felt this strange feeling—albeit more mildly—back at her grandmother's party. But the energy was different in this space, causing the feeling to grow stronger.

The *conguero* on the stage started playing a new song on his congas, and Melanie suddenly felt the urge to move her hips in rhythm with the beat. Before long, the *sonero* slid a wooden stick up and down a *guiro*, while a trumpet aimed at the ceiling added a new depth to the music that sent a tingling sensation up Melanie's spine. It became increasingly more difficult to keep her feet and shoulders still.

Whatever began to rise within her felt instinctual. Second nature and out of her control.

Which explains why after the first stranger put out his hand to ask her to join him in the *rumba* surrounding them, she didn't think twice. It felt as if some strange spirit had infiltrated her body. It must be true what her mother always said: *Colombians don't learn how to salsa; it's in their blood.*

How Melanie was able to keep up with every step and turn that her dance partner expertly maneuvered, she had no idea.

But she did it, and she loved every minute of it. Her smile got wider and wider as she reveled in the sensation of her hair coming loose from her bun and flowing in the current of wind that emerged from the turn variations.

And just one song wasn't enough. Guy after guy wanted a turn twirling the *Americana*. She should be nervous about dancing with so many strangers, but this lively feeling she'd never experienced before distracted her. Not only did she come alive . . . she floated.

After she had danced nonstop for an hour with different partners, her throat felt sapped of moisture. When the guy she danced with pulled away to shuffle his feet in front of her, she decided this was her only chance to get off the dance floor. She gave him a smile, waved, and mimed that she had to go.

She ran to the bar and stuck her index finger in the air, hoping the bartender would notice. Nothing would offer relief from the heat right now but an ice-cold water.

The bartender took the cap off the bottle and handed it to Melanie.

"That's what you're having?" said a familiar voice behind her. She turned to find Sebastian, one of her cousins' friends who'd also been at her grandmother's birthday party.

"I'm nervous to drink anything that's not in a bottle. It's not safe." She wanted to smack her own forehead. What a dumb thing to say. No doubt, he'd now consider her an alarmist.

He was either used to hearing these silly comments from Americans or he was incredibly forgiving, because he responded only with a smile before leaning in to hear her better.

Sebastian had the biggest brown eyes Melanie had ever seen. Even in the dim light of the club, they glistened. His dark brown hair was long enough for a strand to have escaped and tickle his eyebrow. If she hadn't made a vow to reject any and all romantic

relationships until her work life was back on track—and probably even after that—she'd be leaning in closer to him as well.

"Marcela told me you're a journalist, huh?" he asked. Even
his voice soothed her.

"Yeah. I write for a newspaper in Miami." She felt like a
fraud every time she said it out loud. Did she really write for a
newspaper if they didn't publish her articles? At least this guy
would never know the difference.

"Do you enjoy it?"

She struggled to find the right words in response. How can
you enjoy something that always rejects you?

"Um, yeah. . . . It's work, you know?"

"Well, I think that's really cool. And I heard you're here to
write a story about Colombia. You'll be able to give an interesting perspective since you're both American and Colombian.
Don't make us look bad, okay?" He gave her a playful nudge
with his elbow.

She gave a blank stare and nodded, contemplating how she
could change the topic as quickly as possible.

"So, what about you? What do you do?" Melanie asked.

"I'm in the military, on a break right now."

"Oh, cool. Did you always want to do that?"

"Not really. I just didn't know what else to do. And I wanted
stability and decent pay. I can help my mom now, and that's all
that matters to me."

"That's pretty noble of you. You must be very close to her."

"Of course. She moved in with me last year when my dad
passed away. She's done so much for me, there was no question
I'd help support her."

Melanie looked down at her feet.

Sebastian continued, "She loves your mom. My mom . . . she
talks about your mom all the time. She misses her. They were

really tight growing up. She couldn't wait to meet you tonight. I think most people around here feel that way about your family. . . . There's something special about them."

Melanie looked at him and smiled. His words were genuine and sweet, but they also brought an aching pain in her chest.

"Thanks. . . ." Melanie didn't know how else to respond. "So, did your mom teach you to dance? The men around here move so different from the men in America—even in Miami."

"Oh yeah. We learn how to salsa before we learn how to walk. Your mom didn't teach you?"

"Not really. There weren't too many occasions for dancing. She says she's not very good, but I'm not sure I believe her. Before we left the party, she told me she came here all the time, so she's better than she lets on."

"Yeah, my mom has photos of her here with your mom when they were younger. . . . She says everyone wanted to dance with Anita. But that's your mom, right? Always so humble."

Melanie nodded.

"What about *cumbia*?" Sebastian asked. "Did she ever teach you how to dance *cumbia*?"

"*¿Cumbia?*" she asked, immediately regretting it. How could she not know about this type of dance?

"Well, then I think you know what you need to learn before you leave here. I can show you—"

"You guys ready to head home? I know Melanie has some work to do tomorrow," Marcela yelled behind her over the booming congas.

"Already?" Melanie said, turning to face her. She couldn't believe the word had come out of her mouth. Never in her life had she been the one trying to make the fun last a little bit longer. But she wasn't ready to leave the party yet—she wanted Sebastian to finish what he was about to say, and she wanted a little more time in this room that was filled with so many who shared her Colombian blood. Would she ever have another opportunity to be in a place like this?

Watching the people in the club dance, laugh, and chitchat over colorful drinks had first made her feel envious, but now she wanted only to bump shoulders with them. These were people who knew themselves. Knew their heritage and loved it. Melanie wanted to be like them.

Was it too late? She'd spent her whole life running away from this part of her identity. For her, having Colombian parents represented not only poverty and insecurity but chaos too. They yelled when they spoke, showed up to every event hours late, and asked the most intrusive questions. It seemed like, while she lived in chaos, everyone else around her enjoyed a calmer existence. Large homes with tons of space for everyone in the family, birthday parties that started at the time the invitation stated, and an ability to afford whatever was needed.

A few times in her life, she'd attempted to embrace the chaos she'd been born into—whatever that meant—but her patience always wore thin.

That was beginning to change now.

Maybe it was the music, the beauty in the people who surrounded her, the warm way her cousins and their friends had received her. . . . Whatever it was, a longing to be immersed in her Colombian identity began to fill her faster than she could process. She wanted to learn from them. Be like them.

She was one of them after all. How hard could it be?

Marcela's eyes widened at Melanie's plea to stay at the club longer. "*Ayyy*, okay. I thought you might want to get home, but if you want to stay and dance a little bit longer, well, you don't have to tell me twice."

Marcela shimmied her shoulders and pulled her back onto the dance floor. Melanie barely had time to drop her near-empty water bottle onto the bar, but she did turn around long enough to notice the silly grin on Sebastian's face as he watched her disappear into the crowd.

CHAPTER 21

Melanie awoke in her mother's old bed by herself the next morning.

Anita was an early riser. She was likely already in the kitchen whipping up *calentado* and *arepas* with her mother and brother. Melanie wanted to go back to sleep. She'd gotten to her grandmother's home a little before three in the morning.

Her grandmother's birthday celebration had been fun, but the salsa club was a different level of exhilaration. She linked her fingers behind her head and recalled the wild and free feeling she'd experienced almost the entire night as she spun and spun and spun around the dance floor. She stopped caring who watched her or if she didn't quite land a step—it had been the kind of fun where nothing else mattered.

An image of Sebastian's brown eyes and perfectly tousled hair popped into her mind. She hadn't even worried what he might think of her dance skills as he watched her from the bar. Every few minutes, she'd look over in his direction to check if he still watched. He never took his eyes off her.

When was the last time she'd felt that carefree?

I need more of that. I've lived such a rigid life, and look where

*that's gotten me. . . . I'm not succeeding like I thought I would be.
I thought if I remained disciplined and focused on the pursuit of my
career, I'd be in a different place.*

I'm failing, floundering . . . miserable.

*No one else tries as hard, yet they seem so happy. So free. Like
they've found something I didn't even know existed.*

Melanie rolled onto her side and spotted her phone on the
bedside table. She reached for it and opened her inbox. Another
ten emails since she last checked it. There was that tense feeling
in her shoulders again. She opened the emails anyway. Tomorrow, she'd be flying to Bogotá, and she still had the responsibility of bringing home a good story. While she wanted to have as
much fun during the rest of her time in Cali as she'd had the
night before, she'd still have to prepare enough for being in Bogotá.

There had to be a balance she could find.

After responding to a few emails, she reached into the drawer
of the bedside table and pulled out the journal.

As she imagined might happen, she never got a chance to ask
her mother for permission to keep reading the night before. But
there was so much more she wanted to know . . . more she wanted
to read. There was something about reading the details from the
time-worn pages and leather in her hands. Even if her mother
offered to share more, would the storytelling be as absorbing
outside the journal? Would the story*teller* be the same?

She'd read just one more entry, and then for sure she would
ask her mother about it.

Cracking open the leather journal and being careful not to
bend the pages or the cover, Melanie found where she'd left off
and allowed herself to be drawn back into its world.

CHAPTER 22

APRIL 3, 1987
CUIDAD JUÁREZ, MEXICO

ANITA

"I'll meet you in the lobby of your hotel early tomorrow morning." The coyote's voice on the phone was slow and hushed and intimidating enough that Anita didn't want to interrupt him. "I'll be wearing jeans and a black T-shirt. Don't say a word to me while in the hotel. This is very important. There could be officers roaming around. Just follow me outside, where I can give you instructions out of earshot. Be aware of your surroundings, too, in case someone follows you."

The next morning, she put a face to the voice. The sun was just beginning to rise when she followed him outside, carrying her luggage by the strap to keep the sound of dragging wheels from drawing attention to herself. About two blocks from the hotel, he stopped and turned to speak to her in a whisper.

"Are all your belongings in there?" He pointed at her luggage.

She nodded.

"Everything? Even your money?"

She nodded again.

Except she wasn't telling the entire truth. How many naïve

people had stuffed their money into their luggage bag and been robbed on a journey like this?

How did Mamá know I'd need this? she thought as she touched the bag pressed against her stomach. Alba may have never made this trek—never left her neighborhood—but she'd always been clever.

He grabbed Anita's luggage. "Where are you taking that?" she asked.

"I'll get it across the border. You follow him now." He pointed at a man stepping out of a black pickup truck. The same one this coyote climbed into with Anita's luggage.

"Can't I keep my bag with me? It's not very big," she whisper-yelled.

"No. It will slow your crossing. You can't travel with anything."

"What's the likelihood I'll see my luggage again?" Anita asked before silently saying a little prayer that she'd have the chance to document her journey in the journal she'd stashed in her bag.

"If I do my job correctly and you follow my instructions, very likely." He slammed the door shut and started the engine.

"I'm going to cross the street. You stay on this side, but follow me," said Antonio, her new coyote. He was dressed similarly to the last one except his shoes were noticeably muddy—had he just come from a trip across?

Just a few minutes later, there it was: America. She was still in Mexico, but the rising sun allowed her to see the homes on the other side. They were so close she felt like she could reach out her hand and touch them.

A bit farther down, Anita saw the bridge that gave way for drivers and walkers to cross into the United States. In the quiet of the morning, there was just a trickle of cars driving across. Soon, traffic would pick up, and hopefully the black truck would be part of it.

She kept her eyes closely on Antonio. When he started to veer off the sidewalk and into a grassy area, she crossed the street and got closer to him. There was a chain-link fence blocking access to the Rio Grande and a bright-yellow warning sign that read, "*¡Peligro!*"

Mexico would need more than a metal sign to stop her now.

They reached a portion of the fence where a large hole had been cut. The hole was so large she barely had to crouch to get through.

Once through the fence, Antonio stopped for a moment, took in his surroundings, and turned to her and said, "Are you ready?"

She inhaled deeply and nodded.

"Get on my back," he said as he knelt down.

When Anita hesitated, he looked at her again. "Let's go. We don't have a lot of time."

She climbed on like a child climbs onto their father's back. The water reached only to the tops of his ankles, but that would be enough to give Anita away if she'd have the unfortunate luck of getting stopped by a border patrol agent.

"As soon as we're on the other side, you run as fast as you can, okay?"

Anita nodded.

It felt like it took no more than twenty steps to cross the canal. When his feet hit the grass, she jumped off and ran, following him closely, crouched down as low as possible. Her breaths became heavy and sporadic, and for a moment she smiled.

I did it.

I'm on American soil.

She wanted to touch the dirt, bring it closer to her nose. She wanted to know if it felt different here, smelled different. But there was no time. The coyote had told her not to look back, to just run, staying as close to him as possible.

Her heart pounded so loudly she could hear it clearly in her ears. She felt like a fugitive who'd just escaped prison.

Am I a fugitive? I escaped and I'm on the run—illegally. I guess you can call me a fugitive.

A fugitive running for my life . . . or more like from my life.

They ran through a development of homes that were all about the same size and shape. They were pretty but all identical, with nothing to tell them apart except the cars that sat outside. When she straightened her back for a moment, the coyote hissed at her.

"Stay down. Make yourself as small as possible," he said.

Alba would never have been able to make this trip, let alone this run.

At a pay phone on a street near what looked to be a downtown area, the coyote stopped to make a call. It lasted only a few seconds, and within minutes, the man with dual citizenship she'd given her luggage to back in Mexico pulled up in front of them. She was more surprised than she should have been to see him again.

She followed the coyote's orders and got in the truck.

"Where are you taking me?" she asked the driver. He kept his sunglasses on despite the cloudy morning.

"My apartment."

Anita wondered whether her sister Diana had gone to this man's apartment on her trip across as well. Or how many other women, men, and even children had been escorted by this man.

For a split second, Anita thought about jumping out of the

vehicle before they got to his apartment. What if she never left after she went inside? How could she be 100 percent certain this was the man her sister Carolina had hired for her? Who could she trust?

But she was stuck. Without him, she'd be more at risk of getting caught by border patrol. That couldn't happen—not when she'd already gotten this far. She had to keep going. She'd never make it to New York without this man's help. As much as she didn't want to admit it, she needed him. The thought made her cringe. She hated that she needed him . . . needed any man.

"I don't have any other travelers today. It's just you," he said when he unlocked the door to his apartment.

Traveler? Is that what he calls us?

"Usually, these trips are made in groups," he continued. "You're lucky to make the journey on your own."

Lucky?

Anita looked at him with a half smile before taking slow steps inside.

"Normally, this is when I help people change their appearance so they can blend in with *los Americanos*. Sometimes we dye their hair, change their clothes, and practice interacting in a way that doesn't draw attention. But you're an easy customer."

Anita combed through her hair with her fingers. She figured he was referring to her lighter hair color and green eyes. It would be enough to keep border patrol—and other suspicious people— off her back.

"Have a seat," he said, pointing at a card table near the kitchen. "We'll leave in a few hours."

Anita dropped her head and sighed.

"What's the matter?" he asked.

"Huh? Oh, nothing. Just tired."

The man laughed. "Living in America isn't going to be a

walk in the park. I hate to break it to you, but the long days have only just begun."

Anita sat down and stared at the wall. Every hour, she felt more and more numb.

"It's time to go," he said eventually.

She'd fallen asleep at the table, her head resting on her crossed arms. His voice woke her in a fright. Part of her wished it had all been a dream.

She grabbed her bag and checked to make sure her fanny pack was still safely attached to her waist, then followed him back to his truck. They'd been driving about fifteen minutes when Anita spotted a sign that read El Paso International Airport.

Before this week, she'd never been on a plane—never thought she would be. Soon she'd be able to say she'd been on three planes . . . in a matter of days.

The man parked the truck and told her to find a seat when they got inside. He would walk up to the counter to buy her a ticket to New York. After a few minutes speaking with the flight attendant behind the counter, he sat down next to Anita on the bench and opened a big newspaper to conceal his face as he gave her the last bit of instructions.

She nodded, took the ticket from his hand, and then walked in the direction he told her to go. She looked for a sign that said LaGuardia, New York, just like he'd told her. Many of the seats outside the gate were already taken.

"Do you speak English?" said a woman in a long black skirt and a delicate white head covering. She was sitting with a duffel bag draped across her lap.

Anita shook her head.

"Maybe we can help each other, then," the woman said, patting the seat next to her.

"This is where I wait for the plane to New York, right? Is that where you're going too?" Anita asked.

"Yes. *Nueva York*. Isn't that where all immigrants go?" she said, smiling.

"I guess so."

They boarded the plane and found seats next to each other. While she didn't want to talk with this woman the whole flight over—there was so much she needed to process—Anita felt safe sitting near her.

Her stomach churned and her knee bounced. When the flight attendant offered Anita food and a drink, she turned it down. Her appetite had long left her. Instead, she was filled by the view of the city growing smaller and smaller.

Soon, she would see her sister again after three years of being apart. She'd meet her niece, Rosa, for the first time. She'd be an immigrant in a foreign land. That's when it hit her. . . .

I made it.

I actually made it to America.

Her eyes welled up—she was relieved that she'd made it but brokenhearted about what she'd left behind.

CHAPTER 23

2018
CALI, COLOMBIA

MELANIE

Melanie stretched out her legs to rest the journal open on her lap and let out a deep sigh.

She stared up at the ceiling for a few seconds before reaching for her phone. After two rings, Naomi's face shone wide on the screen.

"Whoa—you look like you haven't slept in ages," Naomi said.

"Thanks. . . . I was out late last night with some of our cousins."

"What? You? Out late?" Naomi's eyebrows reached the creases of her forehead.

"Ha ha. Very funny. Listen, I have a question. . . . Am I crazy or did Mom never bring up how she got to the United States?"

"What do you mean? I know she crossed the border and stuff."

"But did she ever tell you details about the journey? Like what it took to get here and the experience of actually crossing with a coyote?"

Melanie watched her sister purse her lips and gaze off to the side.

"I don't know. . . . I don't think so. The report I did in high school was more about her experience once she was here. So, no, I don't think I ever heard the details. Why? Is this about your text from yesterday?"

Melanie's eyes closed momentarily. "How could we have never asked? We just had zero interest in her life before America?"

"I wouldn't say we had zero interest. We were just oblivious, I guess. We had everything we needed. I mean, we were far from rich, but we never lacked anything, so maybe that kept us from any kind of curiosity about what happened before our lives."

"I never thought about it that way," Melanie whispered.

Never lacked anything . . . Melanie replayed her sister's words in her head. It made her slightly nauseous. If anyone had asked her to describe her childhood, *lack* would be one of the first words she used. Yet that still never prompted Melanie to look for answers. Could it be that her apparent lack was precisely what made her apathetic toward her mother and her culture? And perhaps the absence of her father only added to her lack of curiosity. If he'd been around, would there have been more stories to share?

"Do you really feel that way?" Melanie continued. "That we never lacked anything?"

"Yeah. Like I said, we may not have had fancy things, but there was always happiness. Mom did her best, took us to the park every day even when she was dead tired from work, read to us every night, played every kind of ridiculous game we invented. . . ." Naomi put her phone down momentarily to scoop her baby into her arms. "I always appreciated the lengths she went to, to be present with us."

Maybe it was because Naomi had become a mother already or maybe she was simply more compassionate than Melanie felt in this moment, but she was right. Everything she said about her mother was true.

Even after running away from a life of despair in Colombia and being abandoned by her husband in the United States, Anita never let it color the way she parented. Perhaps all she ever did was try to do exactly what her parents had been unable to do for her: provide a safe home where love and joy could grow.

Melanie took a slow, pained breath.

"You're right, Naomi. Hey, I gotta go. I have to talk to Mom. But first let me see that sweet face."

Naomi propped the phone up on her kitchen counter and wiggled Daniel's body in front of the camera.

"Come see us soon, okay?" Naomi said.

"I will. I promise."

Maybe if she'd known, Melanie would have been a little nicer to her mother growing up. That shouldn't be the case. She should have treated her mother better whether she knew these stories or not, but it was too late now to change the past. All she could do was alter the future.

She pulled her knees to her chest and prepared to talk to her mother, not just about the journal, but about her lifelong rejection.

Before she could consider the thought for a moment longer, the doorknob to her bedroom rattled and the door swung open. There was no time to hide the journal or gather her jumbled thoughts into cohesive sentiments.

She was caught red-handed.

CHAPTER 24

"Oh good, you're awake!" Anita popped her head through the door and greeted Melanie with a steaming mug in hand. "Coffee?"

In a split second, Melanie had to make a decision about what she would say and how she would explain the open journal on her lap.

"Are you working?" Anita asked.

Melanie looked down at the journal, hoping it wouldn't be the last time she got to hold it.

"No, I'm not, actually. To be honest, I found this in the night-stand." She closed the journal and lifted it for her mother to see. "I opened the drawer to put my laptop in there, and this journal was inside. I thought it was so beautiful that I opened it and just started reading. . . . I'm sorry, Mom. I didn't know it was yours until I'd already read a few pages. And by then, I couldn't stop."

Melanie looked at her mother, her eyes watering.

"Is that my old journal?" Anita asked.

"It has your name on the back cover. Does it look familiar?"

Anita walked in, sat on the bed, and leaned in for a closer look. She placed the mug of coffee on the nightstand. After flipping through a few pages, she nodded.

"Are you mad?" Melanie asked, wiping the corners of her eyes.

"What?" Anita looked at her daughter, her eyebrows scrunched together. "No, *mami*. Why would I be mad? If anything, I'm embarrassed. This was written ages ago. Who knows what I wrote in here?" She continued to skim different pages of the journal while Melanie took a sip of the coffee. It was strong and satisfying, much like her trip had been thus far.

"I wouldn't say it's embarrassing, Mom. More . . . sad." She paused for a moment, watching her mother read the pages in her hands. Her gaze drifted to her mother's aged fingertips brushing over her penned words. It was hard to imagine all the emotions she must be feeling right now.

"Mom, why didn't you ever tell us any of these stories?"

"What stories did you read?"

"When you left home for the first time, some about one of your boyfriends, and when *Tia* Carolina called you about coming to the U.S. I talked to Naomi and she hadn't heard these stories either."

"Oh my. . . . I might not have wanted you to read some of those."

"I mean, I know they're hard stories, but I feel like I learned so much about you. I should have just asked you about it instead of continuing to read, but, Mom, your writing is captivating. *Abuela* is right—you're an amazing writer. I wish I would have known that too."

Anita skimmed another page, then brought the open journal close to her chest.

Melanie just watched her, not wanting to say anything that might make reopening wounds even more painful.

After a long, deep breath, Anita spoke again. "I don't know, *mija*. I don't know why I never told you. The topic never came up, I guess."

"I take the blame for that. I should have asked you about your life here. I can't believe I never did. I know it was a hard life—well, I know that now—but regardless, I should have been more curious about your story. After all, your story is my story. And it's fascinating."

"I guess I always tried to focus on the positives of my new life in America and even the fresh start we got in Maryland. Leaving my country was hard enough. If I would have talked about these stories, I may have grown resentful, and what good would that do?" Anita paused as she laid the journal back on her lap. "You know, surviving as an immigrant can sometimes take up all the mental energy you have. I didn't always have the capacity to think about anything beyond what we were going to eat."

"It's not your fault, Mom. I should have come here a long time ago and learned about all these things directly from you. At the very least, I should have asked. I never showed any interest, and that's on me."

"Don't be so hard on yourself, *mija*. Even if you had asked, it would have been hard for me to share. Reliving these stories is not easy."

"I know, but this—" Melanie placed her hand over her mother's on the page. "It made you who you are. These stories are important. I feel like I've never known you so well as when I was turning pages in this journal."

"But I didn't want you guys to think of my story as such a sad one. I didn't want anything to hold you back from getting ahead, becoming professionals, and living fulfilling lives. I wanted a fresh start—for you and your siblings. I didn't want you feeling pity or anything like that for me. I don't know. . . . It's just complicated to explain, so that's why I never talked about it."

Anita's eyes began to water. Melanie didn't know what to do

but look into her mother's eyes and search for more of the truth. When was the last time she took a moment to simply sit with her mother? When was the last time she had a conversation with her that didn't involve some kind of tension? How could she have waited so many years to intimately know the person she called "Mom"?

Anita lifted her apron to dry the lone tear that had escaped.

"Mom, all I kept thinking about as I read these pages was that there's this whole woman I never knew existed and that side of you just . . . well, disappeared. All these years, I thought you came to America to make a better life for yourself. To give your family a better future, like so many immigrants do. I didn't know you came here so reluctantly and that you were running away from so much ugliness. And that dangerous journey you took . . . it's heartbreaking. You were so fearless. I don't know what I would have done if I'd been in your shoes."

Anita sighed as if trying to release the feelings the sad stories evoked. She nodded and wiped another tear before placing her hands on her knees for support to stand from the bed.

"C'mon. Let's go to the kitchen. You won't believe the spread your grandmother made." Anita closed the journal and slipped it under her arm.

That wasn't the response Melanie expected from her mother after sharing these revelations.

Is she trying to change the subject? Avoid any more discussion of the topic?

And then her mother smiled.

Why did she smile?

Melanie froze and looked at the familiar expression on her mother's face. It was an expression she'd seen most of her life, but she'd never thought twice about it before. An expression of contentment that for most of Melanie's life felt genuine. But right now, it felt fabricated. Had it always been fabricated? She couldn't help but wonder how long her mother had been covering up so much pain.

"Wait . . . can we talk about this? I was wondering if you had any photos from these years."

Anita faced the bedroom door, her back toward Melanie. She shifted her weight, the floor creaking beneath her feet.

When she reached for the knob, her back still toward Melanie, she responded, "No more questions right now, *mija*. C'mon, we can't keep your grandmother waiting. You know how she can be." She left the room, the journal still under her arm.

It was a sterner response than Melanie expected from her normally forbearing mother.

She should have taken reading her journal more seriously.

Maybe her mother just needed time to process everything that had happened. So, rather than push for more, Melanie followed her to the kitchen, her mind running wild with endless questions. Questions she wanted to ask her mother and questions she needed to ask herself.

CHAPTER 25

Her mother hadn't exaggerated. The spread that covered Alba's table was enough to feed a group of twenty.

In the center of the table was a wicker basket holding more *buñuelos* and *pandebonos* than you could eat in a week. Another dish was piled high with *hojaldras*. There were bowls of white rice that had been colored by dark kidney beans; long strips of *chicharron;* sliced avocados; perfectly seared *salchicha;* eggs, both sunny-side up and some mixed with an elaborate combination of tomatoes, green peppers, and onions; and, of course, her grandmother would never leave out a perfect pile of warm and cheesy *arepas*.

"*Abuela,* are there more people coming over to help us eat this feast?" Melanie asked as she hugged and kissed her grandmother, who had just finished placing the last *arepa* on the table.

"Maybe I'm hoping the better I feed you, the more likely you are to come visit me again."

"Sheesh, you never cook like this when it's just us two," Juan Carlos said.

Melanie laughed and joined her family at the table.

"How do I know where to start?" Melanie asked.

"Let your heart lead you," Alba responded.

"My recommendation is to start with an *hojaldra*," Juan Carlos said. "They're so good while the coffee's still hot."

"What did you think about *La Topa*? I didn't even hear you come in last night," Alba said, placing a flaky pastry on Melanie's plate.

"It was almost 3:00 A.M., wasn't it?" Juan Carlos said. He'd stayed up waiting for Melanie on the couch.

"Yes, thank you for staying up and letting me in. I would have come home much earlier had I known you were waiting for me."

"3:00 A.M.? You must have been having the time of your life, then," Alba said.

"It was so much fun, *Abuela*. I was nervous at first, but then I realized no one was paying attention to me or my skills, so I just danced like no one was watching. I can't even believe I could keep up—well, not as good as Marcela or anyone else on the dance floor, but I held my own. It was the most fun I've had in a long time. I'm glad you made me go, Mom."

Anita gave her a half smile and nodded.

"I'm sure no one had more fun than your cousins. They've been so excited to finally meet you," Alba said.

"I wish I would have met them a long time ago. We have so much in common, and they're, well, so fun to be around."

"Wonderful, wonderful! More reasons for you to visit again." Alba rubbed her hands together like an evil mastermind genius.

Many bites and long moments of conversation later, everyone leaned back in their chairs. Juan Carlos rubbed his stomach and looked as if he could take a nap sitting up. The food coma was imminent.

"What are you going to do with all this extra food, *Abuela*?"

"Don't worry, food never goes to waste here. There's always

someone in need who stops by, and I never send them away without something to fill their stomach."

Melanie smiled at her grandmother, amazed at all she did at her age. She worked her store, kept the community well fed, taught sewing classes to young women, and who knows what else . . . and yet, she never looked tired.

Her mother, on the other hand, had hardly smiled or spoken for most of the meal. When everyone had finished eating, Anita stood and quietly packed away all the food before retreating to her room with the journal tucked underneath her arm. Melanie rested her chin on her fist and watched her walk away with the one thing that had helped her understand herself better than anything else had.

Is she mad at me? Hurt? Disappointed? Will she ever let me read that journal again?

"Why don't you accompany me to the pharmacy? I need to pick up my medicines," Alba said to Melanie, bringing her attention back to the kitchen.

When Alba rejected Juan Carlos's offer to stop at the pharmacy for her on his way home from work, Melanie was sure her grandmother had more in mind than just a walk down the street. She must have noticed the stormy cloud that had appeared over Anita at the breakfast table.

They followed a similar path Melanie had walked the day before with her mother. But this time, she was too preoccupied with what her grandmother wanted to talk about to worry about the fractured roads.

"Is everything okay between you and your mom?" Nothing got past her grandmother no matter how old she got.

"Yeah. I mean, I think so." Melanie contemplated how much to say. She didn't want to tell her about reading her mother's journal without her permission, but then again, her grandmother might be able to help her fill gaps in the stories where her mother might not. "*Abuela,* I found my mom's old journal . . . in the nightstand. I know I shouldn't have read it without asking her first, but I got sucked in and couldn't stop. It's absorbing."

Alba mouthed *Ohhh.*

"Mom found out right before breakfast. I guess that's why she was acting weird at the table. She said she didn't mind that I had read some of the entries, so maybe it was just remembering those stories that put her in a pensive mood. I'm not sure. All I know is that she didn't want to talk about it."

Alba pursed her lips and narrowed her eyes, and Melanie knew by her facial expression exactly what she wanted to say.

"I know, I shouldn't have read as much as I did. But, like I said, I got sucked in. I've never heard any of those stories, *Abuela,* and it's kind of embarrassing. I feel like I don't know my own mother at all." Melanie hadn't noticed that her speech had quickened until all the words had spewed out of her mouth in Spanish with little effort. Was being in her ancestors' country all she needed to get comfortable with the language?

"Well, did you ever ask your mother about her upbringing? About her life here in Colombia?"

The answer was obvious. All morning, she'd already been contemplating doing that. "I know where you're going with this," Melanie said.

"Mm-hmm. Listen, I know I didn't get a front-row seat to your and your mother's relationship. But from what I've heard, you've never been easy on her."

Melanie's cheeks felt warm. She hated to disappoint her grandmother. Her sweet, silly, and joy-filled grandmother. She didn't like the pit growing in her stomach, but she also couldn't deny the truth behind her grandmother's words.

"*Mija,* you can't possibly imagine the life your mother lived in my home. There's so much I feel responsible for . . . so much I regret. But, by the grace of God, we've worked through it all and sought and found forgiveness that has allowed both of us to live in a place of peace. And maybe that's why she never brought up the topic . . . why she never talked about her upbringing. But sometimes I wish she had. Something changes in us when we know the roads someone has walked. It often turns resentment into empathy, which allows for harmony. And I think that's something you and your mother have always been missing."

Melanie nodded and looked down at her feet. There were still no words to offer in response. Everything her grandmother had said was true—Melanie could understand her mother better because she now knew the road she'd walked. Could it be possible, then, to turn all those years of resentment and rejection into harmony, just as her grandmother had said?

"You're right, *Abuela*. Knowing about her journey, I think, would have helped me be less frustrated, always feeling like my mom didn't understand me. No matter how hard I tried, I could never explain clearly enough to make her understand what I needed or what I wanted. If I'd known, maybe I would have had more compassion for why that was the case."

Alba put her index finger in the air before strolling over to a walk-up window outside the neighborhood pharmacy. She didn't have to give her name. The pharmacist knew exactly who Alba was. Gripping a small white paper bag, Alba picked up the conversation from where she left off.

"I don't think you know how much your mother felt that too. She has never wanted anything more than to see you and your siblings thrive. She's done backbreaking work her entire life just to see that through. And look at you. . . ." She reached out and grabbed Melanie's hand. Melanie looked up to meet her grandmother's eyes. "You went to college and got the job of your dreams. The job of *our* dreams. Everything she worked for truly paid off. I know it was hard for you to grow up in a different culture than your mother's and try to find your place there, but look at everything that was possible because of what she did. Don't gloss over that simply because your life wasn't like everyone else's in America."

Melanie looked back down at her feet. All these years, she'd only ever considered how difficult it had been for *her* to have parents who were immigrants. Never once did she consider how difficult it must have been for her mother to feel like she couldn't connect with her own children. To feel like her children were born in a foreign place and spoke a foreign language that, even after more than thirty years in the country, she never quite learned how to master.

Alba released Melanie's hand and reached her arm across her shoulder to pull her in close. "I don't say any of this to make you feel bad, *mi amor*. I say this because sometimes it's difficult to see the world from someone else's point of view. But if we ever get the chance to catch even a glimpse from their shoes, it can change not just how we see them but how we see the world."

CHAPTER 26

Melanie opened the black metal gate to find her mother sitting on a white plastic chair outside the home, a blue notebook in her hand. Her grandmother kissed Melanie on the forehead before continuing inside. She must have known this was a good opportunity for Melanie and her mother to talk alone.

"What are you reading?" Melanie couldn't think of anything better to say to break the awkward tension.

Anita closed the notebook but kept her thumb inside to hold her place. "It's another one of my journals. I'd forgotten how much I wrote. Years and years' worth. There are some big gaps but still a lot here. All the times I've come back to my mother's home, I can't believe I never once opened the bag since I brought it here."

"So, there's more?" Melanie's eyes grew big. What a relief to know the stories wouldn't end on the last page of the leather journal she'd been reading since the day before—that is, if her mother ever allowed her to reopen it.

Anita smiled and nodded. "A lot more," she said. "Look at this." She pulled a Polaroid from the notebook. Melanie walked toward her mother and took a seat on the chair beside her. There were three young ladies in the black-and-white photo, arms linked together.

"Is this you with *Tia* Diana and *Tia* Carolina?" Melanie asked.

Anita nodded. "We were probably in our late teens here."

Melanie noticed the length of her mother's hair in the photo—it reached halfway down her back. It was the first time Melanie had ever seen her mother with long hair. She thought back to the first journal entry she'd read. Perhaps after the incident with her father, she never wanted long hair again. Could a pixie cut be her mother's form of protecting her freedom?

When she looked up at her mother, she noticed her expression had shifted from the one she held during breakfast. Now her eyes looked lighter, as if a huge load had been lifted from her shoulders. There was no time like the present to tell her what she should have told her a long time ago.

"Mom, I want to say something. I don't really know how to say it, so I'll just say it. . . . I'm sorry. All my life, I feel like I've tried to run as far away as possible from you and your culture—*my* culture—and everything it represented. I thought if I could just disconnect from all of it, I could create a different life for myself. One where I was respected and could afford some of the things we never had growing up. I realize now how ridiculous that was. I don't have to push away my culture and my people to create a life I'm proud of. If anything, this culture makes my life richer.

"I'm so sorry, Mom. I'm sorry for all the years I've spent being rude, dismissive, and mean. I was trying to run away from something that I simply can't escape . . . and don't want to. Not anymore, at least. And you know what's sad? I thought pushing my culture away would lead to success, but all it's done is make me a failure."

Anita locked eyes with Melanie and reached for her hand. "Failure? What are you talking about? You were the first in the family to go to college. And that big job of yours—how can you say you're a failure?"

"I've been putting on a front, Mom. I'm not doing that well at the *Herald*. All my articles get heavily edited, and the last one I wrote wasn't even published. There's been something missing from my writing since I started there, and now I'm beginning to think what's been missing is myself. I'm trying to be someone I'm not . . . a writer I'm not."

Anita wiggled in her seat before lifting and turning her chair so that her body could face Melanie.

"You were so brave, Mom. You *are* so brave. And I just wish I would have grown up with an appreciation for everything you did and continue doing."

Anita reached out her hand and placed it atop her daughter's. "*Mija, mija,* it's okay. I should have talked about it more, but I'm a different person now. Sometimes I can't even believe some of the things I did. It's a miracle I'm still alive. But I don't regret any of it. I'm so grateful for the life I have today and for my children and everything they've accomplished. God has been good to me. Truly." She leaned in closer until Melanie could feel the warmth of her breath.

"And you know what?" she continued. "About your writing . . . It's never too late to change who you've been so you can grow closer to who you want to be. I left my country around your age to find something different. It's never too late to change course. I'm sure there's still so much you can do to improve in your job and become the writer *you* want to be. Don't let a few low moments stop you."

Melanie mirrored her mother's posture, leaning forward to

let the words wash over her. No matter how much her mother and grandmother believed in her abilities as a writer, it didn't change how *she* felt. She had one last chance to prove she belonged at the *Herald,* but as her deadline drifted closer, she grew more and more doubtful she could write an article that would be good enough to save her job.

"I don't know, Mom. Maybe I wasn't meant to be a writer."

Anita took Melanie's chin in her hand and gave her a firm look. "Are you kidding me? Anyone can tell from just a glimpse at your writing that you, my dear, were created to be a writer."

"Then why does it feel so hard? I thought by pursuing this dream, success would just come. I know that sounds ridiculous, but everyone's always told me what a good writer I am, so I don't understand why I'm struggling so much. I don't even want to go to Bogotá. There's no way I'm going to be able to write something that impresses my boss. I've written nothing but mediocre work since I started there. I don't know why I thought it would be any different here."

Anita released Melanie's chin and leaned back in her chair. "You're being too hard on yourself. You've gotten this far because you *are* a good writer. No one can say otherwise. But just because you're good at something doesn't mean it's going to come easy. And that's okay because hard work makes victories that much sweeter. How do you think I felt when you got your college acceptance letter? Or when your brother got that soccer scholarship? And watching your sister become a mother . . . it's all so much sweeter because of the sacrifice. You have to keep trying, *mi amor.* I know you can figure it out. You always do. I never had to help you accomplish anything; you've always been so independent and smart. I have no doubt you will figure out how to make things right at work."

"I wish I could believe it for myself, Mom."

"I'll have enough faith for the two of us," Anita said, grabbing both of her hands.

"Thanks. . . . Can I ask you something?"

"Of course."

"What happened?"

"What do you mean?" They both leaned back, eyes farther apart but still connected.

"The woman in that journal is so different from who you are today. I don't mean that in a bad way; I just can't figure out what changed. You were so fiery and fearless. You had attitude and guts. I feel like I've seen some of it come out while we've been here . . . and, don't get me wrong, it's been so fun to see this side of you. It's just so different from the mom I know back home."

Anita shook her head and pursed her lips. "*Ay,* I don't know. I guess I got tired of fighting." She looked away. "I was always fighting something when I was your age—fighting for what I thought was right or what I thought I needed. And then I got to America and realized maybe I didn't know what I needed as much as I thought I did. Learning that humbles you. It helped me be open to something different . . . and I guess *I* just became different in the process."

"But make no mistake, fighter or not, your mother is still the strong woman she's always been. I think strength looks different when you've lived long enough to have the world constantly try to break you," Alba said as she walked out onto the porch with two coffees in hand.

"I don't know if I'd call it strength or quitting," Anita said.

Anita and Melanie received the coffee and invited Alba to join them in a circle.

"Sometimes it takes strength to quit," Alba said.

Anita looked at her mother and back down at the journal in her lap.

"She's right, Mom," Melanie said.

Anita shrugged and said nothing else, so Melanie asked one last question: "Can you tell me more?"

"More?"

"You were on the plane from Texas to New York in the last journal entry I read. You can't leave me on that cliff-hanger. I want to know about your first year in America."

"*Ay, mija,* my memory is so terrible. I'm not sure if it's because I'm getting old or if my brain intentionally chose to block some of those memories."

Anita must have noticed the disappointment on Melanie's face because she stood and motioned for Melanie to follow her.

They walked down the hall to the bedroom where they'd both been staying.

Melanie lingered in the doorway, watching as her mother walked over to the closet. She stood on her tippy-toes and reached into the far back corner of the shelf above the clothing rod. She pulled down a small leather duffel bag and motioned for Melanie to come closer. She placed the bag on the bed and slid it across to Melanie. "Here. If you can carry it, you can take this back with you to Miami."

Melanie opened the bag. Inside was a pile of notebooks in all shapes and sizes—some leather, some spiral-bound, even a few composition notebooks.

"What are these?"

"Those are my journals. All of them. I don't remember what years I paused and what all exactly is in there, but the rest of my journals should be there. If you really want to know everything, you'll find it in them."

"All of them?" Her jaw dropped. How could her mother entrust her with decades' worth of memories?

"If I find anything else back home, I'll send it to you. But that should be all of it."

"Are you sure, Mom?" Her gaze drifted back and forth from her mother to the bag in front of her. How would she ever get any work done now?

"I'm sure. There's nothing in there I wouldn't tell you. It'll be easier for you to read it than for me to keep sharing. Some things are better left in a journal and not on your heart."

Anita retreated to the kitchen, leaving Melanie alone with what felt like a great treasure.

She took out every last journal and laid them side by side on the queen-size bed. Her mind ran wild with thoughts about what other stories she'd discover inside each one. It would take her weeks to get through them all, but it didn't matter. There wasn't one entry among these journals she didn't want to read.

She searched for her phone in her satchel and took a step back to get the entire bed in the camera frame. Then she took a photo and sent it to her sister with a message:

> I think you're the one who's going to have to visit me soon to help me read through all these journals.

Within seconds, she had a response:

> Are those Mom's?

> Yep. She said I could take them back to Miami with me. In case you were wondering, Mom is so cool. You HAVE to read through the journal I've been reading.

> Maybe we can spend Labor Day with you this year.

> I would love that.

She returned her phone to her satchel and stacked the journals back in the bag. She left only one out—the one she'd been reading and hoped to finish. She scooted back against the headboard and opened it again.

CHAPTER 27

APRIL 4, 1987
NEW YORK CITY

ANITA

"*Mamá*, I made it."

Anita could hear her mother release a long, slow breath through the phone.

"*Gracias a Dios*," Alba said. "Thank God. And you're okay?"

"*Sí, Mamá*. I'm okay."

She'd spent the night in tears, but her mother didn't need to know that. In the darkness of her sister's living room—she'd be moving into her more permanent home the following day—she covered her face with a fleece blanket and let the sorrow flow.

"Are you sure you're okay?"

Anita shook her head and cupped her mouth momentarily with her hand. "Yes, I'm sure."

She took a deep breath and continued. "I'm at Carolina's house. It's very nice." There was a wet, moldy smell in the apartment and wallpaper that curled down in every corner. A bucket in the bathroom caught droplets of water from beneath the sink, and it felt like every few minutes, there was another ambulance or police car rushing past their building.

A look around in the daylight revealed a desperate attempt on Carolina's part to make this place feel homey: a floral couch covered with a sheet to hide the secondhand stains, a brown chipped coffee table, and a metal TV stand with cabinets that didn't shut all the way.

Anita was proud of her sister for doing the best she could with what she had—that was all their mother ever expected of them. While it was hard to accept that even her mother's home back in Colombia felt like a more decent and comfortable place to live, Anita was content to know her sister loved her apartment in New York.

"I'm so glad you two are together," Alba said. "If only Diana could be there too. I want you all together—my babies. I can't stand to think of any of you on your own over there."

It was obvious this wasn't the time to tell her mother that she wouldn't be staying in Carolina's home much longer. Maybe her place would be a little bit nicer. She crossed her fingers and chewed her bottom lip.

"We're all adults, *Mamá*. We will be okay. More importantly, how are you?"

"I miss you. I miss all my girls."

Anita looked to the ceiling and covered her eyes. Her mother would only worry more if she knew she was on the verge of tears right now.

"I miss you too. But we talked about this, right? This is for the best. We're all here to help the family. This is our duty to you, *Mamá*, after all you've done for us."

"*Ay, mi amor,* you have no idea how much my heart sings to hear you say that. I am beyond blessed. I just wish we didn't have to be so far apart."

"Me too."

"So, what are your first impressions? Is it like everything we see in the movies?"

Anita swallowed before speaking, hoping to disguise the shakiness in her voice.

"It's even better. Tall buildings, people walking around all day and night, big restaurants on every corner. Maybe one day you can visit. I think you'd like it."

"Wow, *qué dicha*. How cool."

"I have to go, Mom. Rosa is getting up."

"Okay, give that sweet angel a big kiss for me."

"I will."

When the call ended, Anita dropped to her knees and allowed the sorrow to flow once more. She was with her sister, her niece, her family. So why did she feel so alone?

CHAPTER 28

APRIL 15, 1987
NEW YORK CITY

ANITA

"I can't believe it's almost been two weeks since you got to New York. How's it been?" Juan Carlos asked through the phone.

Anita had dragged the receiver and its long, curly cord to her bedroom, where she could talk to her brother in private.

"I don't feel like I've done much and yet time keeps moving. The world doesn't care that I'm not ready to move forward—it goes on regardless. How cruel."

"Yes, life can be cruel. But surely you've found some bright spots. Have you left the apartment at all?"

"I had to buy the calling card to call you, but not much besides that," Anita said.

"You have to get out more. . . . Explore. . . . See the city. . . . Maybe you'll make some friends."

"I'm not ready to do all of that."

"What do you mean?"

"If I start living out there, in America, then it will all be real. I'll have to accept that I actually made it alive and now have an entire lifetime to live here. I'm not ready to accept that yet . . . to accept this is my new home."

"America doesn't have to be your home for the rest of your

life if you don't want it to be. But while you're there, you might as well enjoy what you can. Has Carolina not taken you out? I know Diana is a few hours away from you, but maybe you can go and see her."

"I don't have any money to visit Diana right now, and Carolina is always busy with her family. She's got her two sisters-in-law living in her apartment now too; that's why there wasn't any room for me. I hardly see her."

"Where are you living, then? I thought you'd be staying with Carolina for the foreseeable future."

"Me too. I'm close by. She connected me with a friend named Ana Maria. She had an extra bed—well, it's actually just a mattress on the floor—in her apartment, but I have to share the room with another woman. She's from Colombia too, but she has a mean look on her face all the time, so I don't talk to her much. At least in Colombia, I had a real bed to sleep on."

"Maybe you should try talking to your roommate," Juan Carlos said. "You might have more in common than you think. You need some friends, Anita."

"No, these women are up to something." She lowered her voice to a whisper. "I don't know what they're doing, but I can feel it in my bones that I need to be careful. I can't trust them or their friends. There are these men who come by every few days with envelopes. I try to avoid their gaze when they stop by, but I can feel them staring at me. All I know is I want nothing to do with whatever they're up to."

"Yes, don't get involved with anything that can put you in danger of deportation. Nothing is worth that, okay?"

Deportation didn't sound like the worst thing in the world right now.

"Tell me about America . . . New York. What's it like?" Juan Carlos continued.

Anita sneered at the cheeriness in his voice.

"I thought I was leaving a life of poverty to come to the land of the rich. That's not what it looks like to me. They call this area Jackson Heights. I call it *feo*. Ugly. It's cold. So much colder than Cali. Supposedly it's spring here, but it's still so cold.

"We could have heat in the apartment if we wanted to, but Ana Maria said it's too expensive to use. She told me to wear extra socks instead. She also told me to limit my hot showers and use of the stove. It's a good thing I have no urge to cook or shower."

"I can send you some extra socks if that's what you need," he said.

"I was right all along, Juan Carlos. America is not what everyone says it is. I have yet to see big, fancy mansions, shiny cars, or people who look wealthy. The people here look almost as poor as the ones from our neighborhood. I don't know why people are dying to get here. They're not rich here. They look just as miserable as they were back home."

"You never know. The misery there might be slightly more bearable than the misery in their home country."

"I guess I'll find out soon," she said. "I miss my friends. I miss all our neighbors. At least they make an effort to greet you, ask about your family. The people here are always looking at the ground. They never look up to say hello, good morning, nothing. I guess I can't blame them. After a few months here, I might start staring at the ground as well."

"Maybe you'll meet some nice people when you start working. When do you start anyway?"

Anita rolled over on the bare mattress. She'd managed to get only a sheet to wrap herself in from her sister.

"In a few days. Carolina connected me with an Ecuadorian woman who runs a clothing factory. She says I can put my sewing skills to work and that I wouldn't have to work there long. Just long enough to save some money and get my feet on the ground."

"Maybe you'll enjoy that—you love to sew."

Anita grabbed the sheet by the fistful and pulled it toward her chin.

"I don't know. It might just make me sad. Sewing reminds me of *Mamá*. The beautiful clothes she made us. The classes she used to teach in our living room for the women in the neighborhood while *Papi* was away at work. I wish I would have brought one of the dresses she made me. I'd put it on right now if I had it. But I didn't bring a single one because I was afraid I would lose it on the journey here."

"Maybe that's what I can send you."

"Maybe. . . . I just want a piece of her with me here. I miss her. How is she? It's hard to believe she's telling me the truth when she says she's okay."

"She's good. She misses you, of course. You two are so close. Talks about you every day, and in the morning, I hear her praying for you in her bedroom."

Anita closed her eyes and pictured her mother kneeling at her bedside like she'd seen her do all her life.

"I try not to think about how long it will be before I see her again—or you. I'll have to become a citizen first, and who knows how long that will take."

"Not long if you find a nice man to marry," he said.

"I'm not *that* desperate. I don't even want to get married. For what? I'll find another way to become a citizen . . . a way that doesn't involve moving in with a man. It's like *Mamá* always said: '*Mejor sola que mal acompañada.*' Better to be alone than in bad company."

"I think she spoke from experience."

Anita nodded.

Juan Carlos continued. "Can you make me one promise?"

"Maybe," she said.

"Try to be a little more positive. Good will find you, *hermana*, I'm sure of it. But you have to be open to it or you might miss it right before your eyes. Sometimes God's blessings come in ways we never would have imagined. Keep your eyes open, okay?"

Anita looked up at the ceiling and back down at the mattress. "Mm-hmm."

"C'mon. Do it for me?"

"Okay. Anything for you."

CHAPTER 29

2018
CALI, COLOMBIA

MELANIE

Tears fell from Melanie's eyes and wet the pages of the open journal. She wiped her cheeks with the backs of her hands, not wanting to cause any damage to the already worn pages.

Melanie had left her home and her mother at around the same age that Anita had left for America. The minute she got her offer letter from Northwestern, Melanie packed her bags and said her goodbyes. Not once had Melanie felt as homesick or lonely as her mother felt when she arrived in America. Perhaps she couldn't relate because, unlike Anita, Melanie could visit her mother, or any of her family members, whenever she wanted. Anita didn't have the same luxury. She couldn't hop in a car to hug her mother. Being undocumented, she would have had no idea if she'd ever even see her mother again.

"I'm a spoiled brat," she whispered.

And the thought of her mother being so adamant about not marrying or having kids made Melanie clutch at her shirt near her heart. Her marriage had ended in divorce—yet another disappointment her mother was forced to walk through in a foreign place.

There was a gentle knock at the door.

"Mija." Anita peeked into the bedroom. "Lunch is ready."

"Okay, Mom. I'll be there in a minute."

"I was thinking that after lunch I could show you around my *barrio* a little," Anita said.

"I would love that."

The first line of the next journal entry caught her attention, so Melanie decided to read just a few more pages before meeting her family in the kitchen.

She wiped her cheeks again and continued reading. . . .

CHAPTER 30

APRIL 26, 1987
NEW YORK CITY

ANITA

"How could you have sent me to work there knowing what it's like?"

Anita walked beside Carolina on Northern Boulevard, pushing a small stroller. It was almost May, but the afternoons were still windy and cold.

"I know it's not ideal, but it's just a place to get started. I only spent six months there before I had enough experience to get a job elsewhere," Carolina said.

"Six months? I can't spend six months there, Caro. I'm no stranger to long workdays, but the conditions are cruel. We're so cramped in that tiny trailer. I'm not sure how they managed to fit two rows of sewing machines in there. All the women are practically touching knees, and it only makes them hate one another more. And we're expected to sit there for ten hours?" Her lips pressed into a tight, flat line.

"At least wait until you find something else. You need money coming in."

Anita stuffed her hands into the pockets of her sweatshirt. Her first week in New York, Carolina had taken her to a thrift store to buy a few pieces of clothes that would keep her warm in New York's unpredictable spring climate.

"The manager there . . . she's *una bruja*. She's a witch. From the moment I sat down at my station on my first day, she's been yelling profanities at everyone in the room. But mainly me."

Carolina nodded as if remembering. "Just ignore her."

"She called me *un imbécil*—an imbecile—because I didn't know how to use her sewing machine. I'd never used an industrial machine before. I had no idea it would be so different from the one *Mamá* has at home. There wasn't any training either; she just sat me down and told me to start."

"She slapped my hand once, like I was a child caught reaching into a cookie jar," Carolina said. "Everyone looked. I was so embarrassed."

"How could you let her treat you that way?"

"Trust me, I wanted to stand and slap her in the face. Spit on the machine and walk out of there. But I was pregnant. I needed food. I'd been living off frozen *arepas* for too long."

Anita looked down at her feet—she, too, had been living off frozen *arepas*.

"Being Hispanic, you would think she would have compassion for us undocumented immigrants. But no. We are useless to her like we are to the rest of the world. I wish we could band together and rise up against her—take her down and send her somewhere far, far away. But we're not allowed to speak in the trailer at all. How can we start a revolution if we're not allowed to speak?"

"You and your revolutions." Carolina stifled a laugh.

"They don't pay me enough to put up with their garbage."

"You've gotten your first check already?"

"Yesterday. I don't know what I expected, but the number made my stomach hurt. The whole week of work, ten hours each day, and I only get a hundred twenty dollars? Ana Maria made it clear on my first day in her apartment that rent was three hundred a month and that she would kick me out if I was even a day late with her payment. How do people get by with this kind of pay?"

"By struggling . . . that's how," Carolina said.

"Remember those guys I told you about? The scary-looking ones who stop by the apartment every once in a while? One of them offered me a job."

Carolina stopped in her tracks and pushed Anita to the edge of the sidewalk.

"Don't get involved with them," she said, looking straight into her eyes.

"But he said it was an easy job and that nothing about it was dirty. All I had to do was take cash he gave me to different places around the city and buy money orders of smaller amounts. He said everyone does it—even the women I live with. He pays one percent of however much cash I turn into money orders. He said most people who work for him can make three hundred dollars in a day. That's the kind of money I need to feed myself and start sending some extra to *Mamá*."

Carolina lowered her voice to a whisper and loosened her grip. "You really believe there's nothing dirty about that job?"

"What else am I supposed to do, Caro? I would have stayed in Colombia if I'd known I'd be working in that trailer. I was better off over there."

Grabbing Anita's arm again, Carolina clenched her jaw. "Don't get involved with them. I know the factory sucks right now, but if you start working with those men, you'll end up deported, or worse."

Anita shook her arm free and continued walking forward.

"I know, I know. Maybe I should have gone to Washington,

D.C., with Diana instead and worked as a nanny . . . as much as I don't like kids."

"Can you just give New York a chance, please?"

"Do I have a choice?" Anita said, looking at her sister, her insides filling with regret. "This better pay off, Caro, or I'll never forgive myself for leaving *Mamá*."

CHAPTER 31

JULY 13, 1987
NEW YORK CITY

ANITA

"Anita, can I see you after class, please?"

She'd been in America only a few months, but life already looked drastically different than it did when she first arrived. Not only had she found a better-paying job delivering *The New York Times* to fancy high-rise buildings in Tribeca, but she'd also started taking free English classes at LaGuardia Community College—she'd seen an ad for the class in the paper. Sitting behind a desk with a notebook and pen quickly became what she looked forward to most each week. It didn't matter how much her arms and legs ached at the end of each workday; nothing could keep her away.

The professor was the only American in the class. Based on his head of white hair and deep-set wrinkles, Anita wondered whether he was retired and teaching these classes for fun.

I hope I didn't upset him.

She was embarrassed about her outburst but didn't regret it. It'd given her a wave of adrenaline like she hadn't felt since crossing the border.

When the class cleared out, Anita spoke first. "I'm so sorry, Professor, but he had it coming." She was still reeling about the

distasteful essay a fellow student had written—and read aloud—
about Colombia.

The professor smiled. "You don't have to apologize. In fact,
I agree with you."

"You do?" Anita said, brows furrowed.

"You've always been a tender writer. It was nice to see a different side of you. I can tell you have a lot of passion for your
country."

"Yes, Professor, I do. It drives me crazy when people talk
poorly about my country." Anita could feel her heart beginning
to pick up its pace again.

"I'm so sick of it. So sick of the outside world only seeing
Colombia as a country overrun with drugs and violence. I'm not
naïve; I know that the destruction Pablo Escobar creates hurts
more than just my country. But that's just it—my country is
being destroyed too. Sometimes I wonder if the entire world really thinks every citizen in Colombia is backing Escobar. Like
we even have a choice. He's taken over our police, our prisons,
our government. . . . We're prisoners in our country because of
his power and yet the world still thinks our country is to blame."

"I agree. I like the way you used your writing and your
words—your pronunciation is improving beautifully, by the
way—to help the class see a different side of the story. These are
the things that often push people to resort to violence. But you
resorted to something much more effective, in my opinion."

"Thank you." Anita took a deep breath and hugged her
spiral-bound notebook to her chest. "But why do they have to
do that, Professor? That guy is from Peru—our neighbor. Why
would he choose to write his current event essay about Colombia and how it's causing so much trouble for all of Latin America
and beyond? Why would he blame all the violence, all the ter-

rorism, all the pain on one country—*my* country? As if it was truly a single country working against the world."

"People are always seeking someone to blame for their pain," he said, removing his glasses.

"Why can't the world—just once—talk about something else? I'm so sick of it. I'm sick of the jokes, the stupid comments when I tell people where I'm from, the way they tap their nostrils because they think they're clever. I'm absolutely sick of it. And I won't stand for it any longer. I won't keep quiet."

"And you shouldn't. I think you did a wonderful job helping him see how he may be mistaken about some of these things."

"I hope so. I didn't want him to have the last word."

"Clever title too." The professor looked down at the copy of Anita's essay on his desk. "'The Other Side of Colombia'— I like it. To be honest, I wasn't aware of much of what you said about Colombia. I had no idea it exported so many natural resources, the biodiversity, the culture. . . . I'm a little embarrassed I didn't know those things."

Anita sat down on a blue plastic chair next to her professor's desk. "A lot of people forget about all that we contribute because their perspectives have been clouded by the bad things they've heard. I wish I could stand on a mountain and tell the whole world about these things. I wonder how he would have felt if I had stood in front of the whole class and called the country of Peru a waste of space. Or if I'd said Peruvians can't be trusted or that we shouldn't let them into our countries because they're like a cancer."

"People often think the same thing about where I'm from."

Anita scratched at her temple. "America?"

He shook his head. "I was born in Egypt. My parents immigrated here when I was very young. I remember sitting in classes like this one with my mother. She'd work all day and then sit in a class like this, desperately trying to assimilate."

"I had no idea. Your English is so good. I just figured you were American."

"Sometimes I forget too. I was five when they brought me here."

"So, you know what it's like."

"It's common for people to have misconceptions about a place or people they're not familiar with."

The professor's words made Anita think about something she was ashamed to admit. . . .

I am a hypocrite.

"I guess I'm guilty of the same thing," she said. "I spewed out similar sentiments about America before I moved here." Although a lot of her biases remained, there was also so much Anita was learning about life in this country that she had all wrong.

"No country is perfect—I'll tell you that much. But every country is more than its sins. You still have every right to be a proud Colombian, just like I have every right to be a proud Egyptian."

Anita didn't need her professor's permission to feel pride, but she was grateful for it.

"You're right, Professor. I am Colombian, and I am proud."

CHAPTER 32

2018
CALI, COLOMBIA

MELANIE

Melanie's heart raced.

How could I have been so stupid? So blind?

She found her satchel on the floor and dug through it for the article outline she'd created. There it was—her regret staring right back at her. Numerous figures regarding cocaine produced in Colombia. Bullet points to remind her about the amount of cocaine smuggled into the United States. The number of deaths in Miami last year. Even quotes from American thought leaders speaking on the complacency of Colombian officials. None of it painted Colombia in a positive light.

If she wrote her article according to this outline, it would be no different from the essay the Peruvian man in her mother's journal had written and presented to the entire class, except this time, the words would have a much wider audience. How could she not have seen the potential pain her article would cause her mother—or her whole family?

Even if her mother never said it out loud, no doubt she would be ashamed of her daughter for presenting a one-sided portrait of her country. And not just her mother, but her grandmother, her cousins, Sebastian. . . . Everyone would be ashamed of her.

And she'd be ashamed of herself.

Because what her mother had learned was true: A country is more than its sins. For every piece of media to focus solely on a country's great flaws was to strip it of all that makes it beautiful.

There was that familiar tense feeling in her shoulders again.

What am I going to do now?

I can't write the article I came here to write.

Or can I?

The idea of losing her job made her queasy again. Writing the article how Ignacio wanted it would be the only way she'd hold on to the job for a little while longer. But if she wrote the article that way, she'd join the chorus of voices who'd come before her—and who didn't share more than a singular perception of her country.

Melanie envied her mother's courage to stand before her class—broken English and all—and advance a different narrative. She envisioned herself doing the same . . . sliding an article across Ignacio's desk that didn't tear her country down but built it up. But it didn't feel that easy. Her mother could do what she did because she didn't have a lot to lose at the time. Her job and future weren't on the line, and there would be no reason for her professor to push her out of class. It was an easy response for her mother. But the same didn't feel true for herself.

Ugh. Why did I have to read this right now? This changes everything.

I can't just ignore or paint over the transgressions of this country. But do I have to put them on display when the world is already well versed in them? What would it take to show the good Colombia has to offer and the strides they're making to rid themselves of suffering?

Is that even possible? It sounds idealistic—too good to be true.

Melanie groaned and threw herself back onto the bed. She

buried her face in her hands and did everything she could to keep herself from crying hot, angry tears.

Angry to not have realized how this article might hurt her family to begin with. Angry to have missed out on a richer life on account of her own misguided resentment. Angry to now feel a conviction to *not* write this article.

And now she'd have to face her mother in the kitchen.

She needed more time to process what felt like a wrench thrown into the plans she'd so carefully thought through. What would she do now? It was impossible to unread what she'd just read. It was impossible to put it aside and not take into account how it would now affect her job and entire career.

Would she be able to move forward with this article? With this angle? Was saving her job more important than saving all the strides she'd made in just two days in Colombia?

Why did it feel impossible to save both?

How cruel of the world to ask her to choose between a part of her newfound identity and her lifelong dream. There had to be a way to save both.

CHAPTER 33

Anita and Melanie climbed into Juan Carlos's taxi after enjoying another extravagant meal in Alba's home.

"I can't show you my *barrio* without taking you to my schools. I met so many of my friends there," Anita said. It took less than ten minutes to arrive at *Vicente Borrero Costa*. For the entire car ride, rather than watch the city pass her by through the window, Melanie focused on the back of her mother's head bobbing along as she spoke.

Her mind still reeled about what she would do about her article. Would she have to tell her mom the truth about what she'd set out to write, or could she find a way around it?

Melanie listened as her mother talked about the haven her school had been to her. She didn't need to see her facial expressions to know attending school had been an escape from everyday life.

Juan Carlos parked close to the front entrance. "Let's see if they'll let us walk around inside," Anita said. She stepped out of the car and onto the sidewalk.

The two-story building made of brick had been painted a deep teal color. There was a wall that wrapped around the building—as if for protection—and enclosed the front entrance. It didn't reach the second floor, but there was enough barbed wire lining the top edge of the barrier that reaching any higher would have been unnecessary. Every window on the building was also covered with metal bars. Had it not been for the aluminum letters across the front of the building that spelled out the school's name, Melanie could have mistaken the place for a prison.

Her mother rang a bell below the school's name, which gave them access inside. When they reached the administrative office, she motioned for them to stay behind while she went in to talk with a woman who looked to be about Anita's age. One look into Anita's eyes and the woman tossed her french braid off her shoulder, stood from her small desk, and hugged her. Melanie smiled and looked up at Juan Carlos. Was there anyone her mom didn't know around here?

Anita held her hand and led the woman out of her office to introduce her to Melanie and Juan Carlos, who both greeted her with a kiss on the cheek.

"Fabiola was a student here the same time I was," Anita said.

Fabiola looked at Melanie and said, "No one could forget your mother. She was bossy, but so much fun."

Juan Carlos laughed and nodded as if she'd just described his sister perfectly.

The phone in her office rang, pulling Fabiola's attention away. "Go ahead. Walk around. The students will fill the courtyard in about twenty minutes, so get in while you can. And come say goodbye before you leave, okay?" Fabiola walked back to the office.

The inside of the school was nothing like the outside. As they crossed from one side of the administrative offices to the other, they entered a courtyard—a wide expanse that gave the school a warm, inviting appearance. From where Melanie stood, she could see many of the classrooms. They all had doors that led into the courtyard. This must be where the girls whispered in small huddles while the boys kicked soccer balls. There were a few thin and sparse palm trees on the edges of the courtyard, but the rest sat bare in concrete.

"Come look, this was my classroom my last year here," Anita said, directing them to a room on the far side of the courtyard.

Melanie walked over and peeked through the door. She watched as the young teacher dressed in a knee-length dress and kitten heels walked through the aisles of desks, looking over the words her students wrote in their multicolored notebooks. Melanie didn't move as she pictured her mother in one of those wooden seats. What would she have written in her notebook here? Would she have been honest about her life at home? About her future dreams? Or did she even have any dreams left the year she sat in this room? Melanie turned her head to look at her mother, who peered through the window. Was she thinking about happy memories or reliving sad ones?

As they strolled past the rest of the classrooms, Anita whispered about her favorite teachers. While she no longer agreed with everything they taught about America—like Melanie, she'd also learned that a country is more than its sins—she credited some of her teachers for lighting a fiery spirit in her when she was young.

The school was small enough that they'd walked the entire campus in just a few minutes.

On their way out, the three of them waved as they passed Fabiola.

"I want to show you where I studied once I graduated from here," Anita said. "But ohhh, follow me. Let's get a treat before we get back in the car." She walked across the street to a café with outdoor seating. There was a large glass display at the front of the crumbling building, where Anita waited to be served.

Before Melanie or Juan Carlos could tell Anita what they'd like to order, she turned around with three plastic cups in her hand and signaled for Juan Carlos to grab the white paper bag from the woman behind the cashier.

"We came over here at least twice a week after school for *champús* and *empanadas*. I was in the morning school shift, so I went home for lunch every day. It was always a treat to have this for lunch instead of going home for rice and beans. Go on, take a sip," Anita said.

"Shampoos?" Melanie asked.

"*CHAM-CHAMpús* . . . with *ú*," Anita corrected.

"It's got cooked corn, *panela*, *lulo*, pineapple, orange leaves, and . . . what am I missing?" Juan Carlos asked Anita.

"Cinnamon and cloves."

Melanie took a sip and asked, "What's *lulo*?"

"It looks like an orange tomato, a little bit tart, so the *panela* helps balance it," Anita said.

"Delicious," Melanie said. "All those flavors seem odd together, but it totally works." Something struck Melanie then. She looked down at her cup and realized the drink was filled with ice. For a moment, she considered tossing the juice. But her fear was overpowered by her desire to drink in more of her culture. To be immersed in the opportunity to authentically experience her mother's childhood years.

She took another sip.

"We'd all walk out of here with a *champú* in one hand and an *empanada* in the other." Anita wrapped the bottom half of two hot *empanadas* with small square napkins and handed one to Melanie and one to Juan Carlos. Melanie took a bite, the grease from the napkin seeping onto her fingertips. The *empanada* had been fried to a perfect golden-brown color, giving it the most satisfying crunch. The spongy mixture of beef and potato inside was the perfect complement to the crispy exterior.

They finished their snack in the car. Melanie took small bites, hoping to prolong the bliss as she watched the city pass her by. The median separating the opposite lanes was covered in tall, bushy trees. Traffic was light, the majority consisting of motorcycles zipping by. At a stoplight, Melanie looked up at the rusty bus that had stopped beside them. It was crowded with people— moms cradling small children, workers in uniform likely headed home for the day, and a young couple who couldn't keep their eyes off each other. After passing a large modern shopping mall, they arrived at *Institución Universitaria Antonio José Camacho.*

"I used to come here in the evenings. It's a primary school during the day, but in the evenings, they have classes for adults. I got a certificate in industrial electronics," Anita said.

"Electronics?" Melanie laughed.

"Yes, I know. I need your help to send emails . . . but this was different. I learned how to take electronics apart and put them back together to test for errors in design. Small electronics, like remote controllers."

"Interesting," Melanie said.

This school was about three times the size of the one they'd just left, and much more modern. They walked through a large gymnasium with a stage. People of all ages were slowing filling the room. It looked like they were preparing for a presentation. They passed a cafeteria with TVs and vending machines and a few classrooms, some lined with plastic chairs and small wooden desks and others with large conference room tables.

Outside, they walked through a courtyard similar to the one at *Vicente Borrero Costa,* except it was larger and had twice the amount of palm trees. The concrete was cracked in several places, allowing weeds a place to flourish.

"How long were you—"

Before Melanie could finish her question, a dark-skinned man with a short Afro spoke into a microphone from the gymnasium they had walked through—the double doors that led into the courtyard had been opened, so Melanie could see him clearly. The man organized about six students in a straight line on the stage, introduced them to the crowd, and said they would each recite a poem or essay.

The three of them walked closer to the doors and sat on the edge of a simple stone fountain in the courtyard to listen to the poems the young adults had written. After a few minutes, the students' voices faded into the background. Melanie heard only the gentle trickle of water as she watched her mother, who'd laid a hand against her breastbone.

"Did you ever think about trying something like this?" Melanie asked Anita when the first student had finished speaking.

"Like what?"

"Classes in literature, writing. . . . You mentioned Gabriel García Márquez yesterday. Didn't you ever want to try something like that? To write like him?"

Anita gave a half smile and shook her head. "No, not really. I wrote some poems here and there when I was young, but no, I guess I never considered it more than something to do in my bedroom when I was bored or unsure of what to do with my flooded mind."

Melanie turned back to face the makeshift stage where the students stood.

"When you're as poor and depressed as I was as a kid, these kinds of things don't even cross your mind," Anita said.

Melanie remained silent, looking ahead and listening to a few of the poets.

"These kids have some serious talent, but we better get going. There's a few more places I want to show you before it gets dark," Anita said, shifting her weight forward to stand.

They took a stroll through *Parque de los Gatos,* a beautiful park filled with giant sculptures of cats. Every cat had a different design—colors, props, and even cartoon characters painted on their bodies. They stood tall as if strutting forward on a runway. While walking through the winding path, Juan Carlos took endless photos of Melanie and Anita in front of the hilarious works of art. Melanie's favorite one was a cat who sported a neck brace and bandages. With the weight of all she'd learned the past few days and the uncertainty she still felt about her article, Melanie wondered whether she'd be leaving Colombia in a similar state as the bruised-up feline.

They returned to the car and drove a little farther out of town because Anita wanted Melanie to see one of the many wonders of Colombia: *Cristo Rey.* The statue of Christ was as tall as a six-story building. His concrete arms were outstretched, welcoming both the local and the foreigner.

Melanie looked up and was covered in the shadow of the statue's grandiosity. Her gaze slowly drifted downward to the circular garden and wrought iron fence that surrounded *Cristo Rey.* There were groups of bright flowers every few inches, adding a vibrancy to the concrete frame.

"Come look at this view," Juan Carlos said, motioning for Melanie to follow him to the outskirts of the landmark. She crept toward the yellow railing. When she reached it, she grabbed onto the metal to steady herself. The view took her breath away. The rolling hills below were lush and green—completely untouched. With her hands still on the railing, she shuffled to the other side of the view, where she could see the entire cityscape. Homes nestled in the faraway hills, clusters of tall buildings, and a wide expanse of unrecognizable structures that faded into the horizon. It was all of Cali, and it was beautiful.

"This is one of the most beautiful places I've ever seen," she whispered.

"It really is," Anita responded.

"Why does it feel like I've been here before?"

"Perhaps Colombia has always been in your heart. It just needed a little unearthing." Anita pulled her daughter in to rest her cheek on her head.

Before they could leave, Melanie had to snap a few photos from every angle of this view. No image would do it justice, but she had a feeling there would come a time in the near future when she would need just a glimpse of this place to give her strength.

"You guys ready to get going? *Abuela* is probably working on dinner by now. Let's not make her wait," Juan Carlos said.

Melanie didn't want to leave, but Juan Carlos was right. Alba would worry if they got home too late.

The walk back to the car and the subsequent ride back to Alba's house remained mostly quiet. With the windows rolled down, the sounds of the city were more than satisfying to get them home. It wasn't until they slammed their car doors shut in Alba's makeshift driveway that Melanie finally broke the silence.

"Hey, Mom." Anita stopped in her tracks and turned to face Melanie. "Did you ever think about coming back? To Colombia?"

Anita thought for a moment and then responded. "Well, not really. For one, I didn't get my citizenship for a few years, and I knew that if I came back in that time, I wouldn't be able to go back to America. It was way too expensive to do it once. There's no way I would be able to do it again. But I also met and married your father shortly after arriving there. I think I met him in December of that first year—maybe a little later—and before I knew it, I was pregnant with you. As much as I wanted my children to grow up as proud Colombians in my country, I just knew that would be selfish. I knew your life would be better there even if we didn't have a ton of money."

They walked toward the door.

"I don't know," Melanie said. "After what I just saw, this doesn't seem like the worst place to grow up."

Before Anita could respond, a woman Melanie didn't recognize opened the front door with a concerned look on her face.

"*Juan Carlos, ven rápido. Es Doña Alba,*" she said, running to the back of the house.

Melanie froze. Something was wrong with her grandmother.

CHAPTER 34

Anita took her mother's face in her hands. Alba was propped up with pillows on her bed but looked pale and languid.

"I stopped by to drop off some of my *mondongo*. I know how much she loves it. I noticed her cheeks looked flushed. She told me her chest had been hurting and that she was having trouble breathing. I asked if she wanted to go to the hospital, but she said no. She just wanted my help to get into bed and have some of the soup. I don't know, Anita; I think she needs to go to the hospital, but she keeps saying it's not necessary, so I decided to stay until you got back. I hope that's okay."

"*Ay Dios mio*, of course. Thank you so much, Carmenza," Anita said. "She can be more stubborn than a bull. I'm so glad you stayed to keep an eye on her." Anita gently grabbed Alba's feet and moved them off the bed.

"*Vamos, Mamá.* We're going to the hospital."

"I don't need the hospital. I just need to rest," Alba said in a whisper.

"I love you, but *estas loca*? Are you crazy? You have heart failure. If you're having chest pain, we have to go to the hospital right now. I won't take no for an answer. Soup won't fix a potential heart attack. *Vamos*, get up." Anita took hold of Alba's thin and frail arm and helped her stand from her bed. "Juan Carlos, go start the car; we'll be right out."

Melanie ran over to her grandmother and grabbed her other arm for support. Together, they slowly walked outside to the car. Melanie gulped in an attempt to not reveal the real fear she had within her.

While Melanie knew there would come a day fairly soon when Alba would no longer be around, this wasn't the day or time she thought it'd be. She'd spent only a couple of days with her grandmother—there had to be more time.

Melanie and Anita sandwiched Alba in the back seat and held each of her hands. When they arrived at the hospital, Juan Carlos ran inside the emergency department to fetch a wheelchair.

After Anita checked in with the receptionist, three nurses appeared from behind two automatic doors, pushing a gurney. They helped Alba onto the gurney and wheeled her toward the hidden place they'd come from. Melanie cupped her hand over her mouth and tightly squeezed her stomach with her other hand.

Please be okay, please be okay, please be okay.

This couldn't be the moment she lost her grandmother. She needed more time. More time to talk with her, time to cook with her, time to sit in her presence and just be. It pained Melanie to think she almost didn't come to Cali. What if she'd been in Bogotá already or back in Miami? Would it even hit her this hard to know her grandmother was in the hospital and may not survive this? How would she have been able to live with herself, knowing she couldn't tell her grandmother goodbye?

But that wasn't the case. Thank God that wasn't the case. Melanie stood in the hospital, scared but present and grateful that she'd gotten to spend quality time with her in her home and in her community.

Juan Carlos, Anita, and Melanie found three seats together in the waiting room. A *telenovela* played on the lone TV that hung from the wall across the room. Nobody watched it.

Melanie couldn't stand the waiting. She sprung up from her chair and walked over to the receptionist. "Excuse me, ma'am, what are we waiting for? Can't we sit in the room with my grandmother? Where did they take her?"

"As soon as a room is assigned, I can share that with you, miss."

She nodded at the woman and walked back to her mother. "I wish they would at least tell us where she is."

"*Siéntate, mami.* It's okay. Sit down. They may be doing some preliminary testing. They will let us know when we can go back there."

When the mysterious double doors opened again, Melanie jumped to her feet.

"Carvajal?" said the woman in a short white coat.

"*Sí,* that's us." Melanie followed the woman without waiting for her mother or uncle to keep up.

The walls in Alba's room were white and bare. Besides the steady rhythm of beeps coming from the monitors they'd connected to her, the room was quiet and still. Melanie walked straight to her grandmother's side and placed a hand on the top of her head. Alba lay underneath thin white sheets and was propped up by two stacked pillows. With her eyes closed, she looked comfortable, serene . . . but Melanie's heart wouldn't settle until she spoke to her grandmother once more.

The gentle touch woke Alba, a wide smile spreading across her face at the sight of her granddaughter.

"All of you are going to have to take me out for some *champú* when we get out of here to make up for bringing me here against my will. I'm fine, and I'll prove it to you soon enough," Alba said, looking to Anita and Juan Carlos as well.

"That's a small price to pay to be sure you're okay," Anita responded, walking closer to her bedside.

Alba may have spoken confidently, but no one could deny that she didn't look well. Despite the IV, her skin still looked pale, and no matter how hard she tried, she couldn't keep from shutting her eyes for long stretches of time.

A friendly and chatty nurse came in and out of the room multiple times to check Alba's vitals, draw blood for lab work, and hook her up to a heart monitor. She also performed an electrocardiogram and took what seemed like endless notes on a laptop attached to a cart on wheels. What in the world was she writing?

Alba didn't seem to be phased by any of the several tests the team of doctors and nurses performed. But that wasn't the case for Melanie, or her mom or uncle. Melanie knew she wasn't the only one who thought the worst. Both Anita and Juan Carlos wrung their hands and jumped, just like she did, anytime another medical professional walked in.

"Doctor, please, can you give us an update? What's going on?" Anita said when the doctor came in an hour after the electrocardiogram.

"*Señora*, we still have a few more tests to run, and we have to wait until her lab work comes back. She could be having chest pain for a million reasons, and we don't want to assume anything until we have all the results back. I will update you as soon as I can, I promise," he said.

From the moment the team of nurses and doctors began running labs and different tests on Alba, Melanie noticed that besides them speaking Spanish, the team was just like every other nurse or doctor she'd interacted with in the United States. Smart, capable, and even kind. Why had she been so afraid to end up in a hospital in Cali? This one might be nicer than the one in downtown Miami. She shook her head at her ignorance—so much she'd forever take from this trip.

When the doctor left the room, Anita stood and began to pace. "How could there not be an update yet? We've been here two hours already. They've gotta have some kind of idea what's going on. Are they working fast enough?" Melanie wasn't sure who her mother was asking, so she stayed quiet. "Maybe this wasn't the right hospital to come to. Maybe we should have gone to the university hospital. . . . They would have answers by now. Is it too late? Do you think we can—"

"Anita, come." Juan Carlos stood and wrapped an arm around his sister. "Sit down, okay? Take a few deep breaths. I know this is scary; we're all scared, but we have to be patient and let the doctors do their job." He squeezed her tight. "I'm going to go grab us some coffee. Don't get up while I'm gone, okay? You're only going to make *Mamá* more nervous. It's going to be okay. She's a strong woman; you know that."

Anita nodded but didn't sit down. She walked over to Alba's bed and straightened her sheets, tucking the ends underneath the mattress to create a perfect cocoon.

Melanie was accustomed to witnessing her mother worried about things like overdue bills and angry when she couldn't find the right English counterpart to her Spanish vocabulary, but her mother never openly expressed fear. Thinking about it now after all she'd learned, Melanie realized that fear *had* to be something her mother was well acquainted with. Perhaps, as a mother, Anita had learned how to shove her fear deep down into the recesses of her soul because she had no choice but to push forward and survive for her children's sake. Anita had lived most of her life in survival mode, and when you're just trying to survive, fear takes a back seat. There's no time for it.

But the thought of losing her own mother was enough to tear down the barbed wire fence keeping Anita's fears from exposure.

Melanie stood and walked toward her mother to hand her a tissue. She wrapped her arm around her and whispered, "Mom, Juan Carlos is right. Everything's going to be okay. *Abuela* is the strongest woman we know. She will pull through."

The attempted encouragement only made tears well up in both women's eyes.

"*Niñas lindas,* beautiful girls," said Alba, eyes stretching open, "come closer to me."

Anita and Melanie looked down to meet Alba's gaze. She turned her palms faceup, motioning for them to lay their hands in hers. "Why are you crying, *mis amores?* If I don't die today, the day will come soon. And it's okay, *mi vida.* I promise."

"No, *Mamá,* don't say that; it's not time," Anita said.

Melanie looked down at her hand that was intertwined with her grandmother's. There were more than sixty years between their hands. She brushed her thumb over a deep wrinkle, for a moment drifting to another place.

"*Hija,* I've lived a full life," Alba said. "So full. There may be much in my past I wish hadn't happened, but I have no regrets. My mother used to always tell me to do the best I could with what I had and what I knew and to make changes as I learned and grew. That advice never left me. I've always tried to live that way, and I know you have too. Not only has my life been long, but it's been full. If it's time, I'm okay with that. I'm not afraid."

"But what would I do without you?" Tears poured out of Anita's eyes more quickly than she could dry them.

"You've lived a whole life without me. A beautiful life. Look at all that you've created." Alba turned to look at Melanie, a gleam in her eye, then back to Anita. "When you and your sisters were little, I used to look at you and pray you would grow up to be strong women. Women who didn't take the easy way out but pursued their dreams fearlessly. Women who made better decisions than I made. I know life wasn't always easy for you, but you did it. You did so much more than I did in my life, and I thank God for that every single day. You did all of that without me by your side. You don't need me, *mi amor*."

"But I do, *Mamá*." Anita leaned over to hug her mother while Melanie stroked her grandmother's hair.

"And you, my dear Melanie, you can't even imagine how proud you've made me and all of your family. When your mother and your aunts started having children, I worried all my grandchildren would be too American and that we'd lose our Colombian heritage in one generation. But that was a silly fear. Look at you. . . . You speak Spanish, you come visit me, you eat everything I make you. . . . You're the perfect blend, *mi amor*. I'm so proud of you."

Now it was Melanie who couldn't keep up with the tears soaking her cheeks. She clutched her belly and shook her head. Her grandmother saw a different woman in her than the Melanie who lived in America.

"*Abuela*, I'm so glad I came. You have no idea. Coming here has opened my eyes so much to a world I knew so little about. I love you so much, and I promise I'm going to be visiting you more often now. Maybe I'll spend the whole summer with you next year. So, please, get better so you can go home and I can come back, okay?"

There was so much Melanie had to make up for—she only needed time.

"Well, I can't make any promises, but no matter what happens, my home is always yours. You can always come back—come back to your home."

Melanie leaned down and hugged her grandmother as tightly as she could.

"*¿Señora Carvajal?*" A new doctor entered the room, a clipboard held to his chest. There must have been a shift change in the time they'd been here. This doctor, with thin white hair covering his head and square frames sliding down his nose, looked about ten years older than the last doctor.

"Yes, that's me," Alba said.

"I've been in touch with Doctor Fernandez. He's updated me on what's going on. I have your results. Would you like them in private?" As he asked, he looked at Anita and Melanie, and then Juan Carlos, who walked in a few seconds behind the doctor.

"No, it's okay. This is my family."

The doctor grabbed a black chair on wheels and sat at Alba's bedside.

"Well, I'm sorry to say that it looks like you had a mild heart attack. It's very good that you came in when you did. It could have been worse."

"Okay, so am I cleared to go home?" Alba asked.

"*Mamá, por favor,* we need more information before we can talk about going home," Anita said.

Alba looked at her with a smirk before turning back to the doctor. "Okay, Doctor, what else do we need to know?"

"Well, we'd like to keep you overnight to monitor your heart. We'd like twenty-four hours of data before we send you home. We'll also be prescribing some new medicines to thin your blood and make sure the arteries stay nice and open. You may feel very tired the next couple of weeks, and that's normal. It may be some time before you feel like yourself again. But I want you to take it easy, okay? Bed rest for a week, and then you can ease back into normal life if everything remains well. How does that sound?" The doctor had no idea who he spoke to. Alba on bed rest? There were too many *arepas* to make for her to stay out of her kitchen for a week.

"Of course, Doctor, whatever you say."

Melanie held back a smile. She knew exactly what lay behind her grandmother's innocent eyes.

"Great. Well, family members, you should get some rest. It won't help her much for her caregivers to be exhausted. I always recommend family go home for the night to get quality rest and then come back the next morning. *Señora* Alba, you let me know if you need anything else in the meantime, okay?"

"Yes, Doctor. Thank you."

After he walked out the door, Alba turned to look at her family. "You heard him. Best for all of you to go home and rest."

"No, *Mamá*, I can't leave you here alone. Juan Carlos, why don't you take Melanie home? I'll stay the night with Mom, and maybe you can come in the morning and we can switch until it's time to go home."

"Of course," Juan Carlos answered.

"Mom, are you sure? I can stay too. I don't mind," Melanie said.

"No, *mija*, it's okay. Go home and get some rest. We'll be fine."

Before leaving the hospital room, Melanie kissed her grandmother on her forehead and hugged her mother. Then she reached into her satchel and pulled out the book she'd been carrying around.

"Here, in case you need something to kill time," Melanie said to Anita as she handed her Alba's worn copy of *Love in the Time of Cholera*. "Read it aloud to *Abuela;* she'd like that."

"That's a great idea. *Gracias, mi amor.*"

CHAPTER 35

Melanie's eyes were red and puffy.

Seeing her grandmother in a hospital bed had made her look so frail. Yes, Alba may be ninety years old, but just the night before, Melanie had watched her sway her hips on their make-shift dance floor. Alba took many breaks throughout the night—she'd sit on the couch and yell for someone to bring her water. But after a conversation or two, she'd be back on her feet, looking for another dance partner. That didn't seem like the same woman lying in a hospital bed right now.

With her clothes still on, Melanie got under the covers and wept once more. How could she have waited nearly ten years to visit her grandmother? Her grandma had made the trip to the States back then for her *quinceañera,* but Melanie hadn't felt the need to reciprocate. The past two days might be the final memories she'd have of her grandmother. Although she was grateful she'd decided to come, she was also overwhelmed with grief over the last ten years, when she bothered to call only on holidays. How could she have neglected her family relationships—and all relationships—so much? All for what? For a job she was about to lose.

She pulled the covers all the way over her head and allowed her tears to soak the beige sheet. There's no telling how long she would have lain there—years of regret pouring out of her—if her phone hadn't started buzzing from her satchel on the floor.

It was Genesis. She answered the call without a second thought.

"Gen—" Melanie blew her nose and took steadying breaths.

"Melanie? Is that you? What's the matter? Is everything okay? Are you safe?"

Melanie nodded but then realized Genesis wasn't on Face-Time. "Yes. Well, no. My grandmother is in the hospital."

"Oh, Melanie. I'm so sorry. What happened?"

"I was out with my mom, and when we came home, my grandmother looked all pale and was having trouble breathing. She's still there. . . . My mom is with her."

"*Ay, mija. Que susto.* What did the doctors say? Is she going to be okay?"

"They think so. She had a heart attack and she's very weak, so the recovery will be a while. . . . Or, who knows, she may never recover. But they think she should be home tomorrow or the next day. They wanted to keep her overnight."

"That's so scary. Is there anything I can do?"

"No. Thank you, though. I'm glad you called. I need to talk to you about something." Melanie cleared her throat and sat up straighter.

"Okay. . . . What's up?"

"I can't write the article."

"The article? What do you mean?"

"The article I came here to write . . . I can't do it. I've thought about it a million different ways, and I can't write what Ignacio wants me to write while staying true to how I actually feel about the topic. So much has happened since I got here. I feel like the whole world has shifted on its axis and nothing will ever be the same."

"Are you sure? I'm so confused, though. What changed? You were so ready for this."

"I'm one hundred percent sure. A lot has happened since I've been in Cali. I found these journals, my mom's journals. They're incredible. The writing is absorbing, and the stories just painted a whole new world for me. And it's made me realize I've been living a lie. I feel like my entire life I've been trying to be someone I'm not . . . and in the process, I've pushed away every piece of my culture that makes me who I am. I don't want to write this article because it's so . . . ugh, stereotypical. All people think about when they think of Colombia is drug dealers and gangs and cocaine. Literally . . . think about every movie or TV series you've seen about Colombia—cartels. I can't do the same. I just can't. I would rather lose my job than publish another piece of media that plays into this narrative. This is my country, Gen. These are my people. I can't betray them like that. I can't betray my family."

"Wow, Mel. That's beautiful. So, what are you going to do? I mean, I'm with you. I think I would do the same thing if I were in your shoes, but at the same time, I don't think Ignacio is going to take the news well. Did you get the mass email that just went out?"

"What? I don't know, I haven't even opened my inbox today."

"George, Andrea, and Veronica were all let go Friday. They wanted us to know before we came into the office tomorrow morning."

"No."

"Mm-hmm. I always thought layoffs happened on Mondays, but I guess Manuel is changing things up. Ignacio emailed a few of us senior reporters after too. Said something about Manuel being around more often in the coming weeks. He wants us to meet in his office first thing tomorrow. From his email, Ignacio sounds like he's more on edge than ever before."

"Oh my—"

"I think this is our new norm, Mel. Manuel lurking around checking on every little thing we publish and regular layoffs."

Melanie ran her fingers through her hair and exhaled.

"Maybe he'll understand, no? Ignacio's parents are from Mexico, aren't they? Surely, he'll understand that I can't write a story that bashes where my mother grew up—where I'm from. Maybe I just need to find the right words and catch him in the right moment."

"I'm not sure those moments exist anymore. And, I hate to say this, but I'm not sure Ignacio's job is safe either. I kinda feel bad for the guy, the way Manuel just barges into his meetings and his office lately whenever he feels like it."

"What if I wrote something different? That way I'm not coming back empty-handed," Melanie said.

"Different like what?"

"I don't know. I'll find another story here in Cali."

"I mean, I guess it's worth a shot. Maybe you could connect it somehow to the story you were supposed to write originally— like a different angle. That way you're not completely going off the rails. Although it's probably best to talk to Ignacio so he can send another reporter to Bogotá. I know you prefer the story not be told at all, but the best you might get is him allowing you to tell the other side. It's worth a try."

Melanie stared into the darkness. Genesis's words didn't come as a surprise. She tended to err on the side of optimism, but Melanie could tell she didn't have a ton of confidence in this particular plan. And the thought felt like a bullet to the chest.

"I guess I have to try. But you know what? It's okay if it doesn't work out. I don't really have another option because I can't leave my grandmother. I'll do what I can and see what happens."

"You're brave, *mija*. Braver than me," Genesis said. "I'm proud of you. I don't think I would have been able to do what you're about to do when I was only a year in at the *Globe*. It's admirable. And if anyone can do this, it's you."

"Psh, are you kidding me? My hands are shaking just telling you about it. I wish I could disappear and not have to tell him anything. He's going to be so disappointed in me. I really let him down, Gen. He trusted me with this big story . . . an international story . . . and I completely messed it up. If I don't get fired, it will be a miracle."

"Eh, he'll live. It's best to be honest and get it all out there."

"I guess I have to cancel my interviews and my flights. And I'll definitely have to pay the *Herald* back for my flight here too. It's the right thing to do if I can't write the article like Ignacio wanted. . . . Ugh, my savings account is about to take a major hit."

"Don't be so hard on yourself. Make amends and forget the rest."

"Thanks, Gen. I know in my gut this is the right thing to do. I've always led with my head instead of my gut, and it's time to change that. In the meantime, pray for me, will ya?"

"Getting on my knees right now."

After Melanie hung up the phone, she grabbed her laptop and opened her inbox. There it was: the mass email Genesis had told her about. Her throat muscles constricted. How was it even possible that her name wasn't on this list of layoffs? This assignment was truly her last chance to stay at the *Herald*, yet she was about to draft an email to Ignacio that she wouldn't be able to write what he'd sent her to Colombia to write.

She apologized profusely after sharing about her family emergency but chose to keep the details of her opposition to the article to a minimum. She'd do better to explain it in person with an alternative in hand.

She attached the contact information for all her scheduled interviews and the long document that contained her research before she took a deep breath and hit Send. It was done—she'd burned the ships. There was no going back, but it only made the pit in her stomach grow larger.

It was her own fault she was in this mess. How could she have not corrected Claudia when she assumed Melanie had been to Colombia? She might as well have lied straight to Ignacio's face. What was she thinking? No amount of desperation should have brought her to such a low point. While she was grateful it had all led her here, to her grandmother's home, she wished it hadn't happened because of a lie.

Melanie got up from her bed and walked to the kitchen, hoping to find chamomile tea or some other remedy to calm her nerves.

"You're still awake," Juan Carlos said from the round table in the kitchen, where the family had shared countless meals in just a couple of days.

"Yeah, I was hoping to find some tea or something to help me sleep."

"Cupboard above the fridge. I think my mother has some there. As you can imagine, we tend to choose coffee over tea most days," Juan Carlos said as he stood up. "Here, I'll start boiling some water for you."

"Thank you." Melanie took a seat and watched her uncle fill

a small saucepan with water. "*Tio,* how come you never left here, *Abuela's* house?" Her uncle had never married or had kids, and Melanie suddenly wanted to know why. The longer she stayed in Colombia, the more comfortable she felt asking anything.

"Well, I think I just couldn't leave my mom. My sisters all went to America, and then they took Manny over. They asked me if I wanted to come, but I worried about my mother being alone with my dad. Then, when he passed away, I worried about her being alone. She might be fiercely independent, but she needs the company. Anyway, I have no regrets. It was a small price to pay for everything she did for us."

"*Abuela* is pretty incredible, isn't she?" Melanie said as Juan Carlos poured the boiling water into a white mug.

"The most incredible. And all my sisters turned out to be just like her. And now I finally got to meet you and, wow, how is it possible to have more little Albas? I am totally surrounded by women who could run this world."

Melanie smiled and looked down at the steam coming from her mug. She wanted to believe her uncle's words, but she didn't feel as brave as he made her out to be. She didn't feel as strong as her grandmother and mother had always been.

"I don't know, *Tio.* I'm not sure I'm as capable as those powerhouse women."

"Are you kidding me? I've heard all the stories about you."

Melanie blew into her mug, stirring the curls of steam rising from it. "What stories?"

"The competitions, the awards, the top university you attended, the big job you got right out of college—"

"You mean the big job I'm about to lose?"

"Lose? Why?"

"I came here to write an article that I now know would paint

Colombia in a negative light. I wish I could say I knew that all along, but I didn't. It's kind of embarrassing that it took reading my mom's journals and spending time here with you all to figure it out. And maybe it's why I never told Mom or anyone here exactly what I'd be working on in Bogotá. All that matters now is I'm not going to write it, which means the minute I get back to Miami, I'll be unemployed." Melanie lifted her tea and took a sip.

"Well, if there's one thing I've learned from all the powerful women in my life, it's that there's always another door. If one gets closed, you find another one, even if you have to kick the door down. I think that's why all the Carvajal women have big calves."

Melanie spit out some of her hot tea onto the table and threw her head back laughing.

"Let me see those calves," Juan Carlos said as he leaned over the table to get a look at Melanie's legs. "Oh yeah, those are Carvajal calves all right!"

"You know, all my life I've struggled to find tall boots that fit, and now I understand why. I guess I should be grateful I live in Miami, where I don't need boots."

"Yeah, there's no way those calves are getting into anything."

Melanie shoved his shoulder and gave him a smirk.

"Okay, on a more serious note," Juan Carlos continued, "I have no doubt you'll find something even better if you do end up losing your job. Better to lose a job than lose yourself, no?"

Melanie nodded. "Absolutely. Thanks, *Tio*."

"Okay, I need to get to bed. I'm too old to be up this late. I guess it's just you and me for breakfast tomorrow. I hope you've been watching your *abuela*. I can chop an onion and turn on the stove, but that's about it." He kissed the top of Melanie's head and disappeared down the hallway.

The tea warmed her belly as she sat still at the table. She took small sips while picturing all the different doors her mother had kicked down when she was Melanie's age.

She kicked down the door that said she had to live at home until she was married. She kicked down the door that said she couldn't go to America without a visa. She kicked down the door that said she'd have to do sketchy work to make money as an undocumented immigrant. She kicked down every door that said she couldn't make a meaningful life for herself and her family without a ton of money in America. And she kicked down the door that said Colombia would only ever be known for one thing.

Anita had never been afraid to kick down a door. And now Melanie felt ready to kick down a few herself.

CHAPTER 36

"*D*ios mio, what is that smell?" Anita asked as she crossed the threshold, pushing her mother in a wheelchair. Alba's home was wrapped in a fragrant cloud of peppers and garlic.

"I told you we had a surprise for you," Juan Carlos said.

Melanie stood in front of the stove, wearing her grandmother's dusty-blue apron. "I made *arroz con pollo!*" she announced to the group.

"*¿Qué?*" Anita said, a worried look on her face.

"I found a recipe online. I wanted to surprise you guys when you got home from the hospital."

"*Mi amor,* that is so wonderful, and I'm starving. That hospital food is not worthy of being chewed," Alba said.

Melanie took off her apron and leaned over to hug her grandmother. "You have no idea how happy I am to see you," she said as she gripped Alba so tightly she could have suffocated her beneath the embrace. "What did the doctors say?" Melanie asked, looking at her mother.

"The medicines are helping, so they cleared her to come home. Still, she is on strict bed-rest orders. And we'll need to go back in a few weeks so they can make sure everything still looks okay." Anita leaned forward to look at her mother with a hand on her shoulder. "No more cooking those elaborate meals either."

Alba mimicked her daughter's command and rolled her eyes, which made Melanie laugh.

"Okay, everyone, sit, sit, sit. I'll pass around some bowls," Melanie said.

She scooped a heaping spoonful of the rice-and-chicken mixture into each bowl. It was a beautiful yellow color, and the rice at the bottom of the pan had turned perfectly crisp. With her head lifted high, she placed a bowl in front of each of her family members.

"Okay, everyone, *buen provecho*," Melanie said. She signaled for them to take their first bite and watched as they chewed.

"Mmm, delicious," Alba said.

"The chicken is very juicy," Juan Carlos said.

"You did so good," Anita said.

Content with their praise, Melanie reached for her spoon and dug in. Just a few chews later and she searched the room for a napkin where she could spit out her bite. "You all are a bunch of liars."

Everyone burst into laughter.

"This is the saltiest thing I've ever tasted! Everyone's blood pressure is about to spike. Ugh, what did I do wrong? I followed the recipe perfectly," Melanie said.

"Hmm, it tastes like maybe you overdid the *sazon Goya*. But it's no big deal; I don't mind. I'm not letting this go to waste." Anita may have been doing what any mother would, but the amount of water she poured into her mouth after her second bite said it all.

"Okay, c'mon, we don't have to eat this," Melanie said.

"*Ay, mija,* don't be so hard on yourself. This isn't a good beginner meal. You just need some practice," Anita said before Juan Carlos stood from the table and grabbed whatever leftovers he could find in the fridge to replace their salty bowls of rice.

"I know you're leaving soon, so next time you come, we'll plan for some real lessons in the kitchen, okay?" Alba said.

"Well, actually, about that . . . I'm not going to Bogotá anymore."

"What? Why?" Alba and Anita asked in unison.

"Eh, it's a long story, but they're sending someone else, a more seasoned reporter, so I'm off the hook." Melanie shrugged, thinking about Ignacio's terse reply to her email. He'd wished her luck with her family emergency, but something about him writing "We'll talk when you get back" made her decide to head home no later than Wednesday morning. It also made her want to enjoy her last day and a half in Cali all the more. While she didn't know what awaited her back home, she *did* know that she needed to soak in every second with her family—who knew when she'd be back.

She reached for a cold *buñuelo* and took a big bite.

"Well, I'm sorry they're sending someone else, but I can't say I'm not happy to have you here without work hanging over your head anymore. Now we'll have time to teach you some basics. Maybe we'll start with *empanadas*," Alba said.

"You're lucky, Melanie. I didn't learn to cook until I was married in New York. And I didn't have your *abuela* there to teach me," Anita said.

"Really?" Melanie said.

"Believe it or not, *Abuela* hardly ever asked us to help in the kitchen. Very nontraditional, especially in that time. Normally, from a very young age, the daughters are in the kitchen cooking meals, washing dishes, and doing whatever household chores need to be done. Boys, not so much. They got to focus on school and play outside. But *Abuela* was different. Anytime we offered to help, she would tell us to go read a book or do homework or study. She would tell us that we'd learn how to cook when we got married and so we should focus on our studies instead."

Alba smiled. "I don't regret that."

"Well, it was true. I did eventually learn, so I'm glad I was able to spend my childhood playing and reading and even writing."

"That's so beautiful, *Abuela*."

"It's what my mother did for me," Alba said.

"And you actually did the same too, Mom. I mean, I remember helping you chop vegetables and stuff, but even when we got older, you never made us cook for the family. And now I understand why," Melanie said. Anita nodded and smiled.

"Speaking of schools, you never told me about yesterday. What did you think of your mother's schools, Melanie? Are they anything like the schools you attended back home?" Alba asked.

"Not quite." As Melanie scooped a spoonful of black beans onto her plate, she talked about all the things that surprised her about her mother's life in Cali.

Growing up, Melanie always loved school. Apart from feeling like an outcast when students would comment on her off-brand shoes or wonder why, at sixteen, she still didn't have a car of her own, Melanie considered school to be the one place where she could excel without anyone getting in her way. Money was not required, nor was the participation of your parents. In the classroom, whether taking exams, writing papers, or presenting a short story in French, she felt like she could exceed her teachers' standards. It didn't matter that her parents hardly spoke English or that she lived in a cramped apartment; at school she could be great. And while visiting her mother's school, she got the sense that her mother may have felt the same way. School provided her a safe place to be herself.

Every hour and every day Melanie spent in Cali was like unwrapping a new revelation about her mother. A new explanation that helped her finally understand much of what made her feel lost and alone as a girl.

"Your mom loved school and she was a very good student, but something you might not know is that she also attracted all the boys," Juan Carlos said. "I can't even tell you how many showed up at our door looking for your mom, and I didn't like it one bit."

"Oh, really?" Melanie said, eyeing her mother.

"It's true," Alba said. "All my girls are so beautiful. I feel like I went through ten years of chasing boys away, and Juan Carlos was a big help. Didn't you put tacks in someone's shoes once?"

"What?" Anita said. "Wait, is that why Bernardo never came back around? It was you?"

Juan Carlos belly laughed before responding. "I thought you knew. Hey, I was just doing my job as a big brother."

When they had finished eating, Anita stood and gathered the plates from the table.

"I think I want to go lie down for a bit. Melanie, can you push my chair?" Alba said.

"Of course." Melanie slowly wheeled her grandmother down the hallway to her room, then helped her stand from the chair and move to her bed. Her grandmother couldn't weigh more than 120 pounds right now.

"*Gracias, mi amor.* I'm going to miss you so much when you leave me."

"Me too, *Abuela.* I wish I could stay longer, but my boss will wonder what happened to me."

"I know. It's okay; I'm just so grateful to have spent the past couple of days with you."

"You have no idea what this has meant to me," Melanie said.

Alba gave her a warm smile. "Can you hand me that box over there on my dresser?"

Melanie obliged, walking over to her dresser and picking up what looked like a plain cardboard shoebox.

"What's this?" Melanie asked.

"Something for you."

"For me?"

Alba nodded, opened the box, and pulled out the contents.

It was a long white dress. Alba shook it out so Melanie could see the whole thing. The dress was so long it brushed the floor. Six layers of ruffles covered the bottom skirt, each embroidered with three ribbons in the colors of the Colombian flag: yellow, blue, then red. The sleeves looked like they'd fall off the shoulders and featured a thick piece of lace from front to back.

"It's beautiful, *Abuela*."

"It was your mother's," Alba said. "I made it for her when she was a teenager. When I saw how much you enjoyed *La Topa* the other night, I thought I would make a few alterations to it so it could fit you. I hope you don't mind that I checked the measurements of some of your clothes in the closet."

Melanie's eyes grew wide. She couldn't take her eyes off the dress. "Not at all."

"It's a traditional Colombian dress, and I think it would be perfection on you. Do you want to try it on?"

"Definitely."

Melanie took the dress from her grandmother's hands and crossed the hall to her room, where she could change. When she had put it on and adjusted the sleeves just so, she walked back to her grandmother's room and stood in front of her.

"*Ay, mija* . . . have you seen yourself in the mirror?" Alba asked.

Melanie turned to face the mirror that hung over her grandmother's closet door.

Alba sniffled behind her. "You look beautiful, so much like your mother."

"I can't believe you made this, *Abuela*." Melanie pinched the ruffled skirt and twirled from side to side. She had never felt so beautiful. The white fabric against her skin brightened her complexion and enhanced all her dark features.

It made her think back to the days when she was in middle and high school and would look at her friends' glossy blond hair and crystal-blue eyes with envy. All she ever wanted was to blend in with them—to look like them. In her school, those features were considered beautiful. Her brown eyes were boring, and her black hair faded into the background. The only times she felt lucky to have more melanin in her skin were the days at the community pool when her friends would turn red as lobsters while Melanie contentedly skipped the sunscreen.

How could she have ever felt that way? How could she have ever wanted to look different? This dress wouldn't look the same on those girls from high school. This dress was made for a woman like her—a Colombian.

And now she didn't want to take it off.

"Can I keep it?" Melanie asked.

"*Claro.* Of course. I hope you wear it with pride."

Melanie turned and skipped over to her grandmother to pull her into an embrace.

For once, she didn't feel like she was trying to hide beneath a fabricated exterior. She didn't feel exhausted by the need to create a persona that would make herself more likeable—more likely to achieve, be accepted, do something great.

She simply felt like herself.

"Your mother wore this dress every year to the World Salsa Festival. It's been happening all week, and I was thinking we could go tomorrow, see what's happening. There's always wonderful music, dancing, and the food, of course, is unbelievable," Alba said. "You should wear that dress. You'll be the most beautiful *Colombiana* there."

Melanie walked back to the mirror to get another look at the dress. "Yes. I want to go. But I'm not sure Mom is going to let you leave this house."

"I'll handle her," Alba said.

A moment later, Anita walked into the room with a small tray of pills. "It's time for your medicine—wow. Look at you," she said, catching Melanie's reflection in the mirror.

"She looks so much like you when you were young," Alba said to Anita.

"No. She's even more beautiful." Anita walked over to Melanie's side and looked her up and down.

"I don't think you know how beautiful you are, Mom."

CHAPTER 37

The music coming from the Alberto Galindo Complex could be heard from two miles away. It felt as though each day Melanie spent in Colombia, the music—salsa in particular—got louder and louder.

But she loved it.

She eagerly pushed her grandmother in her wheelchair, laughing to herself at how stubborn the woman could be. Both Anita and Juan Carlos had insisted she stay home and rest—it had only been a day since she left the hospital—but when she threatened to cook another big feast while the rest of the family went to the festival, they decided it would be safer to bring her along so they could supervise her antics.

Melanie didn't need her mother or uncle to lead the way. She followed the music and the vibrating ground until she spotted the stage where couples dressed in neon colors danced more skillfully than she remembered seeing at *La Topa*.

She still couldn't understand how people moved their feet so quickly. How did they stay upright? How were they so graceful while flying through the air? It was as if the bottom half of their body had its own command center separate from their top half.

While their two halves looked entirely disconnected, it resulted in an electrifying harmony like she couldn't imagine.

"Are there reserved seats?" Melanie asked her mother, who trailed behind her.

"No, you kind of just find a spot and claim it."

Like every other day she'd been in Cali, the night was warm and muggy. The temperature sat right in the mid to high eighties all day long. Thankfully, living in Miami had prepared her to accept the frizzy hair and sweaty back—there was absolutely no way around it.

The family found a few empty chairs in the last row facing the stage.

"I guess this is the best we got," Melanie said.

"This is perfect, actually," Alba said. "Plenty of open space behind us to dance."

"*Mamá*, if you get up from your chair, I'm taking you straight home, okay?"

Alba flicked her wrist and turned to Melanie with a look that said, *Does she think I'm scared of her?*

"I may have forced you to get out on the dance floor at *La Topa*, but don't worry, I won't make you get on *that* stage," said a familiar voice behind Melanie.

It was her cousin Marcela with a few of her friends—Sebastian being the only one she cared to recognize. "Marcela! I didn't know you were going to be here." They hugged and exchanged a kiss on the cheek before Sebastian did the same.

"Oh, I never miss this festival. Been coming here since I was little. I used to dream about being up on that stage." Marcela bent over to kiss Alba on the cheek. "But now I'm happy to watch from down here. Aren't they amazing?"

"I've never seen people move their feet so fast. I definitely wouldn't be able to keep up with them," Melanie said.

"Spend a few weeks here and you'll learn in no time . . . especially in that dress," Sebastian said with a twinkle in his eyes. Was he flirting with her? She prayed it was dark enough to conceal her warm cheeks that were no doubt bright red.

Melanie was thrilled for another chance to talk with Sebastian, but his comment reminded her of the unfortunate truth that she'd leave Cali the next morning. She wasn't ready to leave. She felt like she'd just discovered so much about her family and about herself that she wasn't ready to stop exploring. And not only that, leaving Cali meant having to face the realities of her uncertain future.

At this point, she was confident about her decision to tell Ignacio the entire truth. Not only would her article hurt the people who meant the most to her, but she'd seen Colombia in a whole new light. A light so different from the one Ignacio and the other reporters portrayed back at the office—so different from the rest of the world.

What her mother wrote in her journal decades ago still rang true today. She couldn't think of a single piece of media that didn't focus on cocaine when talking about her country. It was true decades ago, and not much had changed. She refused to be yet another steward of an incomplete picture.

But she still hadn't figured out what she would write instead.

What could she write that could replace the original article for the *Herald*? Somehow she would have to connect her new article to the news of the rise in crime and deaths in Miami. She couldn't write something out of the blue and expect Ignacio to see it as a suitable replacement or an addition to the original piece. But how could she talk about more deaths and more cocaine in a positive light? It felt impossible.

Maybe it was impossible. Maybe she would have to show up to Ignacio's office empty-handed. That might be better than showing up with heartfelt words that didn't belong in a newspaper.

She tried to put the thought aside. This wasn't the place to figure everything out. It was her last night in Cali; she should enjoy it as much as possible. Tomorrow could worry about tomorrow.

Marcela and her friends scooted into their row of seats, and Melanie joined them as she moved her hips and clapped her hands with the crowd. She took a moment to look around at her family and their friends.

There were broad smiles on everyone's faces. Marcela's eyes were closed as she swayed from side to side. She lifted her left arm to the sky, tightly gripping her *café con leche*.

Anita had taken a seat on a plastic chair next to Alba's wheelchair, where she could hold her hand and look her in the eye whenever Alba offered commentary on the dancers' skills.

Juan Carlos had been pulled into one of the aisles by a stranger, but he happily danced in their confined space, eyes sparkling beneath the colorful, bright lights of the stage.

Sebastian attempted to have a full-on conversation with the guy next to him despite the blaring music.

Melanie turned her gaze toward the stage, where new couples had shimmied on to show off their moves. The number of sequins and rhinestones onstage right now was enough to light up a small community.

No person sat still. Every aisle and every corner was occupied by audience members who couldn't help but move to the rhythm of the beat.

Since the day she arrived in Cali, she hadn't seen what movies and TV series loved to portray about her country: thugs, drugs, and violence. Yes, there was poverty and need. No doubt there were people in this country suffering from inexplicable injustice and others working against peace and prosperity. But the Colombia Melanie saw now emulated hope, not despair.

She'd seen tight-knit communities. Teachers who longed for their students to get ahead. Neighbors who were more like family. Unmatched talent in cuisine and the arts. In just a few days here, Melanie had seen the other side of Colombia.

The other side of Colombia . . . just like the essay her mother wrote in her first English class in New York City.

That's it. That's what I have to write about!

I can still mention the impact Miami is experiencing right now, but that won't be the whole story. I can make the majority of the piece about the other side of the story.

Ideas flew through Melanie's head, but before she could give her lightbulb moment any more time, Marcela looked at her and said, "Okay, you didn't wear that dress here for nothing. C'mon!" She threw away her coffee, grabbed Melanie's hand, and dragged her to the outer aisle, where people moved and sang along to the music. Some women had even taken off their heels to dance barefoot in the grass.

The energy was electric. But Melanie quickly realized that without a leader to follow, she had no idea what to do. She did her best to follow Marcela's footsteps, but her cousin moved too fast for Melanie to register every move.

Marcela's three-point turns were smooth and graceful, and she knew exactly what to do with her hands when she didn't have a dance partner. Melanie, on the other hand, didn't have a clue what to do with her hands, so she kept them attached to her full skirt while she kept her eyes glued to Marcela's feet.

How much more would I know about the world of salsa if I had been born here like Marcela?

She couldn't give the thought much attention. Sebastian had walked out onto the grassy patch to join them. He stood to her left and mouthed *Like this* as he motioned to the way he rattled his hands in front of his chest. Melanie followed his example, hoping her cheeks weren't turning red again.

As the night went on, more and more expert dancers showed off their moves onstage. Some of the dancers were young children who spun so fast Melanie feared they might fall off the stage.

After a few hours, the host of the festival returned to the stage to close out the event with a few words. Melanie paid close attention as she chugged the bottle of water Juan Carlos had bought her.

The host thanked everyone for attending the festival and celebrating Colombian culture. He went on about what it means to be Colombian: finding joy in the little things, being together with family and friends, enjoying good food as a true gift from heaven, and, of course, salsa . . . because "salsa runs in all of our blood," he said. "It's what connects us and brings us together."

Melanie didn't understand why her eyes began to water.

Why does everything about this trip make me want to cry?

The host's words weren't particularly earth-shattering, but they still triggered something in her. And now she couldn't wait to get back to her grandmother's home so she could start writing.

"I can't believe you're leaving tomorrow. I wish we could have spent more time together," Marcela said as the group walked toward the lot where Juan Carlos's car was parked.

"I know, me too. But don't worry, I'll definitely be back. And maybe you can come visit me too. I'd love to show you Miami."

"I've always wanted to go to Miami."

"Me too. Can I join this trip?" Sebastian asked, nudging Marcela's arm.

"We'll see." Melanie tried not to smile. "I don't have a huge apartment or anything, but I can get an air mattress for you. It would be fun. Maybe we could even find a salsa club in Miami and you can show the Americans your skills."

"You've got something to teach them now too," Sebastian said with a wink.

CHAPTER 38

With the amount of sweat that trailed down Melanie's back, there was no way she could get into bed without washing up.

Even after a few days here, she still hadn't gotten used to the ice-cold showers. She had the option of filling the tub with boiling water for a warm bath—but that just seemed like too much work. Instead, she took a deep breath and jumped around the shower, trying to withstand the icy cold droplets for as long as it took to wash her hair.

After drying her hair, she slipped into her pajamas and crawled into bed. As much as she wanted to take a moment to scribble down all the ideas for her article that had been spewing about in her head throughout the festival, she decided to open another one of her mother's journals. Reading them in her grandmother's home was special. Would it be the same in Miami? Would the words jump off the page and into her soul the same way they had here?

She opened the bag that sat by the nightstand and picked a new journal at random. Her hand traced the golden embroidery on the front. When she flipped through the pages, she noticed each page contained shorter entries than the last journal, and the words were in narrow columns.

Could these be poems? The poems her grandmother had mentioned on her first day here? Perhaps Anita preferred to keep her creative writing in a separate journal . . .

The answer was on the first page of the journal:

POEMS FOR MY DAUGHTER MELANIE

She sighed.

Poems about me? This whole thing just about me?

Turning the page, she spotted the date on the top right of the first poem.

May 27, 1994—Melanie's first birthday.

Niña de ojasos negros
Centellar de estrellas
Sonrisas y alegrías
Hoy el Altísimo
Te concede el privilegio
De tu primer año de vida
Vida que dará
Sentimientos y ternuras
A los padres amantes
Que luchan en la vida
Y que de ti solo esperan
Que siempre los mires
Con esos ojazos negros y
Esa bella sonrisa

. . .

Girl with big black eyes
Sparkle of stars
Smiles and joys
Today the Most High
Grants you the privilege
Of your first year of life
Life that will give
Tender feelings
To the loving parents
Who struggle through life
And from you they only expect
That you always watch them
With those big black eyes and
That beautiful smile

Melanie turned to the back of the page and found a photo of Anita embracing her as they posed in front of what looked like a homemade birthday cake with one candle on top. She stared at the image of her mother. Anita looked so jovial. Young, beautiful, and full of life. It was the same woman she'd seen here in Cali.

And the words. Oh, the words. Melanie pictured her mother sitting in their simple apartment in Queens, her eyes probably watering at the thought of her child growing up too fast, pouring out her heart into this journal. A journal no one would have ever seen had Melanie not come here.

She wanted more.

With every page turned, Melanie found more words of hope and admiration. Words of longing and dreams for her daughter's future. There were even words of pain—pain that likely only a mother can understand.

She read page after page, and then another date stuck out to

her somewhere toward the end of the journal: June 2009. The
year her family moved to Maryland.

Una tarde del mes de mayo
Lleno de sol ardiente
Nace una hermosa niña
Con ojos cafés a la luz saliente
Mira a todos lados y pregunta
¡Instintivamente! ¿Qué mundo es este?

La madre que anhelante
Adivina su temor
La arrulla entre sus brazos
Y le da su protección
No temas hijita mía
Que a tu lado siempre estaré
Sonriéndole a la vida
Y a veces llorando también.

Han transcurrido algunos años
Muy pocos para la experiencia
Pero has sabido vivirlos
Con mucha inteligencia.
Sigue por ese camino
Que la vida te debe mucho
Y no tardará en llegar
El que a tu oído cante en susurro.

Levanta los ojos al cielo
Y al Altísimo siempre da gracias
Por la vida que te ha dado
Llena de esperanzas.
Hoy ya has crecido y
muy lejos de mi te encuentras y

Yo desde la lejanía
Te recuerdo y te bendigo
Para desearte que seas feliz y
Nunca desfallezcas.

...

On an afternoon in May
Full of blazing sun
A beautiful girl is born
With brown eyes that look brown in the evening light
She looks around and asks
Instinctively! What world is this?

The mother who eagerly
Senses her fear
Soothes her baby in her arms
And grants her protection
Do not fear my little daughter
I'll always be by your side
Smiling at life
And sometimes crying as well.

Some years have passed
Too few to be considered experience
But you've known how to live them
With intelligence.
Stay on that road
Because life owes you much
And before long will come
The one who sings whispering in your ear.

Lift your eyes to heaven
And to the Most High always give thanks
For the life that he has given you

Full of hope.
Today you have grown up and
You are far away from me
And from afar
I remember you and I bless you
To wish that you will be happy and
Never falter.

Tears . . . again.

In that moment, she wept for a life with a mother she didn't know. Not only did she wish she could have known many of the stories she'd read about, but she wished she could have known about the raw talent her mother possessed. It would have given them something to bond over—a bridge to connect their lives.

Reading these poems also fired up something else in Melanie. Something that had been buried deep inside the recesses of her heart. She hadn't wanted to shut it away, but she hadn't felt she had a choice.

From a very young age, Melanie had been drawn to the written word.

Nothing made her feel more at home than getting lost in a novel. Anytime she accompanied her mother to the local thrift store, she'd run off to the wide bookshelf in the back and carefully read the spine of every book on the shelf. Whenever a title piqued her interest, she'd pull out the book, read the synopsis on the back, and, if that kept her interest, read the first few pages. Inevitably, she'd search the aisles looking for her mother with a stack of novels in her hands. Her mother always made her leave all but two behind. It never got easier to put those lovely books back on their shelf.

The books inspired her to create her own stories. Sometimes she'd make them up in her head and recite them to rows of dolls in her bedroom. Other times she'd grab a notebook and write her stories down until her mother would come in the bedroom and shut off her light.

She never told anyone about her stories, worried that it made her look nerdy. But her freshman year in high school, she decided to confide in her guidance counselor when they met to create Melanie's schedule and choose her electives. Melanie spilled about her secret passion for creative writing and questioned whether perhaps there was a future for her in writing stories like those she read.

But she was met with a harsh reality.

"That's wonderful, dear," her counselor said. "But I'm not sure creative writing can provide a secure and stable job, unfortunately. The odds of publishing a book—especially one that sells—are just slim. Maybe you could write your stories in your free time, you know, like a hobby. Have you thought about print journalism?"

Melanie stopped listening after the line about a secure and stable job. While her heart longed to write stories, she told herself it would be more important to prepare for a future where she could earn a stable income—something her mother had still not been able to find.

When her mind returned to the room where her guidance counselor continued spewing her advice, she caught a few lines about there being lots of room to be creative in journalism. And something about earning a decent living once you've been at it for a few years. But what rang loud and clear to Melanie was when she said, "You'll be respected. People respect journalists. You don't want to be one of those poor starving-artist types. Of course you don't."

That was enough to convince Melanie that she needed to adjust her vision for her future. *Surely* this counselor knew her stuff. Her mother didn't know anything about the world of writing, so Melanie couldn't seek guidance at home. But this woman in her school—she had credibility. She would know the best route for Melanie to reach her goals of building a safe and reliable life.

That was the last day Melanie ever talked about creative writing. She listened as her counselor raved about the school's journalism elective, where Melanie could learn how to write articles and conduct interviews. She could take the class every year, and if she still liked it her junior year, it would be a great clue to the college and major she should pursue. Melanie nodded along and allowed the counselor to enroll her in the class.

When she got home that night, she stuffed the journals she'd filled with stories underneath her bed, where they would collect dust. She was doing the responsible thing—there was no more to it.

Melanie shook her head at the memory. Where could those stories be? Had they survived her several moves? Had her mother saved them? Why had she listened to that guidance counselor?

As much as it pained Melanie to think about that morning in her guidance counselor's office, perhaps she'd been right. Who did she know who actually made a living with creative writing? Not her mother. Not any of her friends. Not anyone she graduated with from college.

But that reality didn't matter. It didn't do anything to remove Melanie's longing to fill a journal with poems, essays, and short stories. She'd felt the urge begin to simmer from the moment she read the opening entry in her mother's journal on her first day in Colombia, and now it was stronger than ever. The urge called to her, yelled her name to come near.

And it was all because of her mother's writing. Writing she

envied. The words felt so free, like there were no boundaries. No rules to follow. No people to impress. Her mother wrote words straight from her heart. And the best part was that she not only felt like she knew her mother better when she finished reading each poem, but she felt like she knew herself better.

And wasn't that what good writing should do?

My mother's words move something in me. Something a newspaper article has never been able to do.

She laid the journal of poems by her side on the bed and reached for her laptop. Her computer had gotten a break from her writing like it'd never seen before. But that break was over now.

Scooting back against her pillow, she opened the laptop. The first thing she saw was her outline for the article she'd come to Colombia to write. Without a second thought, she deleted the document.

Then she opened a new blank page and started to write.

CHAPTER 39

Sleep escaped Melanie the night before she left Cali. She never imagined all that she would take with her, both tangible and intangible.

Her thoughts ran rampant with ideas for her new article and fueled her to stay up late into the night. Even when her mother crept into the room to get in bed, Melanie stayed awake and continued writing below the dim hue of her laptop.

There was no telling what time Melanie drifted off to sleep that night. Her ringing alarm told her it hadn't been many hours ago. Her eyes were bloodshot, and they pleaded not to be stretched open. She willed her legs to the edge of the bed, hoping the rest of her body would follow.

She'd booked the first flight out that morning, and the night before, she'd begged her grandmother not to defy the doctor's orders by getting out of bed to make another elaborate breakfast for her before the flight. Surprisingly, her grandmother had obliged, but she did manage to reach Melanie in time to stuff a *buñuelo* in her purse before Melanie got in Juan Carlos's car.

"Come close, *mi amor*," Alba said, motioning for Melanie to come down to the level of her wheelchair. "You have made me the proudest grandmother on this planet, you hear me? You are even more wonderful than the sweet little fifteen-year-old I was last with. Whatever happens when you get back to work, I'm confident you will overcome with grit, because that's what us Carvajal women are made of."

"I hope so, *Abuela*," Melanie said.

"I know so, *mi vida*."

Alba reached out her arms and hugged Melanie for what felt like an eternity. Then she held Melanie's face with her two hands and said, "I love you."

Melanie breathed in her words and hugged her once more. "Take care of yourself, okay? I want to come back here next summer, and I need you here to enjoy it," Melanie said before she finally turned around and walked toward the car.

There was no doubt in Melanie's head, whether her grandmother made it another year or not, that she would return to Cali, to this home, to be with her family again. There was no more fear and no more hesitation that this was her second home.

Juan Carlos carried the luggage Melanie had left by the front door to his car. Anita decided to accompany him to the airport, but she would stay another week longer—she never came to Colombia for less than two weeks.

Rather than sit up front with her brother, Anita climbed into the back seat of the bright-yellow cab to sit next to her daughter for the last ride they'd share in her city. "I'm so glad you came, *mija*. Your grandmother couldn't have been happier. And me too." Anita reached out her hand and laid it atop Melanie's, which rested in the center of the back seat.

Melanie looked at her and smiled, hoping to communicate her love and gratitude without using words. She waved to her grandmother, turning her head to watch her for as long as she could. The rest of the ride she spent with her eyes glued to her window, hoping to hold on to the view for as long as possible.

Not many words were exchanged in the car. Instead, the joyous salsa music on the radio filled the space between them, and Melanie, as she so often did, got lost in her thoughts.

It wasn't until they came to a stoplight, just a few minutes down the road, that something caught her attention. There was a young woman in tattered slip-on shoes and a loose tank top covered in dirt who walked up and down the lane to all the cars, offering small plastic bags of sliced mango. Melanie noticed her only when she'd gotten close to Juan Carlos's door.

The girl looked through the rear window and momentarily locked eyes with Melanie.

Melanie gasped.

She turned to look at her mother and then into the rearview mirror to get a glimpse of her uncle's face. Had no one else seen what she just saw? Melanie looked at each of them again before reluctantly looking back out the window at the young woman, who now accepted the few coins Juan Carlos had in his cup holder. She sighed deeply, relieved to see the face of the poor scraggly woman—the *real* face. For a moment earlier, Melanie had seen herself—her own face on the body of this street vendor.

The woman's real face looked like hers—a darker complexion with naturally rosy cheeks and big brown eyes—except *her* face looked more tired, sad, and hopeless. Her eyes were heavy and her hair a matted mess.

Melanie's own eyes watered as she watched the girl, even turning her head when the car began to move again, as if not ready to let go.

A few moments later, her eyes moved from the road to the

headrest in front of her as she contemplated what could have been her reality.

Would that have been me?

The thought of her living the same life as this poor young woman had her mother never left Colombia hit her with great force.

The only reason her family here in Colombia were doing better now was because of the few members who'd decided to move to the States. With their regular financial support, Alba expanded her store and sewing business to reach more clients. Juan Carlos was able to purchase a taxi car that would provide a stable income for himself. And even extended family members, like Melanie's second cousin Marcela, could find help for such things as school fees and uniforms.

It wasn't just her own life that had been affected by her mother's decision to move to a place she never even wanted to visit; everyone's life was different because of it.

Juan Carlos handed the bag of mango to Melanie. "Here, take this for your trip. You'll get hungry. It'll be your last taste of Colombia before you get home."

She met his eyes in the rearview mirror and dolefully said, "Thank you, *Tio*. So sweet." Melanie looked down at the mango in her hand and then turned her head to catch one more glimpse of the young woman. She ran back to the sidewalk, where she would be safe until the light turned red once more. As they got farther away, Melanie turned her body so she could watch the woman a few seconds longer.

"*¿Que fue?*" Anita asked, noticing her daughter focused on something behind her. The sound of her mother's voice startled Melanie and brought her back to the present.

"Huh? Oh, nothing. Do you want some of this mango?" Melanie said, hoping to change the topic. But she couldn't help herself; she turned once more to look behind her. The woman was gone—out of sight.

That was not the last image she'd expected to take with her from Colombia. To see herself on the body of a young Colombian woman around her age, whose fate and future looked so different from her own.

That could have been me.

Destined to sell fruit at an intersection the rest of my life. No college. No job as a writer. No apartment in Miami. Where would I be if my mother had never left? Where would my family be? My grandmother? Would she even be alive?

The little bit of money her mother and aunts earned in America had been more than enough to change her family tree.

Who would have known that in just one generation, with one simple decision, everything could change?

In that moment of deep gratitude, Melanie turned to look at her mother, who stared out her window. She turned the palm of her hand over and gave her mother's hand a gentle squeeze.

CHAPTER 40

When her flight to Miami finally reached thirty thousand feet, she pulled down her tray table and set her laptop on it. She had several hours of undisturbed writing time on this flight, and she wanted to take full advantage of it.

First, she reviewed everything she'd written the night before. Some lines she remembered writing. Others she couldn't believe were her words.

There were lines about the mouthwatering food she'd tasted that she'd never be able to replicate at home. She wrote about the people she'd met in the schools and the bakeries—their beauty, passion for their country, and generous hospitality. There's no way she would have left out the party thrown for her grandmother's birthday, the band at *La Topa*, and the dancing that would have continued late into the night had the event organizers not begun to tear down the stage at the salsa festival. After her own research, she'd also written about notable exports—like petroleum, coffee, gold, roses, steel, and sugar—that the world seemed to forget Colombia created with love.

She'd written about all the things that Colombia should be

famous for but that were constantly overshadowed by drugs, violence, and a government with a bad reputation.

Half an hour before her flight landed in Miami, she put the finishing touches on her article and then pushed her laptop back to get a better look at the whole thing.

It was perfect.

Exactly what she needed to write.

Her writing felt more provocative, distinct, and weighty than anything else she had written for the *Herald*. The article was full of life and felt gutsy for her.

Maybe this was exactly what had been missing from her writing all along. Maybe she'd finally found her voice.

She couldn't wait to show Ignacio.

While she knew he would be upset at her last-minute cancellation, she held on to hope that just a glimpse of these words would erase any anger. This is exactly what he'd been urging her to do. How many times had he told her she tried too hard to be like other reporters? How many times had he told her to bring more soul and creative angles to her assignments? How many times had he told her to unlearn everything her professors had taught her and to let her writing direct itself?

Looking at the open document, she felt like she'd finally done it. She finally understood exactly what he meant, and she hoped he would see it too.

She still regretted not having been honest in the pitch meeting, and she knew she could never do anything like that again, no matter how desperate the situation, but she prayed this article would help her get back into Ignacio's good graces. And as much as she didn't want to admit the truth, she was grateful for everything that had transpired the week before. Had none of it happened, she likely would have never taken the time to visit this country, and she would have missed out on the chance to fall in love with her culture—and with herself.

It was finally clear what had been missing from her writing all along: an authentic voice like her mother's. She looked down at her feet, where the vintage leather bag that carried her mother's journals sat tucked underneath the seat in front of her. The cargo was too precious to place in the overhead bin. She put away her laptop and dug through the bag, looking for the first journal she'd found in her mother's nightstand. The plane was beginning its descent into Miami, but there was enough time to read the only entry she hadn't yet read.

CHAPTER 41

JUNE 2009
CALI, COLOMBIA

ANITA

I can't believe I left so many blank pages in this journal. I wanted to make sure every page was filled before moving on to a new one. It doesn't feel right to leave a journal unfinished.

I'm back in Colombia . . . yet again, without my kids. My mother keeps telling me to be patient with them, but it's hard. Raising children in a place that is not your home has never been easy, but I know now that I made the right decision. Do I wish I could move back here? Finish raising them in my neighborhood? Of course.

But I can't do that to them. Uproot them from all they've ever known.

And to be honest, I'm kind of happy with where we are now. Like, really happy.

Despite the divorce and the move, we're doing okay. More than okay. Some days, I feel like I can take longer, slower breaths. I haven't felt that way in ages. Maybe ever.

Being back in my old home, I'm realizing how much of my life here I spent in fight mode. I was always up against challenges, mainly to do with our lack of resources. By the grace of God, my mother lives a very different life today than she did when I lived here . . . and I'm now realizing that so do I.

It took many years—and a lot of hard work—to get to this place of . . . rest? But I made it. It's kind of funny . . . if I told my kids this they would laugh. They don't think we have much. I know they wish we had a different apartment or a different car or different clothes. But they have no idea where I started. They have no idea what my life looked like here. If they knew, I think they would feel differently. I've brought it up here and there, but words aren't enough.

One day they'll see. . . .

For now, I see. I see how far God has brought me and I'm grateful.

When I left Colombia for the first time, I worried I would lose my culture—become more American than Colombian the longer I lived there. But that hasn't been the case. Maybe when the day comes that I've lived in America longer than Colombia I'll feel differently, but maybe I won't. More than two decades in America has shown me that I can have both—be both.

I can be an American without sacrificing anything that makes me Colombian.

I hope that one day my kids will see that too . . . they don't have to be any less Colombian to be more American.

We can have both.

PART 3

CHAPTER 42

2018
MIAMI

MELANIE

"Who did you end up sending to Bogotá?" Melanie asked with a shaky voice. She stood in the doorframe of Ignacio's office, hoping not to let her fear come through.

He looked up from his computer screen and peered above his glasses. "Myself."

Melanie gulped. "You?"

"What did you expect? It was extremely late notice. All my other reporters were swamped with their own stories. No one had the time to just drop everything and jump on a flight to Colombia. We would have lost the story completely if I didn't go." He shuffled papers around his desk as he spoke. "Now I'm behind on edits, my assistant is scrambling to reschedule all the meetings I had to cancel, and I don't even want to know how many emails I have in my inbox waiting for a response."

Ignacio stopped to look up at her again. "Look, I understand you had a family emergency, but you really put us all in a bind, Melanie."

"Ignacio, I'm so—"

"Come in and sit down." He slipped his glasses off his face

and placed them on his desk. After rubbing his forehead a few times, he continued. "I should have done this last week. . . . I never should have assigned you this story, especially after the last article you wrote. I think we both know I've been putting this off, giving you more opportunities, but I can't any longer—"

"Ignacio, please don't—"

"I'm going to have to let you go."

"No—"

"We'll pay you for the remainder of the week, but please go pack up your things and turn in your badge."

Melanie sat motionless and stared at Ignacio. He'd moved on to editing a printed sheet of paper with a red pen. Bracing herself on the chair's armrest, she almost stood to leave his office, but the sheets of paper she'd stapled together that were now in her right hand reminded her of what she came here to do. She had to at least try. She'd regret it the rest of her life if she didn't.

"I wrote something," she said, meeting his eyes again when he looked up. If she could just have a moment to explain herself—to show him what she'd written—he might be open to giving her one last chance to make amends. She placed the short stack of paper on Ignacio's desk and slid it closer to him.

"As you know, I was visiting my grandmother for her ninetieth birthday. I planned to be in Bogotá in time for the president's address, but you know about the health scare that kept me there longer. Anyway, while I was in Cali, I learned so much about Colombia and my family. I read this incredible journal entry from when my mother was young." The more she spoke about her essay, the livelier her voice became.

"She took an English class shortly after she moved to New York, and the whole class was assigned an essay related to a current event. Well, someone from Peru wrote about the drugs and violence coming out of Colombia because of Escobar, and it killed my mother. She was so angry she went home and wrote her essay about all the things Colombia should be famous for but nobody talks about—"

"Melanie, where are you going with this? I've wasted enough time."

"Short story is, even if I could have made it to Bogotá, I'm not sure I would have been able to write the article I was assigned. I had every intention to write it when I volunteered to take the story until I realized my mother is right. . . . All people think about when Colombia is mentioned is cocaine, and I think it's partly because that's all the media ever talks about. I know it's prevalent—I'm not naïve—but I also know there's so much more to talk about.

"And that's why I wrote that." She pointed at her essay that hadn't yet been touched by Ignacio. "That is my take on what I wish the world knew about Colombia. I do mention the impact Miami is experiencing right now, but I mention it just briefly at the end. I chose to focus on everything else that makes Colombia beautiful. I really think it would be a great fit for our paper."

Our paper. . . . Can I still say that?

Melanie took a deep breath as quietly as she could. It was time to shut up and let Ignacio respond. She couldn't quite read his face. Was he disinterested? Confused? Something else? He glanced at the article for a heartbeat before looking up at her to speak.

"I'm sure this was a great exercise for you, but we don't have extra real estate in the paper. Let me give you one helpful piece of advice: At your next job, stick to the story that is assigned to you. Sometimes young reporters feel the urge to veer off course because some shiny object attracted their attention. Don't be that reporter. Be the reporter who writes a really good article that was assigned to them."

Melanie's mouth went dry, but she knew she had to speak up and fast before Ignacio kicked her out for good.

"So, you're not even going to look at it?"

"I really need to get back to these edits." He moved her paper away from the article he'd been editing.

"Your parents are from Mexico, aren't they? What if someone had asked you to write about how horrible Mexico is for the world? Would you have been able to do it? Wouldn't it have disgraced your family? Please, Ignacio, try to put yourself in my shoes. My family is sick and tired of reading the same narrative about their country. I understand that you have to publish the original article, but couldn't you also publish something like this? It's really good, I promise." She slid the article closer to Ignacio. He slid it back.

"Enough. Don't make this more difficult than it already is. I'm not going to change my mind. Please see yourself out."

Melanie opened her mouth, but words failed to follow.

She wiped her palms on her pants before standing to leave Ignacio's office. She'd almost reached the threshold of his door when she turned around to say one last thing, but she stopped herself when she saw Ignacio back on his computer, responding to an email. Back to business. He didn't need a moment to grieve or process what had just happened. It would be just another day for him. Another employee dismissed.

Had this always been nothing but business for him? Had he ever cared about her? All the time he spent investing in her work and her career had really been an opportunity to make himself look better in front of corporate. He didn't actually care about her; he just cared whether Manuel thought Ignacio hired the right reporters who wrote good stuff. It had always been about him.

She walked as quickly as she could toward her desk, where

she'd gather as much of her belongings as she could carry. From afar, she could see the top of Genesis's head.

Before Melanie could reach her desk, Genesis spotted her and spoke more loudly than Melanie had wished she would in this moment.

"*¡Oye! ¡Que milagro!* I was hoping I'd see you today. Have you— Oh no, what happened, Mel?"

As much as she'd tried to stop them, Melanie's eyes were already watering. She knew there was a possibility of serious consequences when she got back to the office, but deep down she believed she could convince Ignacio that her new article was everything he'd been trying to pull out of her from the beginning: passionate writing with important, even if controversial, things to say.

"Is everything okay? What are you doing? Oh no, please don't tell me—" Genesis watched Melanie gathering the books stacked on top of her desk.

"Yes, he fired me."

"Just like that?"

"Just like that. I asked him to read my new article, but he wouldn't even look at it. Never picked it up. I guess it's understandable. . . . I really screwed this up."

Genesis's eyebrows furrowed. "*Ay, mija.* I'm so sorry. Here, let me help you." She stood and took a few books from Melanie's arms.

"Don't be. I should've known this would happen. It was stupid to think he would care more about me than the paper. You tried to warn me. . . . I shouldn't be as surprised as I am."

"Do you want me to talk to him? I mean, I don't know what I would say, but maybe I can convince him to at least read your article."

"What? No, no. It's okay. I deserve this. I should have been honest from the start and never led anyone to believe I knew anything about Colombia."

"*Ay, mija,* you think this newsroom is full of a bunch of saints? Pfft."

"I know, but still. I shouldn't have done that. But you know what? I'm okay with this. I have to be. I don't regret not going to Bogotá. I wouldn't have been able to sleep at night if I had. So even if my grandmother hadn't had a heart attack, I would have been fired for not writing the article." When Genesis curled her bottom lip outward, Melanie continued. "This was the right thing to do, and I hate that I had to lose my job over it, but so be it."

"Well, I'm proud of you for sticking to your guns. Why don't you leave this stuff here and I'll bring it over to your place tonight? You might draw a lot of attention if you walk out of here right now with all your things in your arms."

"Are you sure?" Melanie said. It felt like a lot to ask of Genesis, but she was right. Everyone would find out soon enough she'd been fired, so no need to draw attention to it on her way out.

"Of course. Leave it all. I'll take care of it. And maybe we can brainstorm what you can do next for work. Sound good?"

Melanie nodded and went in for a hug.

She grabbed her satchel and turned to walk away. It would be her last time ever walking through the newsroom, so as much as she wanted to get out of there as quickly as possible, she also wanted to soak in the view once more.

Slow and measured steps gave her the opportunity to listen to the printer spit out an article that would likely be in the paper tomorrow morning. Someone on the phone sternly asked the person on the other end why they didn't have any records of a suspect's license plate. Three reporters stood in a semicircle around the industrial coffeepot in the break room. And a look over her shoulder allowed her one last glimpse of Ignacio in his office across the newsroom, typing away on his computer.

Would he even miss her? Would he remember her a year from now?

She shrugged.

It didn't matter anymore.

All that mattered was that she'd done the best she could with what she knew and she had no regrets about it.

CHAPTER 43

One person shouldn't have to deal with this many emotions at once.

On the walk to her car, Melanie felt strong and confident for finally having made a decision that felt true to her. A decision that wasn't influenced by anything but her own desire to protect her voice as a writer and her love for her family.

But on her drive home, bitterness took over. After all the time Ignacio had invested in her, how could he not have at least read the article she'd placed before him? How could he just toss her aside like that? She was a person, not some journalist bot who only produced content.

And then when she walked into her apartment, fear and anxiety burst out in full force as she looked around her home. How would she possibly pay her rent next month on top of all her other monthly expenses without this job? Would her student loan go into default? Would her mother have to cover her phone bill or buy her groceries? Would she have to leave Miami?

After she kicked off her shoes and threw her satchel on her bed, her fear turned into grief. It was really over. Her life's work was over. Everything she'd planned had slipped out of her grip until she couldn't even recognize it anymore.

Her feet pounded against the cheap laminate flooring as she walked over to her satchel, which she'd tossed on her bed. She pulled out the white binder and flung it open, ripping out each laminated cover. One by one, she pulled out the articles inside each cover and crumpled the contents in her hands.

It was years and years' worth of stories she'd saved. Content that had inspired her. Content she aspired to replicate in her own way. Content she thought would help her find success and fulfillment in her career. But it had all been a lie. What she thought would bring her dreams to life had betrayed her. None of it had worked. All her studying, all her effort, all her sacrifices had done nothing but leave her disenchanted and unemployed.

She fell onto her bed and let hot tears flow freely from her eyes.

What am I going to do? What am I going to tell my friends back home? My family?

They'd always commended her for her accomplishments and her "cool" job that she miraculously landed right out of college. Would she tell them the truth? That one article she refused to write had been the demise of her career? Or would she have to come up with a more attractive reason, like maybe another job offer better suited to her gifts.

Would another offer even be possible? There's no way Ignacio would write her a reference letter now. Today had likely been her last day ever working in the newspaper business.

Flipping over onto her back made her acutely aware of her throbbing head. Of course, in all the drama that had occurred that morning, she'd forgotten to take in her daily dose of caffeine. The last thing she wanted to do right now was leave her apartment in this state, but if she didn't have coffee soon, her head might very well explode.

She grabbed a hoodie and some sunglasses before she walked the one block to the Starbucks on her street. Thankfully, hardly anyone sat inside. Nothing would be worse than seeing someone familiar right now. Except she did see something familiar.

There, right at the entrance to the coffee shop, was a metal wire stand holding up a tall stack of freshly printed copies of *The Wall Street Journal*. On the front cover was a headline she could have spotted from a mile away: COAST GUARD SEIZES MORE THAN $200M WORTH OF COCAINE HEADED FOR MIAMI.

Melanie's stomach hollowed out and her throat went dry. She hadn't written the article, but that didn't stop someone from writing it. She sighed before walking to the counter and ordering a tall black coffee. When she reached into her wallet to find a couple of bills, a white flyer behind a clear stand on the counter caught her eye. HIRING BARISTAS ASAP!

She exhaled, then asked the blond barista for an application.

It's okay. This will only be temporary. I'll find another place to write.

She took a seat and quickly filled out the form without giving the questions much thought. Her life would be worse off if she didn't have an income soon. She wasn't ready to leave her apartment or Miami. No doubt her bedroom back in her mother's home would be untouched, but she needed more time here to make something of herself. To build something—anything.

When she dropped off the application to the barista behind the counter, the barista smiled at her and let her know they'd be in touch soon—they had many openings to fill.

On her walk back to her apartment, she avoided eye contact with every pedestrian she passed. If only Ignacio would have read what she'd written, maybe she'd be working on revisions right now rather than wondering how she would explain to the world her new job as a barista. She took deep breaths and tried to remind herself that she'd chosen this path and that she would find a way out again. There was nothing wrong with working as a barista, but it wouldn't be the end for her.

Crumpled pieces of paper scattered about her apartment welcomed her home. She walked around the space with her wastebasket, cleaning up her anger. Rather than put the wastebasket back in its rightful place, she walked out to her building's hallway where she could dump the contents in the trash chute. No need for them to remain inside her home—her safe haven.

It was time to shift her energy elsewhere.

A splash of cold water on her face was the last thing she needed before clearing off her desk. Her desk had never served as anything more than a place to eat and store unopened mail. Today, she felt like she needed the space—a fresh place to create something new.

When not even a pencil lay on the desk, she placed her laptop there and brought her lukewarm coffee to set beside it. Her space didn't feel complete until the box of her mother's journals was on the floor beside her desk chair, where she could grab one with ease.

Flipping her laptop open shone a bright white light on her face. When her eyes adjusted to the screen, she saw the article she'd worked hard to produce for Ignacio and closed it. Maybe one day she'd repurpose the article for something else, but for now, she wanted to work on something new.

It didn't matter that her journalism career was in the toilet right now. There was nothing more she needed to do than empty herself of words. Writing remained the only thing that brought her joy—even when it felt like it didn't love her back.

Without any regard for the time of day or her grumbling

stomach, she grabbed the very first journal she had opened when she arrived in Cali and laid it open beside her computer. She turned the pages until she found the opening entry and began transferring some of the content from the journal into a blank document.

Transferring content from a notebook or a voice recorder was always a tedious task. Like dumping a puzzle with a thousand pieces onto the floor, you had no idea where to start or what belonged where. But not this time. Despite the emotional state she'd been in for most of the day, Melanie knew exactly where to start.

She'd never put a puzzle together with such ease. The words almost put themselves together. Just thirty minutes later, she felt as though a cohesive story began to appear before her eyes, and her fingers could hardly keep up with the speed of her thoughts. . . .

My mother never wanted to come to America.

America, to her, was a land of greed and robbery that had stolen much of what made her native country prosperous. Because of America, her land was barren. Broken. Left to rot into poverty.

Her teachers had a name for these *Americanos* who came to their country to steal and destroy: *patas de caucho pecuecudo.* Or "smelly rubber feet." Because their land and their resources weren't taken using heavy artillery, large combat boots, or Humvees, they came stealthily in rubber flip-flops, claiming peace and friendship. Her government went right along with it. They believed in their good intentions. Until they were gone.

Somehow America continued to prosper, while the poor in my mother's country got poorer and poorer.

So, she didn't want to live in America. She didn't want to live and work alongside people who didn't care about the condition of foreign places. She worried her world would become consumed with the smell of sweaty feet in rubber flip-flops. And that people would scoff at her disdain for their country.

She wanted nothing to do with America. But it was America who came to her rescue. . . .

After a while, Melanie finally looked up from her screen and checked the time: 7:00 P.M. In just a few hours, she'd written five thousand words without stopping. And she wasn't even close to being done.

She wanted to keep going. Melanie hadn't felt this exhilarated about writing since the days when she would scribble into notebooks until her mother forced her lights off. How could she have missed the fact that in all the years she spent studying and working in journalism, she never once experienced this kind of exhilaration? She'd felt proud and accomplished and even skilled at times. But writing an article for a newspaper always drained her. Every word felt like pushing a boulder up a rugged mountain.

This kind of writing was different. It came out of her more quickly, and she didn't feel that same exhaustion that came with writing articles.

And when she finally took a break, she was tired—the good kind where you feel more alive than you did before you started. This must be what a runner's high felt like. If only she could get paid to write words like these.

This wasn't the time to dwell on any of that. She wouldn't put pressure on her mother's story to pay her bills. Instead, she would work whatever jobs she needed to work so she could support her love for *this* kind of writing.

There was much more she wanted to write. If it hadn't been for the knock at her door, she would have been delighted to burn the midnight oil.

CHAPTER 44

"*Dios mio*—it's worse than I thought," Genesis said as she pulled on Melanie's messy bun on top of her head.

"Nice to see you too." Melanie swung the door wide to invite her in.

As Genesis crossed the threshold, Melanie caught a whiff of the pepperoni-and-pineapple pizza she'd brought, the delicious smell calling to her now growling stomach. The coffee from Starbucks had been the only thing Melanie had consumed up until now. Not only did her crisis make her lose her appetite, but she'd also become so engrossed in her writing that she'd forgotten about the basic needs of a human being.

"Whoa—I'm starving." Melanie clutched her stomach, then walked into the kitchen to grab two small plates. Genesis put her bag down by the door and took the pizza to the foot of Melanie's bed—the only place to sit in the miniature apartment.

"So, I take it you haven't been using all your extra time to get some spring cleaning done?" Genesis said.

"Ha ha. Very funny. What took you so long to get here? Did you just leave the off—" The office. . . . It belonged only to Genesis now. She had no office but her tiny hand-me-down desk in the corner.

"Well, you weren't picking up the phone or responding to my texts, so I thought you could use a little more alone time before I came over. How are you holding up?"

"I applied for a barista job, so yeah, I've had better days."

"You don't think that's a little hasty? Why not try to get another writing job first?"

"I need a paycheck as soon as possible—I've got bills to pay. And second, I don't know. . . . I'm not sure I want another job at a newspaper." Melanie leaned against a wall post, staring ahead rather than at her friend. "Maybe this barista job will be good for some time."

"Really? So you're giving up journalism altogether? Are you sure about this?"

Melanie laughed. "No, I'm not sure about anything these days. I know I made the right decision not to write the article, but everything else is kind of up in the air. I need some time to think things through. I don't want to jump into another journalism job only for the same thing to happen again. I think I need some time to reevaluate things."

"That sounds like a good plan. All right, the pizza's getting cold. Do you have anything we can wash this down with?"

Melanie rummaged through her refrigerator. In the back of the fridge, she found two Diet Cokes, which she poured into glasses filled with ice.

When she noticed Genesis reading on her computer, Melanie said, "What are you doing?"

"Whoa, this is fourteen pages long? What is it?"

"Oh, just something I've been working on to keep my mind busy. Remember those journals I told you I found when I was in Colombia?"

"Yeah, your mother's journals, right?"

"Yeah, she gave me a whole bunch of them before I left Cali. She's a really talented writer, but somehow, I never knew about it. She kept it a secret. I couldn't believe it. So anyway, I've been reproducing them and combining them into one cohesive story."

Genesis scrolled through the pages that followed. "Girl, this is good stuff."

"Thanks. I don't know what I'm going to do with it; it's just been fun for now. C'mon, let's eat."

Genesis grabbed the computer off the desk and brought it with her as she moved to the floor. "Do you mind if I keep reading? Or is it private?"

"Does it really matter if it's private?"

"Nah, I'm going to read it anyway," Genesis said, causing Melanie to laugh.

The pizza was still hot—just what she needed. It was as if Melanie hadn't taken a moment to breathe and accept her reality until now. She stared ahead at the one-hundred-timeless-novels scratch-off poster she'd framed and hung on the wall in front of her.

Maybe I'll finally have the time to get to some of those. . . .

"Are you gonna read the whole thing, or are you going to talk to me? I thought you came here to cheer me up," Melanie said after finishing her first slice.

"Shh. I'm almost done."

A few moments later, when Melanie had finished her second slice, Genesis lifted her fixed stare from the screen. "Mel, I think you've got something here. What are you going to do with it?"

"Nothing. I told you I was just writing that for fun. I thought it was interesting, and I needed something to take my mind off things. Hey, do you think the coffee shop pays enough to make my monthly student-loan payment?"

"You have to publish this somewhere. People will want to read it, trust me. I couldn't stop. It's absorbing."

"I don't have a job anymore. So please, tell me where I'm supposed to publish that now?"

"I don't know. Maybe I could show it to some friends; they might have some ideas. Or maybe you could launch a blog and publish it like a series. You could publish a new part of the story every day or every week. I can already see three parts in this one document. Probably more."

"I don't think any publication is going to be interested in my mother's personal story. And a blog?" Melanie crossed her arms. "It's not like I have a big following online. Who's going to read a blog I publish?"

"We can figure all that out later."

"I don't know, Gen. When I started thinking about doing a different kind of writing for a living, a blog never crossed my mind."

"People make a good living with blogs. The right kind can still be very popular. And there's more than one kind of blogger, *mija*. There's more than one way to tell a good story." Genesis shrugged and reached for a slice of pizza.

After a few minutes of silence, Melanie spoke again. "Even if I did post it on a blog or whatever, that's not going to help me earn any money. I need a job that pays right now."

"I know. I'm not saying I have all the answers. All I'm saying is you've got some really good content here. This is good enough to be in any major magazine or newspaper right now. Maybe nothing will come of it, but sometimes we writers need to write for the sake of writing. It's not always to earn a prize or make some money. Yes, I know you have bills to pay. But you're smart; you'll figure it out. In the meantime, why not share this with the world? I can already think of five people off the top of my head who would love to read this stuff."

This moment reminded Melanie why she'd gravitated toward Genesis from day one. Even when she didn't have the perfect answer to Melanie's life problems, her words often helped her find peace in the chaotic world around her—something Melanie hadn't quite mastered yet.

"Sometimes we just have to write what we feel called to write and the rest works itself out. You have to trust that you were given these stories for a reason, not for them to just sit in your computer and be forgotten. These are the kinds of stories that move people—that change hearts. Don't keep them to yourself, Mel."

Melanie closed her eyes and nodded to let Genesis know she heard every word.

"I'll think about it, how's that?" Melanie finally said.

"Listen, you don't have to do anything you don't want to—certainly not anything I tell you to do. All I want you to do is recognize that you're a talented writer and, clearly, you've got something important to share. Maybe being fired from the *Herald* was a gift. I know it wasn't part of your ten-year plan, but that's why we have to plan in pencil. It's okay to pivot. The *Herald* may not be the place for you, but it's not because you're a bad writer."

"Thanks, Gen."

"And you know I'm always on your side, so if you decide to do something with this, tell me, okay? Maybe there's something I can help with."

Melanie nodded and then lay down on her back as still as a corpse.

"I have no doubt you'll figure all this out and create something better than what you had at the *Herald*. Just keep your heart and mind open to all the possibilities. And it wouldn't hurt to brush your hair."

Melanie opened her eyes to give Genesis what she hoped was an icy stare.

"I'm just keeping it real, sister. All right, I hate to leave you like this, but I gotta run. I still have some revisions to work through. Call me if you need anything, okay? And try not to eat that entire pizza when I leave." She waited until Melanie nodded in response before walking toward the door. "Oh, and you better not be in this same spot tomorrow when I stop by at lunch, you hear me?"

Melanie gave her one last nod before Genesis walked back to the box of pizza and grabbed a slice to go. When her friend walked out the door, she yelled out one last piece of encouragement for the entire building to hear: "Keep writing, Mel! You're onto something!"

Her voice echoed as she disappeared down the hallway. Melanie wished the echoes could make it through the door and into her heart. She wanted to hold on to those words and believe them for herself because her own head told her something completely different. It told her she'd royally screwed up her entire life and that a blog wasn't the way to fix things. What would the rest of the *Herald* newsroom think about her blogging? What would Ignacio think?

It wasn't the worst idea she'd ever heard, but was it the right one? It felt unlike anything she ever saw herself doing.

But leaving the *Herald* wasn't something she ever saw herself doing either. Everything was different now. Today was the first day of a brand-new life—a brand-new career. Page one of a new book. Maybe a blog was exactly what she needed to kick off this new life.

Or maybe it was the complete opposite.

Ugh. I need just one day without having to make any decisions.

But maybe Gen is right. These words need to reach more people. I want more people to see this reality. To be acquainted with it.

I think I know the worst that can happen if I do this . . . but what's the worst that can happen if I don't?

CHAPTER 45

"So, you're a writer?"

It was only Melanie's second day training at Starbucks. They must have been desperate for more hands because they hired her almost instantly. Melanie hesitated when they officially offered her the job over the phone. Accepting the position would make her new life feel a different level of real. Not only would she be an ex-employee, but she would be employed somewhere else. Kind of like when you break up with a boyfriend. When you start dating someone new, you're *really* broken up with that person. There's no going back.

But there were two weeks left in the month. If she didn't get a steady flow of money coming into her bank account soon, she might have to ask her mom to help, and she refused to get to that point. She hadn't even told her mother she'd been fired yet. Anita was still in Colombia, and Melanie didn't want to ruin her trip by adding worry to her plate. Plus, her mother didn't have a ton of money to spare.

That thought alone pushed her over the edge to accept her new reality as a barista. Not only would this job help her pay her bills on time, but it would give her more time to think things through. The last thing she wanted to do was make a rash decision or end up somewhere she'd want to leave after a month. Starbucks would be her home for now, and it felt better than Melanie expected it would.

"Yeah. Well, I used to work for the *Herald,* but it didn't work out. So now I'm applying and stuff to work for other . . . um, publications. I want to keep writing—just trying to figure out where I can do it next." Melanie tried to remain vague. She didn't want to share the full details of getting fired. Who knows what rumors would ensue from that piece of the truth?

Thus far, Melanie had found that most people kindly moved on from the topic when she offered her vaguest explanation—except for Evelyn.

"The *Herald?* Wow. You mind if I ask why you left? Seems like a pretty legit job if you're a writer. Even *I* read it, and I'm not one to consistently read newspapers and stuff."

Evelyn must be one of those people who couldn't read social cues. Or perhaps she could and just didn't care to do the polite thing.

Melanie paused for a moment, eyes still locked on Evelyn's, trying to gather her words and thoughts into a cohesive statement that would make sense but remain vague. Maybe one more cue would be enough to communicate to her new co-worker that she should stop asking invasive questions.

"I couldn't be myself there. They wanted me to write stories I didn't believe in. So I walked out. . . . Well, I got fired, to be honest. But I'm okay with it. I had a feeling it would happen when I didn't write what I was supposed to write." So much for being vague. Melanie shrugged and moved a stack of coffee filters around the counter next to her.

"Whoa—that's bold. Good for you. I respect that."

Melanie smiled and decided to keep that explanation in her back pocket for future inquiries.

Despite Evelyn's desire to ask the uncomfortable questions, Melanie could already tell she would get along well with her. The bright-purple hair didn't distract from the lightness in her eyes—as though she didn't have a care in the world. As though she was confident in who she was and maybe even liked herself. Melanie wanted to be like her. Maybe being near Evelyn would be the first step toward lightness in her own eyes.

"So, what about you? How long have you worked here?" Melanie asked.

"About a year. But like you, I'm also trying to figure out where I'm going next. I guess it's just taking me longer than I hoped." Evelyn grabbed a soaked rag and started scrubbing at a dried stain on the counter in front of her before continuing. "I'm also an artist. I love to draw—graphic design, murals, all that stuff. I was in law school for almost two years, and then I started painting murals downtown in Wynwood to let off some stress and that's what convinced me to drop out of school. Why keep digging myself into debt when it's the last thing I want to do with my life?"

"Whoa—how did your parents take it?"

"Ha, not good. My dad was especially not happy. He's an attorney; you might have seen his face on bus benches around the city."

"Are you serious?" Melanie laughed.

"No joke. He's got some commercials too. Anyway, when I quit school, I guess I just ruined his fantasy of passing his practice on to his only child. But whatever. I can't live my life according to someone else's dreams, right? And I don't want my face on any bus benches—I've seen the way people mark them up with all kinds of nonsense."

"Has he gotten over it yet?"

"Eh, probably not. I think he still holds on to hope that I'll change my mind and reenroll, but that's never going to happen. I'm so much happier now. This job gives me the flexibility I need to paint when I want to, and it's fun here."

"That's really cool. So, you get art jobs pretty regularly, then?"

"Kind of. I've had really busy months, but I've also gone a month or two without a single gig. That's why I keep working here. Art isn't steady enough yet. But I just can't stop. I have to keep trying. Otherwise, I know I'll regret it the rest of my life. So anyway, here I am, trying to stay afloat while I grind to make that dream a reality."

"Maybe I've seen one of your murals? I love going down there to walk around. When I first moved here, I went there every Sunday morning on my days off and just wandered until I got lost."

"Maybe . . . but mine aren't usually on Second Avenue or even some of those side streets. I'm not there yet. My murals are off the beaten path where there's not a ton of foot traffic. But I'm hopeful that each year, I'll inch closer and closer to Second Avenue."

"That's really cool. Maybe you can show me some of them one day." The words coming out of her mouth struck her. She couldn't believe how much her life had changed in such a short period of time.

She was a completely different person from just a few weeks ago. A person she wanted to continue exploring. Since leaving the *Herald,* she had more time to do the things she never got to do before, like write for herself and spend time with friends.

"A couple of us are actually going down there for tacos after we close tonight," Evelyn said. "You should come."

Tacos? There was no question in her mind.

"I would love that," Melanie said.

She followed Evelyn around the shop all morning like a dog on a leash. There was so much to learn. Evelyn showed her how to work the huge tabletop ovens where the breakfast sandwiches were warmed. Then she learned how to brew a new pot of coffee and where to find more coffee beans when the machines ran low. Melanie would start with the basics before moving on to the lattes and frozen drinks.

When the morning rush hit, she did her best to stay out of Evelyn's way. Evelyn made the job look fun—she was like a master barista with eight arms. She slung drinks across counters while taking orders from her headset and somehow remembering them long enough to make it back to the POS system. When they got really backed up, she'd even run over to the espresso machines and make them screech with fresh beans. Melanie had never worked a job like this, and never in a million years did she think she would.

But she was learning to bend like the palm trees and follow what truly excited her, not what other people thought should excite her. And right now, it excited Melanie to think about being a master barista like Evelyn in a few weeks. While the future remained unclear, she resolved to make the best of the present. She could do that now that she wasn't at the *Herald*. Every minute of Melanie's day used to be occupied before the week even started.

Not anymore. Now she had days off where she really was off.

There were no emails to answer. No voicemails to respond to. And for the first time in years, she wasn't even checking the news alerts on her phone. She had absolutely nothing to keep track of. Any time she didn't spend learning how to craft different coffee drinks, she spent writing words that gave her life.

After about an hour, Evelyn finally slowed down. She threw a rag toward Melanie and told her to join her in the dining room to tidy up before the lunch rush.

"I've seen you out here the past few days, typing like a madwoman on your computer. What are you working on?" Evelyn asked.

"Stories about my mother's life. She's from Colombia, and she crossed the border in her twenties. I was in her hometown recently and learned about so many stories I'd never heard before. Then she sent me home with a bag of journals. I've just been typing them all up and putting them together into one cohesive story."

"Oh, that's really cool. My mom has a similar story. But she came over from Honduras. She rode *La Bestia* to get here. Can you believe it? She had an aunt living here in Miami, so that's how she eventually ended up here. She probably crossed around the same time your mom did—I bet they're the same age. Are you going to try to get the stories published anywhere?"

"I don't know. I haven't even told my mom about it yet. But yeah, I guess that would be cool if I could. I've considered launching a blog." Melanie couldn't believe she'd just said that out loud. She'd been mulling over the idea the past few days but still hadn't come to a decision, let alone told anyone else about it.

"That's a great idea. You should do it."

"I don't know. I've never done anything like that. I have to do a little bit of research first."

"Well, don't kill yourself doing research. Sometimes we learn more by doing. And besides, if you publish it and hate it you can always take it down. It's not like you'd have to paint over a twenty-foot wall like I would," Evelyn said as if she knew from experience.

"Yeah, I guess you're right."

"And maybe I can help with the design. I'm always looking for more graphic design to add to my portfolio."

"I like that idea." Melanie paused and looked over at Evelyn, who picked up napkins and straw wrappings from various tables. "I'll talk to my mom tonight and make sure it's okay with her, and if it is, I'm just going to go for it."

"*Dale.* Life's too short; do what you love."

Melanie laughed and rolled her eyes playfully. It sounded like something her grandmother would have said to her.

CHAPTER 46

Melanie worked on her mother's story every free moment she had—even on her lunch breaks. With only five minutes left on her break, she closed her laptop and pulled out her phone to call her mother.

There were already twenty thousand words in one document. At this pace, she could have a book in a few weeks. It wouldn't be prudent to continue without first ensuring her mother was on board with her publishing the stories on a blog. She prepared herself to accept whatever her mother asked of her, but deep down she prayed her mother would be okay with her story finding a home online.

Outside the coffee shop, Anita's face appeared on FaceTime. They talked about Alba and how she'd been doing since Melanie left. Anita had decided to stay in Cali an extra week to accompany Alba to her follow-up appointments.

"They said she's recovering well, but I don't know; she looks more frail to me. I wanted them to run more tests to make sure, but your grandmother refused, of course. I don't know what I'm going to do with her," Anita said, shaking her head.

"I'm not going to live forever, and just because I'm old

doesn't mean I can't hear you," Alba yelled from somewhere else in the home. "I'm frail because I'm old!"

Anita and Melanie laughed. "Well, she's got a point, Mom. I wouldn't fight her too much; you know she's always going to win."

"*Por Dios,* your daughter is wiser than you," Alba yelled once more.

Anita let out an exasperated breath. "Anyway, how are you, *mija?* How's work?"

Melanie hadn't planned to tell her mother about her recent firing in this moment, but now that she'd asked, she might as well get it over with. "Well, about that . . . I got fired on my first day back from Colombia, actually. I'm sorry, but it's been hard to work up the courage to tell you. I meant to call you every night this week, but I just kept putting it off."

Anita's eyebrows rose to touch the creases in her forehead. "What do you mean? What happened?"

"You remember how I told you someone else was assigned the story in Bogotá?"

Anita nodded.

"Well, that wasn't the entire truth . . . after spending time in Cali, I actually decided I didn't want to write the article. I felt it painted Colombia in a poor light. So the truth is, I told my boss I couldn't write it. But I was already struggling at the paper anyway, so this was just one more reason to fire me, I guess."

"*Ay, mi amor,* I'm so sorry. I can't believe you did that. I'm so proud of you. Are you okay, though? Do you need some money? What are you going to do?"

"No, Mom, thank you. I'm okay. I got a job at the Starbucks by my apartment until I can find something more permanent. I promise I'm okay. I know I did the right thing, and I don't regret it."

Alba appeared behind Anita in her wheelchair with a look of sadness in her eyes. "Was it my fault, *mi amor*? Did my time in the hospital make you stay too long?"

"What? No, *Abuela*. It's not your fault at all. Even if you would have never gotten sick, I would have written an article different from what my boss expected and been fired either way. It had nothing to do with you, I promise. I'm disappointed in myself for thinking I could write this article to begin with. It took being in your home for me to realize I didn't want to perpetuate the same narrative about Colombia that this world loves to share. If I'm going to write about Colombia, I want it to be positive. But I hate that I had to spend time with you to realize that and that I didn't realize it on my own."

Her grandmother and mother both smiled and said nothing.

"Speaking of stories about Colombia," Melanie continued. "I actually called to ask you something, Mom."

"*¿Que fue?*"

"How would you feel about me turning some of the stories I read in your journals into a series of stories for a personal blog?"

"What do you mean? What's a blog?"

"It's like a public journal you create on the internet where you can post your own writing."

Anita's eyebrows relaxed, but her eyes grew twice in size. "*Ay*, I don't know. Those are obviously very personal stories."

Oh no. I should have had a plan B.

"Totally, and I get that you don't want your journals on display for the whole world to see. That's why I thought it would be good to write them from *my* perspective, as I see them. And what they're teaching me about the immigrant experience here in the United States. I would, of course, keep out anything that is too personal to share. You can review each post before it goes live, even."

"I think that's a beautiful idea, Melanie," Alba said. Anita looked at her mother and back at Melanie, who sat waiting for her mother's response.

She exhaled. "Okay—sure, *mija*. That's okay. Don't worry about my approval. I trust you. Write what you want. And when it's done, I would love to see it. You know I love reading anything you write. But, to be honest, I'm not sure anyone is going to want to read it."

"Seriously, Mom? Your story is truly remarkable. To think about where you started, and where you are today because of one decision to move. . . . It's impressive. And it's inspiring." As Melanie said this, her voice got softer.

"*Gracias, mija*. I never thought when I left Colombia more than thirty years ago that I would never move back. I would laugh in your face if you told me back then that I would spend the rest of my life in America and raise three incredible children who are professionals and more successful than I could have ever dreamt of back home. It's truly amazing what God has done with my story."

"I agree, Mom. I wish I would have known all this sooner. And known what an incredible writer you are. I'm sure you never meant for anyone to read your journals, but I'm so glad I did. How else would I have discovered where I got my writing talent?"

"My journal entries don't even come close to the kind of writer you are, *mi amor*." Anita was always so humble. She had no idea the raw talent she possessed.

"That's not true, Mom. It makes me wonder what you may have been able to accomplish as a writer if you would have pursued it."

"I don't know, but I'm pretty happy with how my life has turned out. I really am. I don't need anything to be different."

In that moment, something struck Melanie. She'd always believed her mother embodied weakness and submissiveness. But she'd been wrong. Dead wrong. What Melanie thought was weakness was actually contentment. Anita had known a life of hopeless despair and traveled unimaginable lengths in search of something that would bring her life meaning.

After a lifetime of being beaten down by her circumstances, Anita never crumbled. Sure, she had scars and bruises she'd live with the rest of her life. But rather than succumb to defeat—rather than give up and feel sorry for herself—she got up each day determined to find the good around her. Melanie's mother was the strongest woman she knew.

"Thank you, Mom. For everything you did so that I could pursue this whole writing thing for the two of us."

"Anything for you, *mija*."

"Well, this is your last chance. Are you sure it's okay that I keep writing these stories from your journals?"

"If you want to write about some old American immigrant like me, then go right ahead. I'm not going to stop you. But maybe don't expect to win a Pulitzer out of it."

Melanie chuckled, surprised her mother knew what a Pulitzer was.

"American immigrant. I like the sound of that, Mom."

CHAPTER 47

Melanie didn't have a shift at the coffee shop today, but it had quickly become one of her favorite places to spend her days off.

She loved walking through those big glass doors into a space that had an energy similar to a newsroom—heels clicking around the dining room floor, people yelling into their phones; others sitting at tables scattered with books and loose paper and typing away on their laptops; and, of course, baristas running back and forth in nonslip shoes, trying to meet the demands of caffeine addicts who were never satisfied. If she couldn't be the writer she long desired to be at the *Herald*, she was glad she could do it here.

It still hadn't ceased to surprise her how many people crowded the dining room at nine o'clock on a random weekday morning. There were mainly younger people in jeans and concert T-shirts incessantly typing on their computers, but there were a few middle-aged people in suits as well.

She ordered a black coffee from Miguel, one of her new work friends.

"Is Evelyn working today?" she asked him.

"Yeah, I think she's in the back taking inventory."

"Cool. I'll pop in before I leave," she said.

It was her lucky day—there was still one table open with an outlet nearby. It must be a sign that what she was about to do was exactly what was needed.

When she opened her laptop, the document shone brightly in front of her, the blinking cursor inviting her to keep going. But today wasn't the day to write—it was the day to publish.

She minimized the document and launched the search engine instead, where she typed in "how to start a blog." Her shoulders tensed with just a look at those words. This was the last thing she'd ever thought she'd be researching for herself, but there would be many more firsts to come. This is what she had to do.

The night before, she lay awake, overthinking the whole blog idea yet again. Then she went over to her computer, hoping to find a confirmation that a blog was the right way to go. Something told her she'd find the answer in the Word document she'd been working on for more than a week now.

She was correct. Right there in the first paragraph of the first page of her story.

Her mother never wanted to come to America. But she did it anyway. She went on a journey without knowing what to look for—and she found exactly what she needed. Maybe, just maybe, the same would be true for Melanie.

"I need to share this story," she whispered to herself as she lay back down in bed. By whatever means possible, she wanted people to hear it.

It was no longer a question. This morning at Starbucks, she questioned only whether she knew enough about this blogging world to do it right. After reading the third article she'd found with a list of steps to take, she remembered Evelyn's advice: Sometimes we learn more by doing.

Enough research. Time to get to work.

She decided on the platform that was quickly becoming one of the most popular for bloggers. She loved that with this option, it felt like all the focus was on the actual writing and nothing else, not even the author.

She went directly for the big button in the top right corner labeled Get Started. If she didn't move fast, something else might try to stop her.

Creating a blog turned out to be far easier than she expected.

To begin, she chose one of their basic template designs. A black-and-white color palette and only one page—the home page. It was simple with no frills or bells and whistles, but it was inviting. Even though it would be only Genesis, Evelyn, her mother, and her grandmother who would see this blog to begin with, she still wanted it to look presentable.

At the top of the website, there was an empty rectangular box that prompted her to give her blog a name. She knew instantly what she wanted to call it: An American Immigrant.

Her mother lived more than half her life as both an American and an immigrant. And Melanie now realized that, like her mother, she also felt like both a native of her land and a foreigner. Never quite fitting into either world. They were both American immigrants, and Melanie wouldn't have it any other way.

When it was time to transfer part one of her story to the blog, she reopened the document and reread the first two thousand words to find a natural stopping place. When she found the perfect combination of cliff-hanger and natural ending, she copy-and-pasted the text onto her new blog.

She slid her laptop across her small square table and stared at it, admiring it. There it was. The blog that would house these stories for the world to see. It wasn't fancy, but it was perfect.

There was only one more thing to do: She clicked the little button in the bottom center that read Publish. She watched a balloon of confetti burst onto her screen. Her blog was congratulating her for publishing her first post. A smile struggled to stretch from each corner of her lips, but she only stared at the confetti blankly.

There was reason to celebrate, sure. Why not throw her fist into the air in triumph? But something stopped her. Hitting the Publish button wasn't easy. As confident as she felt about sharing her mother's story, making the blog live felt like accepting the truth about where her writing career stood—an uncertain and less than ideal place.

When the barista yelled, "Tall white mocha, no whip!" Melanie snapped out of her daze.

I guess the next thing to do is show Genesis—after all, it was her idea.

She copied the link to her blog and sent Genesis a one-word text message with a screenshot of the blog's headline.

> Happy?

Within a few seconds, she had a response. Melanie looked at the time and realized Genesis was likely in the daily pitch meeting right now. No doubt Genesis was happy to find a distraction to keep her from falling asleep in Ignacio's boring meeting. After more than ten years in the business, all the excitement of editorial meetings had faded long, long ago for her.

> To be continued? Oh, really? What a brilliant idea to produce a series.

After Melanie responded with a wink, Genesis wrote back.

> You literally just saved me from face-planting on this glass table. Ignacio is attempting to pawn off all your work . . . thanks a lot ☺ How about I send this out in the chat to everyone else in the room?? Literally every pair of eyes in this room is glazed over right now.

> Don't you dare. For your eyes only!

> Love the first piece, and your blog name is brilliant. When can I expect part two? I'm ready for it. But there's no About Me page!!

> Baby steps, Gen. Let me first come to terms with the fact that part one exists. And I'm pretty sure no one who visits this blog is going to look for an About Me page. You and my mother know everything there is to know about me 😄

> Girl, we're going to get more readers than just us two!

Melanie rolled her eyes, smiled, and turned around when she heard a familiar voice behind her.

"Oh no. No, no, no. We need to fix that," Evelyn said, peering over her shoulder.

"Fix what?"

"I'm sorry, but I can't in good conscience let you make that blog public. You need a better design than that. It's lifeless! Black and white? No design elements whatsoever?"

"Well, you're too late. It's already public."

"Uh-uh. Nope, I won't allow it. You're lucky it's time for my break. Let me go grab my iPad." Evelyn was halfway to the back room before Melanie could stop her. When she returned, she brought back two blueberry scones and sat down in front of her.

"Is it really that bad?" Melanie asked, already knowing that, yes, it was really that bad.

"I'm not going to answer that because I care about your feelings. But don't worry, I'll whip something up before anyone sees it."

For a moment, Melanie watched Evelyn scribble on her iPad with a stylus pen. Her friend's hand made long strokes and then vibrated back and forth in smaller strokes like she was shading something in. Evelyn looked up at Melanie a few times as if looking for inspiration. Melanie sipped on her latte and nibbled on her scone until Evelyn finally said, "I really can't work being watched."

"Sheesh, okay, then." Melanie pulled her laptop in closer and went back to the document. Might as well get a head start reviewing the story she'd post as part two. She wanted every post to feel like its own independent story while seamlessly connecting to the ones before and after it.

Almost an hour later, right before Evelyn was set to return to her shift, she looked up at Melanie and said, "Ready to see what I came up with?"

Melanie nodded, pushed her laptop aside, and interlocked her fingers on the table.

When Evelyn turned the iPad around, Melanie's mouth fell open.

"I hope that's the good kind of jaw drop," Evelyn said.

"Oh, Evelyn. It's beautiful. I have no words."

Evelyn's design was unbelievable. She'd drawn a silhouette of a woman, with sun-kissed skin and jet-black hair, looking up at the horizon. Melanie could see only her profile, but it was all she needed to know the woman was beautiful. Her long hair flowed behind her like a superhero's cape, and her chest shot up toward her sight line. Melanie couldn't stop smiling.

Looking at this woman made Melanie long to be like her— sure of herself, confident, and deeply proud of everything that made her who she was.

"Evelyn, I want to be her."

"What do you mean? You are her! This is you."

Melanie met Evelyn's eyes and then looked back at the image.

"It's you, and your mother, and every other woman who's ever followed her heart despite roadblocks," Evelyn said.

Melanie still couldn't find the words to say, her eyes glued to the silhouette of this majestic woman.

"All right, c'mon, let's get it on your website before my break ends." Evelyn grabbed Melanie's computer and worked her magic. In a matter of seconds, Melanie's blog had a new home page that featured Evelyn's art.

"I can't even believe you just did all this in less than an hour," Melanie said.

"What can I say? I'm pretty great."

"You are. One day, I hope I can pay you back for this. You have no idea how much this means to me."

CHAPTER 48

Melanie's phone buzzed repeatedly on the floor beside her arm that hung off her bed. When she picked it up to see who might be blowing up her phone this early in the morning, she rubbed her eyes to confirm her vision wasn't blurred. There were eight messages from Genesis. What could she need at this hour?

She flipped over onto her back and unlocked her phone to read the messages.

The first message was from an hour earlier. It was a screenshot of a tweet from Genesis's account that had been retweeted by a prominent reporter from *The New York Times*. A few minutes after that message, she'd sent a screenshot of the same tweet being shared by a reporter for the *Chicago Sun-Times*.

Genesis chose a poor time to ask Melanie to use her brain. Why was Genesis sending her these screenshots of one of her tweets being retweeted? Before she could read the rest of the messages, she opened Twitter on her phone and pulled up Genesis's account so she could click on the link she'd shared.

"What in the . . ." She couldn't believe what she found. Genesis had shared a link to the story she'd written about her mother on her new blog.

Oh no. What did she do?

As her heart rate picked up pace, she went back to her messages to see what else Genesis had sent her. There were more screenshots of reporters from across the country who had retweeted the link to share the content with their followers. Each reporter added their own impressions of the story. . . .

Good stuff from "An American Immigrant."

Timely & relevant words coming out of Miami.

Love how this elevates the immigrant experience AND the experience of second-gen immigrants like me. A must-read.

Before she could read any more, she called Genesis. Her hands shook too much to send a text in response.

"Are you calling to thank me personally?" She picked up after the first ring, a cheeriness in her voice.

"I can't believe you did that." Melanie's words were laced with disbelief.

"You can't?"

"Okay, maybe I can sort of believe you would do something like this. . . . But, Gen, I didn't send you that link so you could show it to the entire world! I wasn't ready for that. I wanted you to read it first, and then maybe we could talk through it. I thought you were kidding when you said you'd send it to everyone in the conference room!"

"C'mon, Mel. Did you see all the positive feedback it got, or did you miss that?"

Melanie put her phone on speaker so she could take another look at the response her blog had gotten online. "Yes, I see it . . . and I can't lie—this is pretty cool. But I would have worked on it much longer if I'd known you were going to send it to every reporter you know. It still needs a lot of work. I wasn't ready for it to be shared yet. I only sent it to you so you could see that I was still writing, like you asked me to."

"Girl, nobody cares about that stuff. If the writing is good, nobody cares about anything else. Plus, you didn't use your name anywhere on the blog. Nobody knows you're the author . . . not yet at least. I have plans to change that."

"What? Wait—"

"Listen, Mel, I know you. This blog would have never been perfect enough for your standards. You would have worked on it until your fingers bled and still refused to share it. So I did what a friend has to do sometimes. And look what's happened as a result. It's all over Twitter . . . and probably Facebook too. I haven't checked."

"Facebook too?" She dropped her head into her hand. "There's no dipping your toes in with you, is there, Gen? You just push people right into the pool. I guess I better make sure my mom has seen it."

"I know you well enough to not let you just dip your toes in. You worked at the *Herald* for almost a year, and your work never got this kind of traction. I'm not saying that to hurt you. What I'm saying is that this story clearly resonates with people. And on top of that, your writing has never been better, even with a few typos. Maybe it's because you've been writing the wrong things all along. Maybe *this* is the kind of writing you should have been doing."

Genesis had a point.

Despite the established readership of the *Herald*, her work had never made this many rounds on social media before.

But here was a small portion of a story she'd written, and almost instantly it gained the kind of traction reserved for senior writers of the big coastal newspapers. The ones with big followings and household names.

"So, who else did you send this to? You've sent it out to your twenty thousand followers. . . . Is there anything else I should be aware of?"

Genesis chuckled before responding. "What if I told you I also emailed it to practically my entire contact list?"

"What? Please, please tell me you're kidding."

"I started by adding any reporter I could think of who was a second-generation American like us. And, let me tell you, there's a lot of them. Then I decided this wasn't a story only children of immigrants would connect with, so I also added every other reporter, producer, and editor in my contact list."

Melanie grunted, and then Genesis added, "What's the point of a network gained from more than ten years in the business if you're not going to tap into it?" Genesis paused, and when Melanie didn't respond, she continued.

"Melanie, I figured if you didn't believe what I told you about this story and this blog that maybe you would believe the feedback of countless other writers. I didn't ask you first because, at this point, I know you well enough to know you still haven't learned how to get past other people's opinions—mainly negative ones—of you and your writing.

"And while I want to respect your say in this matter, I also desperately want you to see another truth. That you *are* an excellent writer and have just been stuck in the wrong place to do your writing. Maybe you're being called to write in a completely different way and through a completely different avenue. I know you saw Twitter, but can I read you some of the email responses I got?"

"Sure."

"This one says, 'This is like word for word my own experience. I've always wanted to write about it but just never got the chance to, I guess. Feels so good to read someone else doing it. These are the stories I wish more people read about! So, who's the author? Is it anonymous on purpose?' And this one is from Brenda at the *Post:* 'Can I send this to my editor? I wonder if we can republish something like this, especially if it's going to be a series. Unless the *Herald* is already working on that?' That one made me think . . . this is the kind of content we should be publishing at the *Herald.*

"It's an important topic for the *Herald*'s readers—I think I remember Ignacio once saying sixty-eight percent or so are either immigrants or second-generation Latinos. I know that's probably out of the question now, but—"

"Yeah, he refused to look at the article I wrote for him. It wasn't exactly this, but close."

"Well, whatever. Forget him. Melanie, do yourself a favor and keep going. Trust me. Go back and do whatever editing you want to do to your blog. But whatever you do, make sure you post the next part of the series sometime this morning. People are literally asking you to. You still love me, right?"

"Yeah, yeah. . . ."

"Where did you get the design from anyway? It's gorgeous."

"Oh, a new friend from work designed it for me. She's crazy talented. She paints murals in Wynwood."

"Super cool. Okay, I gotta go. Show your mom! She's going to love it. I'll call you later with more good feedback about your blog. Oh, and let me know when you've published part two."

Before Melanie could say anything more, Genesis hung up the phone. This was just like Genesis—to take matters into her own hands and, of course, produce magic.

She let her phone fall to the ground and buried her face back in her comforter. Even though the feedback had all been positive, she felt so exposed by the sheer number of people who'd read her blog. She hadn't prepared herself to feel this vulnerable. Knowing hundreds—maybe thousands—of people had read her words felt akin to standing naked before a crowd. This wasn't like the articles she'd written for the *Herald*—these stories were personal. They were about *her* and her family—a family that still felt so new to her. Had she sat with these stories long enough?

Knowing she hadn't put her name anywhere on the blog gave her a sense of peace that there was still a way out if she needed one.

Did she really want to share even more? Would people call her a fraud? She had only recently fallen in love with her heritage; how could she write about it already?

Probably none of it mattered. There's no way Genesis would let her stop. And when she really took a moment to think about it, she didn't want to anyway.

Her blog had reached the hands of practically all the reporters in the business she respected the most. How could she not give them more, especially when it involved such an important societal issue?

The only problem was that the pressure was now on. She couldn't sit back and produce anything mediocre. As a steward of her mother's story, she had a responsibility to do it well. Not just for her own mother, but for all the families across the United States who had a similar story.

Melanie stuck her head out from underneath the comforter, grabbed her phone from the floor, and started reading once more through the comments her blog had received on Twitter.

She flipped over onto her back and scrolled and scrolled until she reached the last comment:

I need to know what happens next! Don't leave us hanging, "American Immigrant"!

As if this post was an outstretched hand from the Divine, she pulled off her comforter, sat up in her bed, and grabbed her laptop from the floor. She would post the next article in a few hours, and this one would absolutely get proofread.

CHAPTER 49

Melanie could hardly believe she could fit two other humans in her tiny apartment, but it had become a regular occurrence to have both Evelyn and Genesis sitting on the floor by her bed. It might be prudent to start saving for a small love seat where people could sit.

"Is this your natural hair color? I would have guessed you were more of a brunette," Melanie said as she tousled Evelyn's newly dyed jet-black hair. She'd added bright-red glasses—without a prescription—and a magnetic septum ring to her look too, probably because the black hair wasn't enough to express her eccentric personality.

"You're right about that. The black is for my latest mural. I usually change the color of my hair to match the project I'm working on. I have almost twenty photos of myself standing in front of my work with matching hair. . . . It's gonna make for a banging home-page image for the portfolio I'm working on."

"Love it. When can we see the mural?" Genesis asked.

"Actually, I'm finishing up tomorrow morning. I have one tiny addition I need to make. You guys want to come?"

Genesis and Melanie nodded.

"Good, because I'd already planned on a ride from one of

you. The Metro has been trying my patience lately." Evelyn grabbed a plate from Melanie and opened the paper box of steamy Chinese takeout.

"Okay, so what did you guys think of part three?" Melanie asked.

Evelyn spoke first, mouth full of food that was still too hot to eat. "Mmm, so good. Loved it. Sent it to my mom." She gave her a thumbs-up, and Melanie wasn't sure if that meant her mom liked part three or if the Chinese food was delicious.

"Thanks. Finish chewing, and then I want to hear more. Gen?" Melanie said.

"Agreed, couldn't be better. You're really striking the right balance between how the immigrant experiences life in another country and how their children learn to live in a third culture, so to speak. I think it's really empathetic to both sides."

"You're not just saying that, are you?"

"No, girl. You know I wouldn't lie to you. It's really, really good."

Genesis had a point. She had never lied to Melanie about the condition of her work—she'd never dare to sugarcoat things. She was like a tough older sister who loved you but didn't care if you liked her. At the sound of her reassuring words, Melanie released a breath she felt like she'd been holding for hours.

"Okay, here we go . . . and part three is"—Melanie hit Enter on her keyboard—"live." She took a moment to look at the words on her screen that were now public for the world to see. "I have to admit, that's kinda fun. Publishing when *I* say so, not someone else."

"I'll toast to that!" Evelyn said, holding up a plastic cup filled with Diet Coke.

"You need to start thinking about revealing your identity," Genesis said.

Melanie looked over at Evelyn, who scarfed down another mouthful of chow mein while nodding. "What she said," Evelyn added through bites.

"I don't know. . . ."

"People are starting to speculate online. There's even a hashtag about it."

"What?" Melanie said.

"You haven't been keeping up with your blog on social media?" Genesis asked.

"I'm nervous that the first negative comment I see will make me question everything I'm writing," Melanie said.

"*Por Dios,* Melanie! Well, for your information, someone started a hashtag: #AnAmericanImmigrantIs. And everyone is throwing out guesses. People started out by saying it obviously must be a female Colombian writer, but then other people started saying the female voice might be a disguise and that it's actually meant to throw people off about it being a man's voice."

"That's ridiculous," Evelyn spat out. "Please don't let a man get the credit, Mel. You have to come out and set the record straight."

Melanie laughed and shrugged. "I don't know. It's kind of fun being anonymous. Feels like a happy accident."

"I'm with Evelyn on this one," Genesis said. "Plus, if you reveal your identity, you can start taking media interviews, which will help promote the blog even further. And it might even result in advertising to get you some kind of income from it."

"One of my friends in Chicago—I sent him the link directly so he knows I know the author—told me he'd connect me with their local affiliate TV station, which would be open to running a story about you for Hispanic Heritage Month. They want to talk about your time in Cali and how it was the impetus for launching the blog. And another friend, who has a podcast called

Latinas Together, is dying to talk to you too. I think you'd be the perfect fit for her show, but I've had to push her off because you're not out yet. She's pinging me like every day about it. I think she's hoping to hear first whether you reveal your identity."

Melanie could feel her eyes grow wide. Her mouth agape, she couldn't believe what she heard. How could her little blog garner this much media attention in such a short period of time? Living in Miami made her feel like her story was similar to most of the people around her. What could be so different about her story to make people want to cover it on their media outlets?

If she revealed her identity, there was no doubt Genesis would be the perfect PR agent. She had influence in the journalism space and, clearly, the energy to run her own media company.

"Whoa," Melanie finally said.

Her on TV? And podcasts? It was the kind of exposure Melanie wouldn't have even dreamt of when she worked at the *Herald*. It might have taken her years to ever be invited to share her work across other media platforms.

"Well, there's no rush, I guess," Genesis said. "But it might also be a good idea to strike while the iron's hot. I'm not saying the buzz is going to die down, but maybe I am saying the buzz might die down. Eventually, people will move on to the next exciting thing and you'll have lost your chance to make headlines. Just saying. . . ."

"Honestly, I'm not sure why you wouldn't want to capitalize on this kind of exposure. I would kill for that for my murals. I can barely get people to like my posts on Instagram," Evelyn said, laughing.

"I know, I know. I just want to think about it, that's all. I don't want to draw attention away from the stories. Maybe if I reveal my identity, people will talk about it for a day and then move on and forget about the rest of my posts."

"Yeah, I get that. So maybe you can wait until you publish the last story in the series. Do you have any idea when that will be?" Genesis asked.

"I have like four or five more to post in the next few days. I don't think there will be anything else to write after that, but I'm not a hundred percent sure yet. I'm still working on it."

"Cool, then you have about a week to make a decision," Evelyn said.

"Yeah, no pressure," Melanie said. "You gonna hog that chow mein or can I have some of it?"

Evelyn slid the paper box toward Melanie, and the three women sat in a circle enjoying their dinner in the cozy space.

When her friends retired to their homes for the night, Melanie sat down at her desk and opened her computer to Twitter.

She'd been mostly honest with her friends that night. It was true that she hadn't looked at the comments about her blog online since the first time it went viral because she wasn't sure what kind of impact a negative review would have on her. But she wasn't desperate to read the positive reviews either. Until now, of course, since Genesis had piqued her interest.

It was the right decision not to look at the comments sooner. She was still recovering from a life of crowd-pleasing. Today, she felt stronger. Strong enough to see for herself what her friends had told her.

All her life, she'd cared deeply about other people's opinions of her work. And for once in her life, at a time when she couldn't feel more confident about her passion project, she didn't want to be driven by other people's approval of her. She didn't need it. More than anything, she wanted to be happy with herself and her work no matter what other people thought about it.

The last thing she needed was for the positive or negative comments to be what fueled or hindered her writing. The fuel should come from within her—she wanted to write no matter what someone else thought about it.

What she'd said to her friends about being anonymous was true too. Yes, people were starting to speculate about who the author of the blog was, but from scrolling on Twitter right now, she could tell nothing got more attention than the storytelling, the word usage, the metaphors, and the thought-provoking questions at the end of each piece.

It surprised Melanie more than anyone that she actually preferred the anonymity. Just a few months ago, she couldn't wait to see her name in bold black letters in a printed newspaper or on a website with a good reputation. But none of that mattered to her anymore. All that mattered was that she had a place to write in her authentic voice and a place to tell stories that were really important to her. Whether people knew she was the author was beside the point.

There was one truth she couldn't deny. If she revealed her identity, she might be able to make a little money from her work. It didn't have to support her completely, but it would help her make headway on the savings she'd drained paying the *Herald* back for her travel. Not to mention, being the author of a popular blog would likely help her land a full-time writing gig in the future.

What should I do? What would my mother have done? My grandmother? What would make them—and me—proud?

CHAPTER 50

Genesis arrived outside Melanie's apartment the next morning with Evelyn in tow. The three had become fast friends thanks to Melanie's newfound love of exploring the city when she wasn't working or writing.

Melanie threw on a white Northwestern baseball cap with some shorts, a plain blue T-shirt, and white leather sneakers before she met her friends downstairs. The storm that swept through the city the night before caused a thick layer of moisture to gather atop Melanie's arms the second she stepped through her building's front doors.

She stopped for a moment on the front steps and looked up at the palm trees that soared high into the clouds. They were as still as statues. Had they always been there? Each day Melanie spent further removed from her life at the *Herald,* she saw something she hadn't noticed before. Miami was truly paradise, and she was glad her eyes were now open to notice.

"C'mon, daydreamer! Get in the car," Evelyn yelled from the passenger seat.

"Here—we stopped at Versailles. Thought an unveiling deserved the good stuff," Genesis said as she handed Melanie a white Styrofoam cup with the unmistakable green logo on the front.

"Lifesaver," Melanie said. "So, who'd you paint this mural for anyway? Who's the client?"

"Well, I actually commissioned this one. Found a sponsor and everything," Evelyn said.

"Really? Who is it?" Genesis asked.

"You'll see."

Evelyn directed the way when they reached the Wynwood neighborhood. The sidewalks were already flooded with tourists and locals taking photos in front of the walls, sipping coffee, and waiting in line outside the hottest brunch spots. Distinctive graffiti brought this part of Miami to life. Each block featured a vibrant hue of colors stretching across every inch of the walls, not a corner left untouched. They drove by statues of sea creatures erupting from the ground and a feline that was painted in bright yellows and reds. The cat took Melanie back to Cali, strolling down the winding path along *Parque de los Gatos*.

They'd reached a quiet, empty street when Evelyn instructed Genesis to find a place to park. Melanie looked around and noticed there weren't any murals on this block.

"All right, follow me," Evelyn said when they'd all jumped out of the car.

They walked two blocks and turned a corner before Evelyn began to slow her strides.

"Ready?" Evelyn said, waving her hand for them to come closer. Genesis and Melanie nodded in unison and followed her through an alley. When they reached the end of it, they walked out onto the sidewalk and turned to face the wall.

"Wha . . . wha . . . how?" Melanie's head tilted back to see the entire wall that had been covered with black and white paint. There, in front of Melanie, on a tall concrete building that looked abandoned, was a thirty-foot replica of the woman Evelyn had drawn for Melanie's blog. It was as if Evelyn had copy-and-pasted the design on her iPad onto this enormous wall.

"Wow. This is truly remarkable," Genesis said. "You've outdone yourself, girl."

Melanie nodded. It didn't matter that this street didn't seem to attract much foot traffic. The image was striking, and soon enough, she hoped, people would walk the distance to see it. "But I don't understand, Evelyn. How did you do this?"

"I told you. I got a sponsor."

"But who . . . who would pay you to do this?"

Evelyn pointed at the bottom right of the mural, where there was a small social media handle. Melanie instantly recognized the name of the business because it was Evelyn's last name.

"Your dad's law firm paid for this?" Melanie said.

"Yep. Took some convincing, but you know, I'm good at that kind of stuff. I told them thousands of people would be posing in front of this mural soon and posting it on social media, so it would be easy marketing for them. Plus, it's always been hard for the president of the firm to say no to me," Evelyn said as she gently elbowed Melanie's arm.

Melanie pulled her in for a tight hug. "I can't believe you did this for me. It's perfect."

"Well, almost perfect. I brought you here for the finishing touch."

Before Melanie could respond, Evelyn took off her backpack and pulled out a can of black spray paint. Then she walked toward the mural, shook the can, and climbed onto a ladder that had been left by the wall. She began to spray the paint, and after a few seconds, she stepped off the ladder and moved it out of the way so Melanie and Genesis could see what she'd written: An American Immigrant Is ___.

"Now it's your turn. I want you to fill in the blank. It's time to reveal the author behind the blog." Evelyn reached out and handed Melanie the can of spray paint.

Melanie looked down at the can in her hand and back up at the mural.

She could feel the gazes of Genesis and Evelyn behind her, probing her to move forward.

After a moment longer, she put her arms down by her side and walked toward the wall.

With her shoulders back and her hair tickling the nape of her neck as it blew behind her in the gentle breeze, she took a few steps up the ladder, shook the can, and firmly pressed down on the nozzle.

The upward zigzag motion said it all.

Genesis and Evelyn looked at each other and smiled when they confirmed the first letter was an *M*. But when Melanie started to climb down the ladder after writing the second letter— an *E*—they looked at each other again with puzzled expressions.

"Is the can out of paint? I could have sworn I brought a new one with me just in case," Evelyn said.

"Nope, I'm done," Melanie said, strutting toward where her friends stood.

"Me? What do you mean, me?" Genesis asked.

A trickle of black paint made its way down her forefinger. "I don't need anyone to know it's me. Because it's not just me. It's you"—she looked at Genesis and then at Evelyn—"and you too. It's so many people in this city and so many people in this country. We're all American immigrants, and when people walk by this mural or pose in front of it, I want them to see themselves in it. I want them to connect with the story and with this part of their identity."

Genesis and Evelyn looked at the mural once more as if seeing it for the first time, their eyes growing bright.

"I love it," Genesis said without turning her stare from the wall.

"Me too," Evelyn said.

"Good. Then let's be the first to take a selfie in front of it."

CHAPTER 51

There's nothing more demeaning than undressing in front of someone who suspects you're a criminal. But that's how every single Colombian was treated in the eighties. The ironic thing is that my mother *was* a criminal. But not the kind they were looking for.

She wasn't trying to traffic drugs or even artillery. She was sneaking into a country that promised a better life. What kind of life she was hoping to find, even she is still not quite sure. All she knew was that she needed something different. Very different. And her mother needed money. A lot of money.

America seemed to be the only place she could find both. So she took on criminal status and a fake identity. She memorized lines and addresses and fake ambitions. She averted her eyes and held her breath when they asked her to undress in the airport in Mexico City. And she clenched her fists and bit her tongue when they transferred her to a hospital for an ultrasound of her stomach because a strip search did not suffice.

Didn't the immigration officers know they weren't the only ones who hated the drug lords who lived in Colombia? Didn't they know her country also tried endless tactics to exterminate them? Didn't they know there were probably more illegal immigrants than drug traffickers in their midst? Probably not. Because they had every right to be afraid of our people. And my mother had every right to be afraid of theirs. So she did as she was told and didn't question their commands.

What would you have done? Where would you have gone?

I like to think I would have given those slimy immigration officers—who probably would have let my mother continue through without additional searching had she slipped them a couple of twenties—a piece of my mind. Refused to undress completely and certainly refused an ultrasound of my stomach when I had nothing hiding in there. Or maybe I would have followed their instructions and saved my reproach for when I was safely on the other side. Who knows what I would have done, because even a fighter like me knows when to bow. Knows when a desperate situation excuses momentary cowardice.

Or is it even cowardice? All my life, I've pulled down, shouted at, punched, kicked down, berated, and pushed through any barrier that dared get in my way. And even if my opponent gained the upper hand against me, I always went down swinging. And isn't that the life of most of us first- and second-generation immigrants? If we didn't live it, we grew up listening to our parents recount the literal blood, sweat, and tears they shed to force themselves into a better situation—because a lot of times, anything is better than what they're living in their country.

Except for me. I'm different. I didn't grow up listening to those stories. Not because my mother didn't have them—it's obvious she did—but because I never cared to listen. Or I never stopped fighting invisible battles long enough to know my mother had a story to tell. A story that would have probably changed a lot about how I lived my own life in this foreign country. This foreign country that I may have been born in but that never fully embraced me. I was too "ethnic" to be American. But what they didn't know was that I was too American to be "ethnic"—to be Colombian. And so I lived as though I didn't have citizenship in either place, even though, ironically, I had citizenship in two countries . . . two countries that rejected the full me.

But this story isn't about me. It's about the stories we don't know exist because we don't bother asking, searching, digging. We breeze through life as narcissists, believing our stories begin with us. How absurd to believe that, to believe that the stories that come before us leave no mark on ours. How self-centered to think our ancestors have nothing to offer their descendants.

Recounting these stories of my mother's journey from Colombia to America has been like turning a dial on a prescription lens you've worn your whole life. You thought you could see clearly enough, so you never complained. And then an eye doctor forces you to sit in his chair so he can check the strength of your vision through the lens you've always worn. And he scoffs and asks how you possibly could have survived so long with such muddied vision . . . but all you can do is look up at him and shrug and suggest that maybe you would have tripped eventually and been forced to see the eye doctor. Forced to check your vision. Forced to see through a new lens that reveals a whole new world.

Thanks to my mom, I now see a better world.

A truer world.

What stories have you been missing?

—An American Immigrant

Melanie looked at her computer screen, hit the Publish button, and sighed deeply. It was official. She had written the last part of the series featuring her mother's story. If she tried, she could likely find much more to write about her journey, but for some reason, she felt done.

This last article felt like the perfect way to end the series. And maybe one day she would come back and add to it or arrange it in some other special way. But for now, she was content with what she had written and how she had shared it. And the timing to finish just felt right.

She scooted back in her desk chair and stared at her screen a moment longer. What now? Every spare minute she had the past few weeks had been dedicated to writing and publishing these stories. Now that she had finished, what would she write? What would she spend her time doing when she wasn't remaking lattes for picky aficionados?

With the traction each article had gotten, it felt strange to be done. Each post that was published got shared by hundreds and even thousands of readers across all the major online platforms. The rumors about the real identity behind An American Immigrant had even died down.

While most people would try to keep the hype going for as long as possible—ride the wave of success however long it lasted—that didn't feel right to Melanie. Writing for the sake of getting more shares, more readers, or even a possible income. She wanted every word she wrote to have meaning and purpose—to matter. She wouldn't fall prey to the platform-obsessed culture. She would write only when the story truly needed to be told.

The thought of what would come next for her blog hardly permeated her mind. Sure, she considered it. But the thought didn't linger. For the first time in her life, she wasn't planning what the next year or five years might look like. She wasn't even planning what the next week looked like. She left her calendar and her heart open for what might come *to her*.

She had never felt so free, and she had never been more confident that she would know exactly what to do next when the time was right. No planning needed.

Melanie stood from her desk chair, gently closed her computer, and slipped it into her satchel. She had ten minutes before her shift started, so she slipped into her polo and tightened her black cap, which was already turning a different color from the wear, and left her apartment to make it to work on time.

Before tucking her satchel into the small silver locker in the break room, Melanie felt her phone vibrate in her back pocket. It was a message from Genesis. There were no words, just a link to an article from *The Florida Post:*

HERALD FIRES EDITOR IN CHIEF. *NO WORD YET ON WHO WILL STEP UP TO THE COVETED POSITION. . . .*

Melanie gasped so loudly she instinctively covered her mouth, preventing any other exaggerated sounds from coming out. But it was too late. Evelyn heard it and walked over to find out what could be so exciting.

"Did you win an Emmy or something?" Evelyn asked. She'd been rotating giant bags of coffee beans in the back stockroom. Doing that every morning must be the reason she was cut like a rock.

"Evelyn, thank God it's you. Look! Can you believe it?" Melanie shoved the screen of her phone about an inch from Evelyn's face.

"Geez, I'm not blind," she responded as she pushed back her head and Melanie's hand to get a better view. "Whoa, is that for real?"

"Must be. Genesis sent this to me."

If it hadn't been one minute before Melanie had to clock in for her shift, she would have run out of the store to call Genesis and get more details from the inside. But the call would have to wait until her lunch break.

While she worked the register, Melanie tried not to occupy her mind with the possible details of how Ignacio had been fired. She reprimanded herself in her head for slightly hoping he'd been let go in some public, embarrassing way. It was punishment enough for him to be fired; no need to pray he'd been embarrassed too.

When it was finally time for a fifteen-minute break, Melanie stepped outside, in her apron and all, and called Genesis.

"No way. No way that really happened!" Melanie said, cupping her hand over her mouth again.

Genesis vividly described how Manuel had charged into the building and walked straight into Ignacio's office without even stopping in his own office first. Everyone could see that whatever he had to tell Ignacio was urgent.

While Manuel's words were inaudible through the glass walls and shut door, the entire office could sense his obvious chastisement. The flailing arms, the scrunched-up noses, the killer glare Ignacio gave Manuel until it was his turn to speak. Ignacio didn't stand a chance. Within seconds, he grabbed his briefcase and stormed out of the office, avoiding eye contact with anyone. Nobody knew where he was going, but everyone knew it wasn't good.

Genesis originally thought that it was nothing more than another blowup with the publishing company that would resolve after everyone cooled off. But when she arrived the next morning, Ignacio's office had been completely cleared out. The framed copies of archived editions of the *Herald* left faded spots on the walls of his office. He must have come back late in the night to pick up all his things. Genesis told Melanie she didn't blame him—she wouldn't have wanted anyone to watch her leave with a box full of belongings either.

"It was insane, Mel. And sad. Honestly, I kinda felt bad for the guy. I know he fired you and everything, but we started on the same day. We'll always have that shared experience, and I guess I just hated seeing him be embarrassed like that in front of the whole newsroom. It was pitiful."

"Wow," was all Melanie could utter.

"But that's not all, Mel."

"What? There's more?" Melanie's eyes stretched wide and she combed her hair with her fingers, awaiting what else Genesis could have to share.

"Manuel called me into his office this morning." Genesis spoke in an oddly mysterious way.

"Oh no."

"I thought the same thing, but it wasn't anything bad."

"Okayyyy. You're killing me here. So why did he call you in?"

"Well, he asked me if I would be interested in the editor-in-chief position now that Ignacio is gone."

Melanie squealed for the third time. It was a good thing she'd decided to call Genesis outside. Only the patrons in the drive-thru line could hear her. "Shut up! No way. You said yes, right? Please tell me you said yes."

Genesis laughed and Melanie could tell she was just as excited to share the news as Melanie was to receive it. But Genesis still tried to keep her cool for some reason. Maybe she was in the office or something.

"I know. I didn't even think Manuel knew who I was. I mean, I've been here more than ten years, but he's so new and he rarely makes rounds in the newsroom or attends any of our editorial meetings. And to be honest, I'm not sure he even reads the *Herald*. So, as you can imagine, I was shocked."

"Wow, that's amazing. Like, really amazing. But you didn't answer my question. You accepted, right?"

"Yes. I accepted. It still doesn't feel real. And it's kind of strange to step into a role that was held by someone who fired you."

"Oh, whatever." Melanie flicked her wrist as if Genesis could see. "Gen, you're going to be so good at that job. You're like everything an editor should be. It would have been a dream to work under you."

"Well, maybe it doesn't have to be a dream," Genesis said.

Did Melanie hear her correctly? What could she possibly be talking about? Even with Ignacio gone, there was no way she could ever go back to working in a newspaper.

"Please. . . . You know I can't come back to the *Herald*. I've accepted that journalism is not for me."

"I know. But I don't mean come back, come back. I mean come back as a freelancer. Or more like a columnist."

Columnist? Am I hallucinating?

"Your series did so, so well. I think people are pretty upset you just published the last article. No one was ready for it to be over. Sooo, I've been thinking . . ." Genesis dragged out her words again as if trying to find the right ones to persuade her friend. "What if you kept going? But since you're done telling your mother's story, maybe you could write a regular column for the *Herald* about the immigrant experience. Every two months, you can find another person who immigrated to the United States—not just from Latin American, but anywhere—and you can interview them and tell their story in a series format like you did on your blog. You would have complete editorial freedom. I mean, I'd love to sit with you and strategize on content ideas, but I want this to be from your voice, no one else's."

Melanie had to sit down.

If she hadn't just jumped at the sound of a car's horn in the drive-thru, she would have wondered whether she was dreaming.

"Are you still with me, Mel? What do you think about the idea? Oh, and I guess it would be time to officially reveal your identity. Maybe we could do it in the first column."

"Um, wow, Gen. I mean, thank you. I'm kind of speechless. That sounds amazing, of course. But . . . I don't know. I've loved writing about my mother, but I never considered writing about other immigrants. It's not really what I ever pictured myself writing about . . . but I guess everything is different now."

"You're not writing stories about immigrants, *mija*. You're writing stories about people. And you're so good at that." Melanie was silent again, so Genesis continued. "Hey, I think this could be really cool. Think about it. There's no rush. I'm the boss now, so we can launch this whenever you're ready, okay?"

When Genesis hung up, Melanie put her phone on the metal patio table and stared down at her hands.

A columnist, at the *Herald* of all places? Only people with huge platforms and a bunch of letters after their names got that kind of privilege. Could there really be a place for her too?

She looked back at the doors to the entrance. Would she have to leave this place? It surprised her to think this, but she wasn't ready to leave Starbucks. Coming here five days a week had become therapeutic in a way. A few hours of working with her hands allowed her imagination to run wild. She met interesting people who inspired characters and stories. Being here was like a creative exercise she got paid to do. So even if this columnist position paid well, maybe working at Starbucks would only make her a better writer—a better columnist.

Maybe the missteps that brought her here hadn't been missteps after all.

CHAPTER 52

FOUR MONTHS LATER

Fluffy white foam danced on top of the hot cappuccino as Melanie passed it to the woman dressed in all black and dark sunglasses. It was the last drink she had to make before she got to take her thirty-minute break.

She shook out her apron, removed her hat, and laid it on a chair in the break room so she could get a little work done for her side gig. With her lightweight laptop open on the table, she launched her email, knowing she'd have a message from Genesis requesting one last review of the suggestions she'd made to Melanie's latest installment of the new *Herald* column, An American Immigrant.

It had been four months since the *Herald* had hired her as a columnist, and her last two series had been hits. The first series featured a woman from Haiti who had traveled on a thirty-five-foot boat with about a hundred other migrants. The latest series covered the stories of unaccompanied minors from Honduras and El Salvador.

She clicked on the message from Genesis, which read,

Another fabulous column. Really love this one. People think they're just coming to the United States for work, but they have no idea the unthinkable fear they're running from. Great work, Mel. Have you found your subject for the next one?

Melanie smiled at the email. It still felt like a miracle to be associated with the *Herald* again and working under her mentor. It was everything she never knew she needed.

After responding to Genesis's message with a confirmation that she had already scheduled a meeting with her next subject, she noticed another message in her inbox from an unknown email address. It had come in from the contact form on her blog. The subject line read, Author query.

Author what?

Her curiosity led her to click on the email immediately.

It was a short message. To the point. But there were three sentences that stood out to her like bold, highlighted letters:

I've been following your work. I'm a big fan of your column and the original blog. I'd love to talk to you about turning your mother's story into a book.

Melanie gasped. She looked around to see if anyone else had read these words too. Then she grabbed her laptop and held it tightly to her chest as if attempting to embrace the most wonderful words she'd ever read. She stared at the wall in front of her, but her mind was running wild with thoughts and questions.

"A book?" Melanie whispered into the empty break room. "Did someone just ask me if I wanted to write a book?"

She placed her laptop back down on the round table and decided she'd better search the name of the person who had emailed her to make sure this wasn't some cruel prank.

A quick Google search of Charlotte Roman confirmed she

was a literary agent with a long list of accolades and successful authors she'd represented across her twenty years in the business. Even better, she was based in Miami.

But what could she possibly want with me?

She knew the series about her mother was still getting clicks online—she'd already received a few inquiries about advertising on her blog—but could that be enough to warrant a book deal? Would people really be interested in even more stories about her mother?

Being an author had always been a part of Melanie's life goals, but her original plan was that it wouldn't happen until she'd worked and built her reputation in journalism for at least ten years. Then enough people would know her work and want to buy her book—probably a book about creating a life plan or something similar. She knew she'd have to walk the walk before writing a book about it.

But everything had changed so drastically. So quickly. Nonfiction was her plan all along, but not this kind of nonfiction. This was unlike anything she ever thought she'd write, let alone publish for the world to see.

Can this really be a book?

I'd have to add to it—it's not long enough.

Who would even buy this?

Ugh—enough of that. . . .

She silenced the endless thoughts and questions racing through her mind. There was no sense in dealing with them before she'd even talked to anyone about her idea. The agent had asked for a meeting in the email; it's not like she had sent her a contract she wanted signed that night.

I can do a phone call, she concluded. She responded to the email, trying not to reveal her nerves through her words.

Hi Charlotte, thanks for reaching out. I'd be happy to chat. I can meet at Panther Coffee tomorrow at noon if that works for you.

She typed and retyped and retyped her short message a dozen times before finally hitting Send. And as soon as she heard the swoosh confirming her message was on its way to Charlotte, she ran back out to the floor, called Evelyn's name as softly as she could, and waved for her to come to the break room. She couldn't wait until Evelyn was on her break too. She had to share this news with someone immediately.

"What's going on? Is everything okay?" She had a worried look on her face.

"I have to show you something." Melanie pulled up the email and pointed at the screen.

"Whoa. Is that a literary agent?"

"Yes. Can you believe it?" Her voice became squeaky with excitement.

"I can totally believe it. The series was a hit. And your new column has so many loyal readers. To be honest, I thought at some point the hype would die down. But it hasn't. Every time you publish another column, it's all over Twitter for forty-eight hours. And for good reason—your writing is out of this world. You know I'm not much of a blog or column reader, and even I can't wait until the next installment."

Melanie didn't know how to respond to Evelyn's compliments, so she looked down at her laptop to reread the email for the umpteenth time.

"You know if you'd gone to Bogotá and written that article for the *Herald*, there's no way this would have happened, right?"

Melanie nodded.

In this moment, she couldn't have felt more grateful for these few months she'd spent working as a barista and publishing her work on her own blog.

She'd made the right decision after all.

For once in her life, she'd followed her gut, not a curated life plan that she'd created and edited in her early twenties. If she had listened to that—to her plan—she'd be sitting at her desk at the *Herald,* miserably working on another story about something she didn't care about or, worse, something that made her feel like a traitor. Who knows how long she would have endured that life—probably forever—just to avoid going off script? But not anymore.

The embarrassment of getting fired had been worth every ounce of pain.

Within a few hours, Melanie had a response from the agent confirming their meeting. She couldn't focus on anything else that day. The possibility of publishing a book felt unreal—better than a dream come true.

When Evelyn went back to the floor, Melanie stepped outside to call her mother to tell her the news. She wondered how her mother would feel about her story being published as a book that could potentially reach even more people than the blog had.

"Wow, *mjia. Dios es bueno.* Look at that. . . . Your first time coming to my country with me and you get a book deal out of it," Anita said.

"Well, it's not a book deal yet. Just an informal meeting to learn more."

"Oh, it's going to be a book deal. I have no doubt about it."

"So, you don't care if your story were to reach more people—possibly be sold in bookstores and stuff? That doesn't make you nervous?"

"Nervous about what? How can anything make me nervous after what I've lived through? Plus, maybe the stories will give other people out there hope. Help them to keep going even when life tries to knock them down."

Yep, that's my mother. Always looking for ways to serve other people. Melanie felt the pangs of regret once more for having lived with her mother for so many years and never once having asked about her story.

At the end of the day, she realized her mother's story was pivotal to her own story. She couldn't appreciate where she'd come from until she knew the strength, the sacrifices, the loneliness, and the many valleys her mother had to walk for Melanie to be where she was today.

If it weren't for that story—for everything her mother did—what would have become of Melanie?

She had a flashback of the morning in the taxi when she was on her way to the airport in Cali. The young woman at the intersection who looked her age and who strikingly resembled Melanie, selling bags of sliced mango.

I'm not that woman today because of every decision you made to come here, Mom.

She didn't say it out loud, but the thought permeated her mind and her heart.

"Maybe this book will help more people understand people like us," Anita continued.

"People like us?"

"Immigrants who live in two cultures, two worlds. Fully Colombian but also fully American."

Melanie smiled and nodded as if her mother could see. Before she hung up, she thanked her mother. For her vulnerability. For her stories. For every decision she'd made, thinking of her children more than herself. For her love.

EPILOGUE

ONE YEAR LATER
CALI, COLOMBIA

MELANIE

"**N**aomi, pay attention! You're going to miss everything," Melanie said from the passenger seat of Juan Carlos's taxi cab.

"Sorry, Daniel spilled his milk. Okay, I'm paying attention. Whoa, what's that?"

"Oh, you're going to love that place. They have the best *champús*," Melanie said.

"The best what?" Naomi asked.

"You'll see," Melanie responded. "*Tio*, how much longer?"

"Five more minutes, but I can make it two if you're brave."

"*No, señor*, please follow the posted speed limits," Anita said. "We can't have an accident on the first trip to Cali I get to experience with both of my daughters."

Melanie looked back at her mother, who sat on the other side of Daniel's car seat. "Next time, we won't take no for an answer from Alex."

When Melanie turned around to face forward again, she squealed. "There she is!"

"*Abuela*," Naomi whispered with a hand pressed against her window.

Melanie nearly jumped out of Juan Carlos's car before he'd

put it in park. Within seconds, she was caught in the warm embrace of her grandmother, breathing in *arroz con leche* once more. Released from the embrace, Melanie stepped back and said, "I'm sorry it took me so long to come back."

"*Mi amor*, it's only been a year. That's nothing compared to the ten years I waited before. Thank you for coming, *mi vida*." Alba caught sight of Naomi removing a car seat from the cab. "Wow. I can't believe my eyes. Is that my Naomi?"

"And your great-grandson, *Abuela*." She placed Daniel in Alba's arms.

A stream of tears poured out of Alba's eyes. "What a treasure to be alive to see this sweet face in person." She turned her gaze to the sky and smiled before placing a kiss on Daniel's forehead. Anita walked over and kissed Alba's temple without a word.

"Okay, let's get inside. I want a piece of the big spread I saw *Mamá* putting together before I left for the airport. Let's dig in while it's still hot," Juan Carlos said, arms full of luggage.

"So, you haven't slowed down with the cooking, have you, *Mamá*?" Anita said, shaking her head. "You are one stubborn bull."

Melanie and Naomi looked at each other and smiled before following Alba, who still carried Daniel on her hip. It didn't look as if she'd be putting him down anytime soon.

At the round dining table, Melanie reached into her satchel, which leaned against the leg of her chair. "*Abuela*, I have something to show you." She pulled out a book with a black-and-white silhouette of a woman who stared into the horizon. It also featured her name in bold black letters.

"Oh my. . . . Is that what I think it is?" Alba asked.

Melanie nodded. "I wanted to show you in person."

Alba reached out to receive the book. She stared at the cover before allowing Naomi to take Daniel from her arms so she could flip through the pages.

"Can you believe it, *Mamá?*" Anita said from the table.

Alba flipped through a few more pages before looking up at Melanie with misty eyes. "*Claro que sí,*" she responded. "Of course I can. Melanie, you have made me prouder than you can even imagine. Not because of your accomplishments, but because of your love. This is a beautiful expression of your love for your family, and I will treasure it forever." Melanie walked over to Alba and pulled her in for another embrace.

"I hope you brought enough copies for your cousins," Anita said.

"And Sebastian," Naomi chimed in with a sly smile.

"Sebastian, eh?" Alba said.

Melanie sat back down, feeling her cheeks turn bright red. "We're just friends, *Abuela.* We've kept in touch . . . through email. I sent him some early drafts of the book, you know, to get a sense of how a modern-day, young Colombian would receive these stories."

"That's wonderful. I'm so glad I invited him and Marcela, then, to help us—"

"Wait, what? He's coming? Here?" Melanie asked, wide-eyed.

"I thought we'd need help finishing all this food," Alba said. "Plus, Marcela has told me how much he's been looking forward to another visit from you."

Everyone laughed.

"Is there some sort of matchmaking going on here? Because I can assure you, Sebastian and I are just—"

There was a knock at the door.

"That must be them." Alba walked to the front door.

Melanie took a sip of water before running her fingers through her hair and dabbing at the excess oil on her cheeks.

"It would have been nice to know she'd invited them," Melanie said.

"You're just friends, no?" Anita said, bumping Melanie with her shoulder.

Before Melanie could respond, Marcela walked into the kitchen, looking beautiful as ever in a maxi dress and wedge heels.

"Melanie! It's been too long," she said, pulling her in for a kiss on the cheek.

"Ugh, I know. I'm so sorry your travel visa wasn't approved. You'll have to try again. I'll see if anyone at the *Herald* has connections."

"That would be amazing. I have to see Miami before I die."

When Marcela moved on to greet Anita and meet Naomi for the first time, a familiar face came around the corner and entered the kitchen in a more composed manner.

"Hi, Melanie, it's been so long," Sebastian said as he kissed her on the cheek.

"It's only been a year. I should get some credit for not taking another ten to come back."

"That year felt like ten to me," he said. Melanie could feel the eyes of her family burning a hole into the back of her head. Unsure of how to respond, she smiled and left the room to look for extra chairs.

Once everyone was seated at the table, they caught up on what had happened in one another's lives over the past year and relived Melanie's last visit.

"Okay, *La Topa* sounds incredible. You have to take me, Marcela," Naomi said.

"There's a killer band playing tonight. Let's all go," she responded, looking around the table. "Maybe even *Abuela* can make a celebrity appearance."

"*Ay Dios mio*, I might be able to dance circles around you in my living room, but *La Topa* is a different beast. My bones aren't strong enough for that dance floor anymore, but I'd be delighted to watch *Danielito* for you, Naomi."

"That settles it," Marcela said. "I'll have to go home and change, but we'll come pick you up later tonight?" Melanie and Naomi nodded.

Marcela and Sebastian stood up from the table, and Melanie followed them to the front door to see them out.

"You go on. I'll catch up with you," Sebastian said to Marcela. She looked at Melanie and smiled before nodding her head and continuing onto the sidewalk.

"Marcela always hogs the conversation," he said, laughing. "I just wanted a second to tell you I've loved every single one of your columns, and now your book. I mean, wow, you must be so proud." He held up the copy of the book Melanie had given him over lunch. "And to think it all came from spending a few days here. Imagine what you could write if you spent a month or even a year here."

"That would be a dream," Melanie said, looking out into the neighborhood.

"Well, actually, let me take that back. I wouldn't want you to move here for a long period of time."

"Why's that?" Melanie said, tilting her head.

"Because then I couldn't see you."

"What do you mean?"

"I'm moving to the United States, Melanie." He slipped his hands into his pockets.

"Are you serious? But how?" A wide smile emerged.

"I never got to pursue higher education—I went straight

into the military. I started looking into my options and found FIU in Miami. I've been accepted as a foreign exchange student. I thought Miami would be a perfect transition because at least I could find people who speak Spanish and because, you know, I already have a friend there."

Melanie was speechless. She tried to act cool, but what she really wanted to do was jump up and down in celebration. The idea of getting to talk to Sebastian in person, face-to-face, on a regular basis, as opposed to waiting for an email, made her heart soar.

"Is that close to where you work or live?" Sebastian said.

"Huh? Oh yes. FIU is very close to where I live, actually."

"That's great. Maybe I can be your next subject."

"My next subject?" Small creases appeared on her forehead.

"For your column."

"Oh, right." She looked into his eyes and smiled. "That's a great idea."

She watched Sebastian walk away and disappear into the bustling neighborhood. Still smiling, she turned around. When she looked up, she stopped in her tracks.

Are you kidding me?

There they were: her mother, grandmother, and sister peeking through the curtains of the front window. Giggling like a trio of schoolgirls.

She shook her head and laughed, slightly embarrassed but grateful they were all together, and excited for what lay ahead.

AUTHOR'S NOTE

I'm embarrassed to admit that I didn't know the story of my mother's border crossing until my freshman year in college. But from that very day, I've dreamt about putting not only *her* story to paper but mine as well.

Outside of Anita's journal entries, much of *An American Immigrant* is fictional, although Melanie's story and journey throughout the book are inspired by my experience growing up in America with immigrant parents. I wanted to tell both stories: the story of the immigrant who starts over in America, and the story of the children they raise, who often grow up feeling like they don't completely fit into either culture. As an adult, I look back on my growing-up years with fondness and feel grateful to have parents who were immigrants, though I didn't always feel that way as a child. To this day, they teach me about endurance, pride in hard work, and gratitude for life's small pleasures. And, as you can probably tell from the book, the food—oh, the food—is one of the best parts about growing up in a Colombian family.

When I started writing this book in 2021, I wanted nothing more than to travel to Cali with my mother and see her past life for myself. But with a newborn baby and strict Covid restrictions on international travel, I had to settle for hours of conversation at my dinner table with my mother instead. She vividly described everything for me, and the stories were endless. I couldn't believe how much I didn't know!

Even halfway through writing the book, there were fun revelations—like finding out my grandmother was a talented poet. Yes, the two poems you read in this book were actually written by my late maternal grandmother, Alba Rosa Restrepo Ortiz. My mother found the poems taped to old photo albums, and I knew I had to include a few of them somewhere in the book. Only God knows how much I wish I would have known she was a writer before she passed away.

The character of Alba, whom you grew to love, was modeled after my grandmother. She spent her last ten years with us in America before she got sick and passed away. While I knew her up close only for a short time, I quickly fell in love with her stubborn, fiery, and playful spirit. I wanted to honor her legacy through the Alba I portrayed in this book.

There's so much more I could say about why I wrote this book (I could fill another novel), but I'll leave you, dear reader, with just this one thing: My greatest hope writing this book, beyond honoring my mother and grandmother, was to inspire people to dig into their own roots and find all they can to love about where they came from.

Why?

Because, speaking from experience, these kinds of discoveries have the power to change the trajectory of your life.

READERS GUIDE

1. Anita and Melanie had different growing-up stories and made different choices as young adults. What parallels can you see between their personalities and their lives? What differences? Which woman do you identify with more?

2. As the daughter of immigrants, Melanie felt stuck between two worlds. Think about Melanie's reasons for why she was so hesitant to embrace her Colombian roots while growing up. What did you learn from this? What resonated with you?

3. Have you felt freedom to embrace your heritage? In your family, are there stories and traditions that have been handed down through the generations? In what ways have you celebrated your heritage? Or how do you want to start that journey?

4. When she first arrived in Colombia, Melanie still had a bit of fear. How did her time there change her perception? What was an experience you had that changed your view of a person or place?

5. By reading her mother's journal, Melanie experienced a different side of her mother. Have you experienced a similar kind of revela-

tion about someone you are close to? Think about your own life—how have you changed from who you were years ago that might surprise people today?

6. Melanie quickly realized she missed out on many opportunities to get to know her Colombian family, especially Alba, her *abuela*. How did Alba help Melanie on her journey of self-discovery?

7. Friendships played a key role in helping Melanie after her life initially seemed to fall apart after returning from Colombia. Evelyn and Genesis both encouraged Melanie in her creative talent. In what ways did that stand out the most? How have friends supported you in hard times? How have you been able to support your friends?

8. Anita didn't want to leave Colombia but left for reasons beyond her control. Her *abuela* stayed, even through hard circumstances. How are themes of sacrifice and love portrayed in the novel?

9. Despite growing up in a different country, Melanie quickly got along with her cousins and friends, like Sebastian, in Colombia. Why do you think they all got along so well?

10. The women in the family played key roles in the novel as each character faced her own struggles. How did these struggles (Alba staying, Anita leaving, Melanie struggling with identity) help shape them? Which character's struggles do you identify with?

11. Through her writing, Melanie wanted to honor her mother and her mother's experience of immigrating to America—as well as honoring all immigrants. Why is it important for us to engage with stories like Anita's and Melanie's?

ACKNOWLEDGMENTS

When I had my first baby and left corporate America, I thought I would spend my son's nap times working as a freelance copywriter, helping influencers and educators grow their online businesses. But that lasted only about two months.

One day, while sitting in the passenger seat of our car, my husband looked over at me and said, "When are you going to stop writing for other people and start writing for yourself? You need to write that book you've always wanted to write."

This book is in your hands today because of his encouragement, support, and unending belief in my dream. I love you, Daniel!

My dream was also made possible because of endless family, friends, and colleagues who sacrificially supported me through the process.

I'm grateful for my sister Diana, who accepted every one of my distressed phone calls. Thank you for listening to all my ideas and offering some ideas of your own (many of which ended up in the final draft!).

Thank you to my mother-in-law Frances for reading early drafts and for all the days you offered to play with my babies so

I could write undisturbed. And to my father-in-law Rick, thank you for preordering a bunch of copies! I love you both more than words can say.

To my writers' group, Mandy Johnson, Rachel Miller, Meredith Boggs, and Kelsey Chapman, your encouragement and presence in my life was the constant I needed in this crazy rollercoaster journey. Thank you for patiently listening to every rant, for lifting my spirits through every rejection, and for offering honest critiques of my writing. Every writer needs a group of friends like you.

To my father, who also crossed the border in search of a better future, I know you sacrificed so much throughout my life so that I could be the writer I am today. Thank you. Perhaps one day I'll write your story too.

Endless thanks to my literary agent, Kristy Cambron, for reading my manuscript and believing it had the potential to change hearts. I'm so grateful for your partnership and advocacy of this project.

To my editor, Jamie Lapeyrolerie, thank you for giving this book a chance when it landed on your desk. Your tireless work improving my manuscript was a great gift. And to the entire team at WaterBrook, thank you for making this writer's dreams come true! It's been a joy to work with all of you.

I can't forget you, dear reader. Thank you for picking up this book. I hope the story inspired you to discover what you might be missing about your own heritage.

And finally, to my mother, thank you for allowing me the privilege of writing down your story.

ABOUT THE AUTHOR

Johanna Rojas Vann is a wife, mother, and professional writer with a passion for stories that highlight the complexity and beauty of diverse families. As a second-generation Colombian American, she hopes to use the power of story to foster an appreciation and understanding of minority families in the United States today.

Johanna lives and writes in Nashville, Tennessee, where the coffee is good and the people are even better.

An American Immigrant is her debut novel.